The Four Redheads: The Wrath of Satan

Other "Redheads" books by Yard Dog Press:

The Four Redheads of the Apocalypse
The Four Redheads: Apocalypse Now!
Redheads In Love

Linda L. Donahue
Rhonda Eudaly
Julia S. Mandala
Dusty Rainbolt

The Four Redheads: The Wrath of Satan
Linda L. Donahue, Rhonda Eudaly, Julia S. Mandala, Dusty Rainbolt
First Edition Copyright © Linda L. Donahue, Rhonda Eudaly, Julia S. Mandala & Dusty Rainbolt, 2016

Published by Yard Dog Press @ Create Space

ISBN 978-1-937105-98-3
The Four Redheads: The Wrath of Satan
First Edition Copyright © L. Donahue, Rhonda Eudaly, Julia S. Mandala & Dusty Rainbolt, 2016

Yard Dog Press
710 W. Redbud Lane
Alma, AR   72921-7247

http://www.yarddogpress.com

Edited by Selina Rosen
Copy & Technical Editor Lynn Rosen
Front cover photo by Stuart Jones of Rose and Dagger Photography Studio
Photoshop by Julia S. Mandala & Linda L. Donahue
First Edition September 1, 2016
Printed in the United States of America
0 9 8 7 6 5 4 3 2 1

Dedication

In loving memory of Ed Drevecky III. We miss you!

Acknowledgments

We thank all the members of fandom who worked to spread the word about *The Four Redheads of the Apocalypse* and the subsequent books. We have met people from Boston to Seattle and beyond who have read, or at least heard of, this series. That is largely because you all recommended it to your friends and relatives, or dragged complete strangers into the dealers' room and forced them to buy it. In small press, word of mouth is the best marketing tool we have. Thanks for being such great supporters. Thank you also for coming to our "press conferences" and participating as reporters, and for coming to the variety shows. Thanks also to our wonderful "minions" who have helped out in these events over the years—Tamisan Eber, Kathy Turski, Carla Sullens, Candace Hales, Todd Caldwell, Sam Gayle, Robyn Winans, Bobby Hitt and a host of others. We couldn't have done all this without you! And special thanks to Selina Rosen for being our Satan and wearing those high-heeled boots. Not only is she awesome at the live events, she is an inspiration to us in writing the character.

Special Note

No disrespect was meant in our use of characters based on persons living or dead. We respect and admire them, especially Jesus, Pernell Roberts, Wil Wheaton, Donald Trump and Tom Hiddleston.

Chapter One

Bunny sat at the Redheads' usual table at the Sulfur Well bar. She checked her Cartier diamond wristwatch. The other Redheads were late. She checked the calendar on her phone: Meeting with Redheads ... Sara Lee has news.

Zoe waltzed up, wearing a spaghetti-strapped, black evening gown with beaded olivine trim. Since marrying Jake, her steps had been lighter—though Jake failed to earn Satan's approval to take Zoe's job as Death. God and Satan both liked Bunny's boyfriend Adam for War ... but getting married was a big decision.

Zoe flagged the waiter, flashing her sparkly wedding ring. "Bring me a glass of sweet moscato." Glancing at Bunny, she said, "Make it a *bottle*."

"Hey." Bunny wrinkled her nose, version nine of her nose-wrinkling expressions, to indicate she knew she'd been insulted.

Butterflye teleported into the bar. With her leopard-print shoe, she squashed a bug that crawled from under her teal tiger-print gown. She preferred teleporting around Hell, saying the hot pavement was ... well, hell on her shoes.

Butterflye grabbed the waiter by his collar. "A double scotch. Pronto!"

He scurried off, mumbling, "Yes, ma'am."

"And don't *ma'am* me," Butterflye called in his wake.

"I hate that word," Zoe said.

"There should be a better word for women who are no longer misses," Bunny commiserated.

"We are too misses," Butterflye said, folding her arms. "We're single. Well, three of us are."

"Technically, you're a widow and a divorcee," Zoe said.

"Don't remind me." Butterflye snatched the scotch from the tray and knocked it back with a gulp. "Not bad for this place. Just a little kerosene taste." To the waiter, she snapped, "Keep 'em coming."

"I'd drink too, if I had your luck with men." Bunny stirred her fruity drink with a skewered pineapple slice.

Butterflye scowled. "Not all men are bad. My Ossie was wonderful, much nicer than your Ares." When her second scotch arrived, she paused a nanosecond to savor its aroma before slamming it back.

"People always say bad things about Ares. No one knew him like I did." Bunny pouted. Wasn't it wrong to speak ill of the dead? Everyone said Ares had neglected her and treated her like a prisoner. Yet it wasn't his fault that being War had kept him so busy.

"Let her have her fantasy," Zoe said.

Sara Lee strolled up in a vivid red gown with sparkling silver sequins. "Ladies," she said, "soon we won't have our jobs to complain about." She took a seat. "I've found another loophole in our marriage contract."

After the original Four Horsemen of the Apocalypse fell into oblivion in an unfortunate ice-fishing accident, the marriage contract saddled their wives with the jobs.

Butterflye groaned. "Why do you keep reading that damned contract? The ending isn't going to change."

"To find a way out," Sara Lee said. "If your job sucked as bad as mine, you wouldn't ask."

"Would you rather be Plague-Pestilence?" Butterflye squashed a roach with her scotch glass before it could scurry across the table.

"It'd mean any food and drink I touch outside my domain wouldn't turn to dust." Sara Lee hovered her finger over Butterflye's scotch.

Butterflye pulled her scotch to safety. "Okay. You've got it rough, but at least you don't deal with bugs and pus." She shuddered. "If we could at least *trade* jobs, I'd happily switch with you, Sara Lee." Eying Bunny, she added, "Actually, I'd switch with Bunny, if I got her unlimited expense account."

"I do have it best," Bunny said. "War's an easy job."

Zoe hummed. "I'm not sure I can afford to give up my job. Jake and I couldn't live very well on just his salary. Maybe I should put him up for a raise."

"We'd have pensions," Sara Lee said. "*Big pensions.* Apparently, Satan felt generous towards the original Horsemen when the original contract was written—you know, before actually she met us."

"Just how big is this pension?" Zoe asked dubiously.

"Biggest one in Hell," Sara Lee said.

A cautious, yet hopeful glimmer lit Zoe's blue eyes. "How's it work?"

"I just hope *this* loophole isn't as disastrous as your marriage one," Butterflye mumbled into her scotch glass.

Sara Lee bristled. "It's not my fault Larvy turned out to be a jerk. And it's not like my romance worked out either." She looked at Bunny and Zoe with a touch of envy. "Besides, it didn't turn out bad for *everyone.*"

"I'm not complaining," Zoe said, smiling. "So what's the deal?"

Sara Lee leaned in close. "It turns out we can just *give* away our jobs, as long as it's to someone from our own bloodline."

"Do they have to be dead?" Butterflye asked.

"From the same bloodline is all that matters." Sara Lee's lip curled. "Of course, a dead relative will already know that the job and Hell suck. Then again, if we pawn the job off on a living relative, he or she would have to die to become a Horseman."

Butterflye waived away the problem. "We all have to die sometime."

"This loophole doesn't help me," Bunny said. "I haven't kept up with my family. My father abandoned us when I was three. And my mother always left me with the nanny." Bunny tapped her chin. "Maybe my half-sister is still alive—although she'd be ancient by now."

"When was she born?" Sara Lee asked.

Bunny shrugged. "Late 50s, early 60s?"

Butterflye grunted. "Then she's hardly ancient," said the oldest redhead at the table.

"Back on topic," Zoe said. "When would we have time to con a relative? It's not like these jobs sell themselves."

A look of defeat settled across Sara Lee's features. "That's why I was late. I tried to talk Satan into giving us some extra comp time on Earth—but no luck. We'll just have to do it during our existing comp time or the time allotted for doing our jobs."

"This new scheme sounds hard," Bunny said.

"You go to Earth all the time, pretending to work," Sara Lee said. "Take a little time out of your shopping schedule to get to know your sister. Convince her she wants the prestige and power that goes with being War."

"If it's so great, why don't I want it?" Bunny asked.

Sara Lee heaved her large bosom with a patient sigh. "No job means no time wasted with training?"

Bunny wrinkled her nose—variation six. "Semyaza's fun

when we talk makeup, but otherwise he's boring. I *would* miss training with Michael and Adam though. And we wouldn't have our minions anymore." Wreak and Havoc did lots of the little chores she preferred not to bother with. "Oh, and would I lose my dogs and horse?"

"I'm sure your sister would let you keep the Poodles of War," Sara Lee said. "Don't forget the biggest perk of all: we won't have to work for Satan anymore." She straightened. "I almost forgot. As Satan was booting me out, she said to send Bunny to her office."

"Then I'd better go." Bunny teleported to Satan's office. She poked her head through Satan's open doorway. "Hiya, Satan. You wanted to see me?"

Satan wore a big, self-satisfied grin. "Come on in, War. We need to chat."

"I always knew you liked me." Bunny stepped around the smoldering remains of someone and took a seat before Satan's desk.

"Ignore the mess," Satan said. "He'll recorporealize— eventually." She leaned on the desk, knocking over a stack of soul requisition forms. "I called you in for two reasons. You want the bad news first?"

"There's good news?" Bunny asked. "Now *that's* surprising."

Satan smirked. "Good for me." Glowering—her mood shifting faster than a strobe light—Satan snapped, "You've got to do something about Pernell! How's he slipping in and out of Hell? I can't run this place like a vacation hotspot! It sets a bad precedent for our denizens."

Bunny blinked. "Who's Pernell?"

"Forgot him already?" Satan snarked.

"I don't know what you're talking about."

Satan groaned. "That's right. You call him Hoss."

"I'm seeing Adam, not Hoss. Really, Satan, you should be better about remembering names."

"Well, isn't that the pot calling the kettle *pink*." Satan squinted at Bunny. "Speaking of pink, what is that gawd-awful color you're wearing?"

"Popcorn pink."

A low rumble spilled from Satan's throat. "Why do I always fall for it? Oh, well. Bunny, popcorn isn't pink."

"But if it *were* pink," Bunny explained patiently, "it'd be this shade of pink."

Satan clenched her hands into fists. "Whatever. What can I do to be rid of you?"

Bunny thought hard. "If you didn't want to see me, you shouldn't have sent for me. As I see it, this is your fault."

"Hell." Satan's expression suddenly brightened. "That's right. I almost forgot. Before you distract me again, I'll make this short and O-so-sweet. Your unlimited expense account has been frozen."

"I didn't think anything froze in Hell."

"Clearly you haven't visited every circle." Satan waved her hands. "No sidetracking! Now that you have minions, I'm taking away your *carte blanche.*"

"So I can't spend whatever I want?"

"You catch on pretty fast for a dumb, redheaded blonde. It's time you worked on a budget like the other Horsewomen." Satan shooed Bunny. "Go. Now."

Bunny perched her hands on her hips. "You can't take things back—that's breaking a promise."

Satan laughed. "What do you think I do all day, every day? Why else would I have so many lawyers on staff?"

"What's the point of being War without an unlimited expense account?" Bunny demanded. Suddenly, Sara Lee's plan looked a lot more attractive.

"Frankly, I don't see the point of you being War at all."

"Then you think I should give my job to a relative too? You sound like Sara Lee."

Satan's eyes grew round. "Oh? Sara Lee's found a new loophole?"

"You should know. She was just here about it." Clearly, Satan's memory was as bad as Bunny's was.

Brimstone smoke rolled off Satan in waves. "She tried to get you bitches extra comp time—like any of you've done a good enough job to deserve a break." Then Satan shrugged. "Well, Zoe's not *so* bad."

"Sara Lee wanted the time so we could talk a relative into taking our jobs. It's all in the contract," Bunny explained.

Satan snorted. "Yeah, that's just what I need—four people from your bloodlines who'll probably be just as useless as you all."

"At least it'll be a change," Bunny said consolingly.

"I don't know," Satan drawled. "Better the bimbo you know…" She gazed at the ceiling where scorch marks made patterns of dead bodies bent in tortured positions. "I guess I should look at this damned loophole." Sighing, she retrieved a copy of the wedding contract from a file cabinet and flipped through it furiously, her eyes flicking across the lines. Satan was a champion speed-reader, a necessity, given the length of her contracts. "What I really need are successors more like your husbands were—"

An evil smile spread across Satan's face, and she flipped past about fifty pages. "The succession clause. Yes! I never considered using it this way! How could my lawyers have missed this? The loophole of all loopholes! The Horsemen all had brothers."

"That won't work," Bunny said. "It has to be one of *our* relatives."

Satan flashed sharp teeth. "I'm not talking about *that* clause. Wow. I never thought I'd see the day when I thanked you. But thanks for the inspiration. Now run along. I don't need you anymore."

"What about my expense account?" Bunny demanded.

"It's *finito*. Deal with it."

Without an unlimited expense account, there was no point in being War. Bunny just hoped she could connect with her sister Kitty and convince her to take the job.

"Bunny, wait!" Satan called. "I've changed my mind."

Bunny spun around to see Satan beaming from her desk. Feeling hopeful, she asked, "I get my expense account back?"

"Hell, no! I'm just rescinding my 'no more vacations on Earth' rule. I'm giving all four of you damned Redheads an actual, *mortal* vacation on Earth, just like I used to give your husbands. Hell—take the whole month of October off." Then she muttered, "It's not like there'll be much difference with you bimbos *off* the job." Again she shooed Bunny. "Now get your popcorn pink ass out of here."

Bunny's mood brightened. "Thanks, Satan."

From behind, Satan chuckled, then let out an excited, "Oblivion!"

Whatever that meant.

Zoe scrolled through reports from Reaper. The monthly intake numbers trended nicely upward. Her minions logged decent hours without running into overtime. She hadn't received a threatening message from ... well ... anyone for a while. Maybe she was finally getting the hang of the blasted job.

"Heads up, Boss. Incoming."

Before Zoe could acknowledge her assistant Bambi's intercom warning, the door to her office flew open and slammed against its stops. As Satan stomped into the office, Zoe leaped to her feet.

Wow, instant jinx. Way to go, brain. Satan seemed to have a whole swarm of bees in her proverbial bonnet. Zoe swallowed hard and tried to think of what she might've done.

"What can I do for you, Boss?" Zoe tried to keep the tremor out of her voice.

"Like it wasn't enough you had to marry that goody-goody, pansy reaper boy—"

"Jake. His name is Jake," Zoe said.

"Do you think I give a flaming, flying crap what his *name* is? Now look what you made me do. I've lost my train of thought." Satan gestured vehemently, waving an envelope. Her eyes flicked to the paper and her rage refocused. "Oh, yeah, this. Lynn tells me it's *non-optional*. We must give you"—she choked—"a wedding gift. This is it. Don't say I never gave you anything."

She slapped the envelope down with such force Zoe jumped back and tottered on her elegant but sensible heels. She didn't fall and squeaked out a "thank you." Satan stormed out, leaving Zoe staring at the door, trying to process the situation.

Bambi stuck her head in a moment later. Her once-classic, blonde French Twist stuck out in all directions from the force of Satan's passing. "All clear, Boss? ... Boss?"

Zoe finally blinked and waved her in. "What just happened?"

"I was hoping you'd tell me." Bambi leaned on the back of a black, high-backed guest chair. Her deep-cut, blood-red dress hung off one shoulder and her impressive cleavage canted asymmetrically. "The volume shorted out the intercom. All I heard was tone."

"It has ... she said something about a wedding gift." Zoe poked the envelope with the end of her Montegrippa Chaos fountain pen.

"You're acting like it might explode."

Zoe was pretty sure her assistant meant it as a joke, but it fell pretty flat. "It's from *her*, so I wouldn't discount anything. Maybe I should call Jake."

"Oh, come on, Zoe! You're *Death* for crying out loud! What do *you* have to be afraid of? Open the envelope."

Bambi's snap spurred Zoe into action. She snatched up the envelope and pried open the flap. Nothing damaging happened, so she pulled out the cardstock. As she carefully unfolded the page, something fluttered out. Her eyes widened as her jaw dropped and her brain shut down again.

"Boss? Are you all right?" The longer Zoe sat there unmoving, the more concern crept into Bambi's expression. "What is it? What happened?"

Bambi reached for the card, breaking Zoe's self-inflicted spell. Zoe snatched the card from her assistant's reach with one hand and reached for what fell out.

"Get Jake and Reaper in here as quickly as possible. Faster, even. Go!"

Bambi fled the office. Zoe leaned back in her chair and let a smile slowly play out as she fanned herself with card.

Bambi's voice soon broke the silence. "Boss, they're here."

Zoe looked up from her computer monitor and did a double-take. Bambi had repaired her French Twist and evened up her cleavage and the hang of her dress. Sometimes Zoe hated her assistant. "Bring them in, and you stay too. This affects you as well."

"Right away."

Bambi retreated. Zoe thought she heard a gulp before the door swung open—much more gently than before—and the trio paraded in, Reaper leading the way. He'd changed his hair again. He'd added blond highlights and low lights into his "natural" tousled look that took more time and more product than Zoe's hair did, to give him a rakish, Hollywood look. Reaper looked wary and intense but dapper in his tailored black silk-blend button-down and slacks. Her chief soul-gatherer was a clothes horse—so unlike his brother, and now love of her afterlife, Jake.

Jake Grimm—yes, of *those* Grimms—tended to be less flashy than his brother, Wilhelm—a/k/a Reaper. Jake liked cotton and khaki. He tended to wear cargo pants and polo shirts or t-shirts and shorts when he could get away with them. That suited Zoe just fine. Though the Redheads were known for formalwear in most cases, when out of the public eye, Zoe liked her yoga pants. In fact, she wished she could be in them now instead of the vintage black suit from the Audrey Hepburn Collection.

Both men made her job as Death infinitely easier, which

made her entire afterlife infinitely better. She loved and appreciated them both for it—in vastly different ways. Bambi, a now invaluable member of her team, brought up the rear.

"Come on in and take seats. Bambi, close the door behind you."

"Enough mystery, Zoe." Reaper slouched in one of her guest chairs in a practiced, hipster way while regarding her with intense concentration. He'd been watching way too many CW television shows lately.

"Don't get your man panties in a twist," Zoe said. "It's my news and I'll tell it my way."

Reaper stuck out his tongue in a stunning display of adult behavior. She loved rattling her new brother-in-law. He turned to his brother. "She talks to you like that?"

"Never. She doesn't have to. We have an adult relationship based on respect and trust."

Zoe beamed at Jake. She didn't care that he was ribbing Reaper; he was right, and taking her side. The smug rebuttal also meant his shy exterior shell was crumbling.

"Bambi, did you tell them about *her* visit?"

Her assistant shook her head. "There wasn't time."

"She just barked at us to get in here." Reaper gave Bambi a look Zoe wasn't sure was pissy or proud before turning back to his boss. "So curiosity is about to kill the cat. Figuratively speaking, maybe."

Zoe was tempted to drag out the moment, but thought better of it. If she pushed it any harder, Reaper would be even more annoying. She zipped through the whirlwind encounter with Satan, ending with the card.

"She left us a freakin' *wedding* present. Jake, she's giving us a vacation—honeymoon. On Earth. For the entire month of October."

"That's not far off," Reaper said.

"We'll have to work up a game plan. I'm counting on you and Bambi to take care of business." Zoe met Reaper's gaze steadily. "I know we've had our bumps in the past, but we're in a good place now, right, Reaper? I can count on you?"

Reaper nodded, all business. "We've got it covered."

"Why me, Boss?" Bambi asked.

"You know more about where the bodies are buried—literally and figuratively—than any of us. I can't do this job with you, and if Reaper's half as smart as he thinks he is, he won't either."

"Um, Zoe, I have a question," Jake said, holding up a finger to be recognized.

"Yes, dear?"

"A month on Earth? That means we're mortals, right? With mortal problems that'll require money. How will we pull that off?"

Zoe's smile spread wider. "That's where it gets even better." She held up a plastic rectangle. "There was also a very generous pre-paid credit card included with the note."

Bambi's brow furrowed. "That doesn't sound like *her*."

"It's not at all like her. Satan said Lynn insisted."

"Ah," Bambi said. "So what now?"

"You and Reaper work out the logistics of this end."

"Sure." Reaper's quick agreement and great effort to *not* look at Bambi set off bells in Zoe's brain. She just wasn't sure if they were *warning* bells or *wedding* bells.

"Jake and I have plans of our own to make. Let's meet back here tomorrow and see what we have." Zoe dragged Jake out of the office.

"You're just leaving them in your office, unsupervised?" Jake asked as the door closed on the black and chrome, skull-festooned office.

"You want to plan a honeymoon with them present?"

He shuddered.

"Didn't think so. Besides, you need to know something else about this trip I'm not ready to talk to them about."

"Oh?"

"Sarah Lee found another loophole." Zoe did her best to ignore Jake's groan. "Yeah, I know the others haven't worked out so well, but this one... If we find a blood relative to transfer the job to, we can retire and get a pension. We can use the honeymoon trip to do that."

"Why don't you want Reaper and Bambi to know that?"

"In case things go horribly wrong."

"Because that's never happened."

"Exactly.

As Zoe left final instructions, she felt a little like a parent leaving teenagers at home alone for the first time. "I know you two will be fine. If you run into any major—and I emphasize *major*—problems, find us. But I fully expect to not hear anything.

Right?"

"We've got it covered, Zoe." Reaper seemed confident.

"Keep an eye on him, Bambi."

"You got it, Boss."

Zoe turned to leave, then stopped. She snapped her fingers, turned and pointed a well-manicured fingernail at Bambi's nose. "Don't let him redecorate my office while I'm gone. I like it the way it is. And if for some reason you can't stop him, make sure you put it back the way it was before I return."

"Will do, Boss." Bambi grinned. "So, what do you guys have planned?"

"Road trip!"

"Okay, people, listen up," Sara Lee said to the minions gathered in her living room.

Her deceased husband, Oscar Mayer, had liked to work from home. Photos of his "greatest hits" adorned the walls—starving Ethiopians, supermodels and little children in China and India. Beside those hung Sara Lee's four framed "Pillsbury Bake-off" awards, a photo of Oscar and her at Disney World, their favorite vacation spot, and one of him and his brother Jimmy Dean at a baseball game several years before Oscar met Sara Lee. She'd enjoyed having Oscar around all day, but now that she held the job of Famine, she wished she had a place where she could get away from the "office." Not that she spent much time working. She just hated being reminded that she wasn't working.

Wreak and Havoc, sitting on her worn velvet couch, carried on an animated debate about MPG vs Firepower in the tank they were building out of an old Buick Roadmaster. Candace, the Master Trainer from Hell, and Tammy, a former Marine drill sergeant, exchanged ideas on the best way to "whip" souls into shape. Bobby sat on the broken recliner, fiddling with his phone. In all, it looked as unproductive as any business meeting on Earth.

Sara Lee sighed. Some days, it wasn't worth getting out of bed.

But this would not be one of those days! She pulled out a digitally enhanced police whistle and blew with all her strength. An eardrum-shattering shriek filled the air.

The minions wrapped up their conversations, wiped the blood from their ears and slowly turned their attention to Sara

Lee. They were worse than cats. *Hmmm.* Maybe next time, she should try an electric can opener.

"Here's the deal," Sara Lee said. "I've found a new loophole..."

The minions groaned and rolled their eyes.

"When it fails, you'll just fall into another deep depression," Tammy said, tossing her auburn pigtails. "Then *I'll* have to deal with a mopey, binge-eating bitch."

"So, nothing new," Wreak whispered to Havoc.

Sara Lee's smile hardened in Tammy's direction. "Maybe you'd like to go back to Hell's Kitchen."

Tammy looked as hopeful as a puppy by a treat jar. "You think they'd take me back?"

"You can't go back, because I'm leaving you in charge," Sara Lee said.

"Whoopee," Tammy said in a dead monotone. "My fondest dream come true."

"Hey, what about us?" Wreak asked, waving his Stetson fedora across Sara Lee's vision.

"We have seniority," Havoc reminded her.

"Exactly the same amount of seniority," she said. "You can't both be in charge—says the *mopey, binge-eating bitch.*" Besides, Wreak and Havoc, with their many interests, weren't exactly known for staying on task.

"Yeah, whatever," Candace said, folding her arms across her black leather bustier. "Tammy may be in charge Down Here, but *I* expect you to get an hour of cardio every day and to strictly follow the Paleo Diet."

Sara Lee almost laughed, but the looped bullwhip that Candace gripped stopped her cold. "Uh, sure." Another lie couldn't get Sara Lee in any worse trouble than being in Hell. And she was Going on Vacation to Earth!!! That meant real food that didn't turn to dust, as it always did outside her domain, or wilt and rot, as it always did inside her domain. Fudge cake, french fries, beer—no, a mudslide! Alcohol *and* chocolate—

Before Sara Lee could slip into a food-fantasy coma, Candace cracked her bullwhip an inch from Sara Lee's nose. "I see that smile," Candace said. "That's not for grass-fed beef and organic green vegetables. That's a sugar smile!"

Sara Lee tried an innocent look. Her face wasn't up to the challenge.

"So what's the loophole this time?" Bobby asked, his gaze locked on his phone.

"Huh?" Sara Lee blinked away the visions of sundaes dancing in her head. "A blood relative has to agree to take the job. None of my dead relatives are dumb enough to fall for that, and the only one I know who's still alive is my brother."

Her gut clenched. She wasn't sure how to *approach* her little brother, let alone convince him to take this crappy job. After all, she'd been dead for over twenty-five years, and she'd died to be with Oscar. The family reunion could be a tad awkward.

A tiny voice in the back of her head—a voice that sounded a lot like Jesus—said, *You don't really want your little brother to go to Hell, do you?*

She smirked. *Better him than me. Oh, wait. I'm stuck here anyway.* But she could get rid of this stupid job. And, as Butterflye said, everyone died sometime.

Ever since Sara Lee made the sacrifice of setting her boyfriend Nathan free when he offered to marry her and become Famine, Jesus's voice had been showing up in her head with alarming frequency. She hoped it would pass. Or maybe this was what people meant by "no good deed goes unpunished."

Candace smacked Sara Lee's shoulder with the looped whip, then handed her a huge ball of yarn and some knitting needles.

"Where did those come from?" Sara Lee asked.

Candace readjusted her black leather corset. "Never mind that. Use them. If your hands are busy knitting, you won't be shoveling food into your mouth."

Milkshake. Straw. There was a way around almost anything.

"So what do you want us to do while you're gone?" Tammy asked.

"Just keep an eye on the machine." Sara Lee nodded toward the door to the room housing the strange contraption Oscar had built to control the global climate—an Earth model with snow-globe thingies attached to it. Except that they contained all kinds of weather, not just snow. "Maybe see if you can get that one globe unstuck, the one I think is causing global warming."

"I thought that was axis wobble," Havoc said.

"Besides, isn't global warming good for famine?" Bobby asked, not looking up from the tiny screen.

Sara Lee shrugged. "Depends on how far it goes. Frankly, I don't know who to believe about the causes, but I don't want to step on Zoe's toes. Plus God made us promise not to try to end the world again. If it looks like global warming will destroy all life on the planet, we'll need to slow it down."

"Good luck with that," Wreak muttered.

Sara Lee gave him *The Look*.

He raised both hands, palms out. "Okay, okay. We'll try to get some WD40 smuggled into Hell."

Like duct tape, WD40 was a banned substance. WD40 alleviated annoying squeaks and squeals, and Satan found that petty annoyances, cumulatively, tortured the damned even worse than pitchforks and brimstone. Or Bunny and Butterflye's "singing."

Still looking at his phone, Bobby chuckled.

Sara Lee snatched it from his hand. "What's so damned interesting?" A Hell YouTube video of Satan played on the small screen. Looking in her mirror, Satan sprayed on perfume and sang, "I feel pretty, O so pretty..."

Sara Lee snorted and tossed the phone back to Bobby. "You should back that up somewhere before Satan has it pulled. That's priceless. I wonder who got that video."

Wreak and Havoc exchanged innocent looks.

The front door slammed open, sending down a rain of plaster dust. Satan stood in the doorway, a malicious grin on her face and an evil glint in her eyes. Same old, same old. "What have we here? A nerd convention? Not you, Candace."

"Staff meeting," Tammy said.

"More like a crutch meeting. You all enable her moodiness. Not you, Candace. It's about time someone cracked the whip on this sorry excuse for a Horsewoman." Satan turned her glare on Sara Lee. "Shouldn't you be packing?"

"I'll go naked if it means getting out of here sooner," Sara Lee said.

"I'm evil, but not so evil that I'd inflict your naked lard-ass on the world," Satan said. "Now pack a bag, so I can make you mortal and teleport you to Earth."

Satan's cooperation—no, more like eagerness—concerned Sara Lee. Sure, Satan longed for the Redheads to leave their jobs as much as the four of them did. But helping others wasn't exactly in Satan's nature. Sara Lee decided not to question her good luck.

Bobby laughed, his gaze still on the video and oblivious to all else.

Satan snatched the phone from his hand. Watching the screen, her face went crimson and steam hissed from her ears.

"What in the Nine Circles of Hell is this? When I find out who's behind this, I'm gonna make them wish they'd never died."

"Um, we all kind of wish that," Tammy said, as Wreak and Havoc whistled tunelessly.

"Can I please have my phone back?" Bobby asked hesitantly.

Satan smiled. "Sure. Here you go." She dashed it against the floor, shattering the case and screen into a dozen pieces. "Now get back to work, you good-for-nothing maggots!"

Chapter Two

A flash of lightning and poof of smoke exploded at the front of a security line inside the Port of Galveston. Satan, dressed in red fatigues, stepped out of the haze, followed by Butterflye Plague-Pestilence. Wide-eyed, Butterflye scanned the room.

"Where am I?" Butterflye asked the Ruler of Demons.

The walls of the cavernous room held murals of sleek white cruise ships and heavily airbrushed photos of happy passengers dancing in discos and kissing dolphins. The security line snaked around temporary barriers like living intestines. Satan tried to smile. "It's a Come-As-You-Are party, and you're going on vacation. Take your suitcase. I had your nun pack it."

Butterflye tugged at her enormous rolling trunk, embellished with her trademark sequined blue-cheetah pattern, which by design, would be unmistakable on any airport conveyor. The bag refused to budge so much as an inch.

At the sudden appearance of the pair from Hell, an eighty-year-old woman behind them in line fainted. Her equally ancient husband kneeled down and waved his hat across her face.

"Y-you're sending me on a cruise?" Butterflye stammered.

"Surprise, Plague!"

For a moment, Butterflye was speechless. Two minutes ago, she'd been sitting at her desk looking through pharmaceutical information sheets. Satan walked in and, boom, Butterflye was in line with thousands of strangers.

"I know the last few months have been rough," Satan said. "You need to get away and think about what you want to do with the rest of your life."

"Satan, as you're so fond of reminding me, I'm already dead."

"For the rest of your death, then. I made reservations for you to go on a month-long cruise."

Butterflye clutched her purse defensively, as if protecting her nonexistent firstborn. "Did you *make* reservations or did you *pay* for reservations?"

Satan feigned a hurt look. "You don't trust me?"

Butterflye continued to guard her handbag.

"It's not coming out of your budget. Technically, Bunny paid for it before I revoked her expense account." Satan got a faraway look and chuckled. "That was great."

Visions of a coffin-sized cabin and an all-you-can-eat Spam® bar filled Butterflye's head. "I know the other girls would jump at this opportunity. But I can't imagine anything more depressing than going on a romantic vacation alone."

"Look, I want you to forget about that perverted ex-husband of yours."

For a moment, as Butterflye slipped into the past and relived that glorious moment in divorce court when Satan decorporialized that sleazy rat to the subatomic level, she smiled. Even after all this time, some of his body parts still hadn't come together.

"Satan, I don't want to be around a bunch of honeymooners."

"You know, Plague, I've always liked you—" Satan started.

"Plague-Pestilence."

"What?"

"I go by Plague-Pestilence."

"Fine." Satan smiled a terrifyingly sweet smile.

Before she could return to her train of thought, the old man behind them left his unconscious wife on the floor, sucked his dentures into place and challenged Satan. "Hey! You jumped line. You know what we do to people who cut in line around here?"

Satan dropped her head to the man's eye level. "What?"

He stuck out his chest. "We feed them my wife's cooking and watch them writhe in pain!"

Satan grunted as she shifted the weight of Butterflye's five carry-on bags. "You know what we do to smartasses where I come from?"

"What?" The old man moved closer.

After a moment of uncomfortable silence, the geezer passed enough gas to power the city of Milwaukee for six hours. He grabbed his belly, abandoned his wife and dashed toward the nearest restroom.

Satan laughed. "That never gets old." She stepped over the motionless woman and returned her attention to Butterflye, who had her hand over her nose.

"Now where were we before we were so rudely interrupted?" Satan tapped her chin with her forefinger. "Oh, yeah." She nodded at the oversized wall photos with her horns. "Look at those people enjoying themselves. That could be you. Have fun. Let down all that damn red hair of yours."

Butterflye tested the air to see if it was safe to breathe again. "I don't *want* to go." She smoothed her dress. This Old Thing, as she called it, would be considered high fashion on anyone's red carpet, but the cobalt-blue Scala original was Butterflye's everyday work attire. While she'd been accused of being overdressed, her floor-length frock was purely functional. The yards of fabric caressing her ankles concealed the swarms of cockroaches that shadowed her every step back in Hell. "Thanks for the offer of a vacation, but I just want to get back to work."

"And you will, but give yourself time. I spared no expense. This is"—Satan looked down at the booking information—"the Helvetica Cruise Line."

"There's a cruise line named after a popular typeface?"

"Really, Plague." Satan forced another smile. "I mean Butterflye. The other Redheads would kill to have me send them on a cruise. You're looking a gift devil in the mouth."

Butterflye eyed her boss's fangs. "Not unless I have to."

Satan dropped the stack of papers into Butterflye's hands. "Here's your boarding pass. You're booked on, let's see, *Squalor of the Sea.*"

Butterflye's passport sat atop the papers. The scarlet cover bore a gold embossed pitchfork engulfed in flames and block letters that read, "The Kingdom of Sheol."

"Really, I'd rather..." Butterflye continued to struggle with the trunk. Satan pushed her out of the way and yanked the luggage off the floor with no more effort than picking up a puppy.

"Consider yourself on furlough. You can come home in a month. Enjoy your cruise." Satan pushed Butterflye toward the next available security bay, then disappeared in a cloud of flaming vapor. In Satan's absence, the trunk slammed atop the X-ray conveyor belt, startling the strapping security guard manning the device. Butterflye dumped her carry-on bags and purse into six different plastic tubs. The conveyor belt strained under the weight of her possessions, but rolled them though the X-ray chamber. The guard monitoring the screen slept as Butterflye shuffled her luggage through the appropriate stops.

Behind Butterflye stood a particularly attractive man with a thick five-o'clock shadow. And it was only eleven-thirty in the morning. Black glasses perched above his enormous nose and square mustache. The man bore an amazing resemblance to one of Butterflye's favorite dead movie stars, Groucho Marx. The stranger handed his passport to the guard.

"First name," the guard asked.

"Stanley, but my friends call me Stanley."

Stanley emptied his pockets and walked into the X-ray chamber. The outline on the screen displayed the silhouette of a man, as well as a bazooka, Uzi, battering ram, flamethrower, torpedo, pipe, knife, candlestick, scimitar and a chicken, none of which the X-ray guard caught. Instead of examining the video display, the guard turned his *Naked Pussies* magazine lengthways and pulled down the foldout, exposing two hairless Sphinx cats grooming each other. He waved Stanley on. The door slid open and he exited the compartment.

Stanley reclaimed his possessions from multiple plastic bowls, pocketing brass knuckles, two grenades, a Saturday night special, switchblade, icepick, hammer, rope, Bowie knife, ninja throwing star and a tampon. As Stanley returned the smaller items to his overnight bag, the security guard scrutinized the pocketbook of the middle-aged woman behind him in line. "Hey, what's this?" He held up a bottle of prescription eye drops. "That's more than three ounces."

An armor-clad bomb squad moved in. A German shepherd thrust his nose in her crotch and growled at the trembling woman. The guard nodded to a bomb technician who dragged her out of line and behind a transparent wall. A gray Extra Terrestrial strip-searched her. A second ET entered the room with an anal probe.

Butterflye watched the commotion as she put her shoes back on. She quickly made her way toward the gangway. "Man, they're strict."

She handed the uniformed greeter her still-smoldering boarding pass. He scanned it. As he handed Butterflye her Have-A-Blast card, the monitor beeped. "Hmm. There seems to be a discrepancy between the stateroom listed on your boarding pass and the suite assigned to you." He raised his hand. A moment later the third officer arrived.

"I knew it." Butterflye dug through her purse and pulled out her wallet. "How much do I owe? I had a feeling Satan would stick me with the fare."

The officer placed his hand on hers. "Ms. Plague, I'm afraid your money is no good here."

"Oh, great! Are you telling me she cut off my credit card again?"

"No," Number Three said. "I'm telling you that all aspects of your cruise are paid for up front with no additional cost required. I see you're also scheduled to go on three shore excursions."

"Really? Where am I going?"

"It looks like you're going skydiving, on a shark encounter, and on a submarine sea life adventure. Sounds like fun."

She imagined the nausea she'd experience plummeting toward the Earth at 190 miles per hour. "Lucky me," she said unenthusiastically.

"I'll take you to your stateroom." The third officer flagged the waiter holding a tray of bubbling champagne flutes. "Would you like a glass of Moët?"

"Sure." She reached for the glass, then hesitated. "How much is it?"

"On the house."

She took a sip, then noticed Stanley had managed to stay near her in line. From behind the glasses, Stanley winked at her. Butterflye smiled back. He must be a fan of her music.

"Follow me." The third officer picked up Butterflye's carry-ons. "Your trunk will be delivered to your room in a few minutes."

Butterflye kneeled to retrieve her purse. Suddenly the waiter who'd given her the Moët fell back, a throwing star lodged deeply in his throat.

"Wow. People need to be careful with those things. Someone could get hurt," Butterflye said to no one in particular.

Carrying only a glass of champagne and her handbag that could have put Arnold Schwarzenegger in a truss, Butterflye trailed behind the officer to the lift. Instead of descending into the bowels of the ship as Butterflye expected, the glass elevator rose higher and higher, making the people below appear the size of ants.

"I'm surprised," Butterflye said. "I expected to be below the waterline, just above the engines."

"I think you'll find these accommodations more acceptable."

As they approached a door labeled "Presidential Suite," an armed ship's security guard held a guy wearing a Trump Signature silk suit in a choke hold. The cruise director and two other ship security guards struggled to restrain the irate man. They hauled the flailing passenger past Butterflye.

What kind of riffraff travels in this part of the ship? I hope they're not violent.

"The Presidential Suite should be mine, not some Miss Universe wannabe's!" the struggling man shouted, pointing in fury at Butterflye.

"I don't give a rat's rear what your boarding pass says," the guard said. "The manifest says you're on Deck Zero, far aft, interior."

The man pulled his cell phone from his coat pocket. "I'm calling my guys."

"Whatever floats your boat, Mr. Rump."

"That's Trump."

"Whatever."

Trump poked his phone and glared at the screen. "Where the hell are you guys? You're supposed to be protecting me!"

"We're in the hot tub outside your suite," a man said, sounding flustered. "You were asleep—"

"You're fired," Trump yelled.

"Um, you can't fire us," the man said. "We're assigned as your detail by—"

"Then get your lazy butts out here and do your damned jobs!"

Within moments, the door to the Presidential Suite opened and three men wearing only earpieces, *Squalor of the Sea* towels and holstered pistols, darted out. A fourth man forgot his towel, but covered his assets with a wad of black suits, ties and white shirts. The men followed Trump and the ship security guards toward the elevator.

"This isn't over yet," Trump said, stuffing his phone into his back pocket.

"I'm sorry for the disturbance, Mrs. Plague." The third officer swiped her Have-A-Blast card and reopened the door.

"Was that Donald Trump?" Butterflye asked

He returned the card to her. "Yes. He thinks he's God."

"That's funny," Butterflye said. "Sara Lee said God appears to her dressed kind of like Donald Trump."

As the third officer gave her a discrete sidelong glance that labeled her eccentric, Butterflye peeked inside. The suite name notwithstanding, she already knew what she would see: a room slightly larger than a Kleenex® box with bunk beds and bathroom with all the amenities of a portable construction toilet. Instead she found a massive suite, with a wall of picture windows, which gave an unimpeded view of the Port of Galveston. A grand piano sat in the corner.

Butterflye stepped inside and did a three-sixty. She felt like Dorothy entering Oz. Her living room was bigger than hers at home. The cabin held a bar, a sixty-inch curved-screen TV, and a bedroom with a king-sized bed. "Are you sure this is my stateroom?

"Absolutely. I hope you're pleased with the Presidential Suite."

"Wow, Satan certainly was generous. I have a balcony?"

"A patio. It runs the entire length of your suite." Number Three opened the sliding glass door. "You have a hot tub out here and the most impressive vista on the ship." He switched on the bathroom light. "There's also a Jacuzzi in the master bath."

"Wow. Look at all the mirrors!" Butterflye gave her makeup a quick check. "Oh, no. Is that a gray hair?" She turned back to the officer. "Are you sure this is my room? I can't believe my boss would spring for something this luxurious."

"No mistake. This will be your home for the next thirty-one days."

"Excellent." She handed him the empty champagne glass. "Would you be a dear and freshen this up for me?"

"Of course. I'll send your steward." Heaving and grunting, he carried her bags into the bedroom. "Your trunk should arrive any time. If you need anything, anything at all, just ask your steward, Fred."

"Fred? Thank goodness. When I've taken other cruises, I've had problems understanding the steward's English."

There was a knock at the door. A strapping Helvetica steward wearing a name tag that read, "Fred, New Jersey" stood just outside.

"Weajwejld dsrkrjwaaw oawtjwes sktj, Mrs. Plague. Awer serw ji erea klje?"

"That's Plague-Pestilence," Butterflye corrected him.

"Huh?" He pointed at her trunk and a shiny red child's suitcase, shaped like a car. "Dwe a dier dert drwl?"

"In the bedroom."

He deposited the luggage, grabbed the empty flute and turned to leave. "Tre giem dopler winces broeke. Novuem feil dyr."

"Hey, that little Volkswagen bag isn't mine. I think you delivered it to me by mistake."

Fred nodded knowingly, but Butterflye suspected he didn't understand her any more than she did him.

"Elog weriu axdrol oewrip."

Fred and Number Three exited, leaving Butterflye alone in her own little Heaven, at least for thirty-one days.

Out of curiosity, she unlatched the red VW suitcase. It looked just like a 1960s Beetle with yellow plastic headlights. It was stuffed full of toddler t-shirts, diapers and one very ugly crocheted baby bonnet. "I'll have to find out who this belongs to later." She opened her trunk and pulled out a couple of outfits to hang up. No telling what she'd find in there. After all, Satan surprised her with a cruise-as-you-are party. On top of the pile of wadded up clothes, Butterflye found a present wrapped in taped-together requisition forms with a couple of bloody hand prints on it.

"Aw, isn't that sweet? Satan wrapped it herself."

Butterflye pulled the gift out of the trunk. A note, scrawled in red, said, "Better not open before Halloween."

Butterflye poised her fingers over the corner of the wrapping, then stopped. She'd honor her boss's wish and unwrap it the last day of her cruise. Knowing Satan, she'd have sensors to alert her to a premature revelation. Butterflye placed it, out of sight, out of mind, in the top drawer of the burled oak dresser.

She returned to unpacking the trunk. Beneath her trademark leopard Scala gown, the gold sequined Michael Kors blouse seemed to come alive. One brown antenna popped out from beneath the spaghetti straps, then another. Butterflye jumped back and shrieked. Finally a two-foot-long Madagascar hissing cockroach emerged as if being born. He flexed his wings and scrambled out of the trunk.

Butterflye clutched her chest. "Oh my God, Ralph. You nearly scared me to death." She giggled at the irony of her statement.

He scurried over and rubbed his head against her legs.

"Ralph, you shouldn't have come. They don't permit pets on this ship."

He looked up adoringly at his Butterflye. *Damn those puppy dog eyes.* He pressed his antenna down against his head and spread his mandibles.

She stroked his shell. "Oh, all right. We'll think of something."

"Suppose someone grabs you like this," Adam said, wrapping an arm around Bunny's waist.

Bunny countered by cupping his neck, then kissing him. Adam's hold melted into an embrace. She loved it when Adam substituted for Michael as her Heavenly trainer.

Up until he sighed. A lot of people sighed in frustration, Bunny noted.

"No, no, no," he said. "That's not how you break a hold."

"You loosened your grip," Bunny argued.

"Sure, a kiss works on me, but I'm trying to teach you to defend yourself against anyone. You gotta take this seriously."

Bunny smoothed the beaded lace bodice of her orchid pink gown—which looked orchid white, since she was in Heaven where all clothes were white. "I'm pretty sure *my* kiss will work on *anybody*."

"Because I understand women," he started, adding the mutter, "as well as any man does," before continuing, "I won't argue the point. But as often as you visit Earth, you need to know basic self-defense—especially since Satan is giving you a vacation. You do remember the dangers, don't you?"

"I know. Die on vacation and it's poof forever."

"Then let's practice," Adam said firmly.

"I can use a sword," Bunny said. It wasn't all that different from twirling a baton.

Adam lifted an eyebrow, and his mouth twisted into his patented half-grin/half-smirk. "Sweetheart, are you doing any better with Semyaza's training than Michael's?"

"Why do you ask?"

He rubbed the back of his neck, one of his nervous habits. "Some of the things Michael says concern me."

"Michael says I'm dangerous with a sword."

"I was there, darling. He said, 'You're a danger to yourself.'"

Bunny wrinkled her nose in dislike, her number one signal she was about to be mad.

Adam picked up on the warning, because he raised his hands in surrender. "We've practiced enough for the day. Just remember what I said. *Anything* can be a weapon. If you're ever caught unaware—and someone does attack you, however unlikely that is—look around for something heavy and blunt, or something sharp, or something that will give you reach."

"That sounds silly, but fine, *anything* can be a weapon." As the words bounced around Bunny's brain, she mused a bit. "If *anything* can be a weapon, then *everything* belongs to War."

"It doesn't work like that," Adam said.

"Whatever. I'm bored with talk about weapons."

"All right," Adam said, "how about we talk about names?"

"Names are a good idea," Bunny said. "I'm all for them. Without them, we'd just call everyone 'Hey, you.'"

"That's not what I meant. I was hoping to convince you to call me Pernell."

Bunny wrinkled her nose again, this time in confusion, tinged with a faint recollection of having heard that name before. She studied Adam, a striking cowboy in black—currently turned white. She thought of other famous cowboys, all named after Indian tribes: Cheyenne, Sioux, Bronco and Maverick. "Oh, I see. It's an Indian nickname, like Cheyenne or Maverick."

"Bunny, it's just my name."

"I get it. But Cheyenne, Bronco and Maverick had *real* names besides. Like Adam is your *real* name."

Adam let out a slow breath and seemed to be counting. "If it helps, Pernell is slang for 'cowboy in black.'"

"I thought that was Johnny Cash."

"He's the Man in Black," Adam said.

Bunny shrugged. "I only know he sang a lot of songs about cowboys—like 'A Boy Named Sioux.'"

A harried angel, her gown spotted with the remnants of breakfast—eggs, syrup and sausage—hurried toward them. A little breathless, she said, "Bunny, your minions are looking for you."

After searching her memory, Bunny recognized Angelina with the crooked halo. "Did they sneak into Heaven?"

"No," Angelina said. "Somehow they hacked Peter's computer and sent a message that they got your voicemail. They also sent a hundred spam emails and a wicked computer virus." The angel grinned. "You should see Peter. He's so mad, he's about to burst out of his leather pants."

"I guess I'd better go." Bunny gazed into Adam's honey-brown eyes and lingered. "I suppose Michael will be back next week."

He grinned wolfishly. "You'd be surprised how many emergencies can come up requiring an archangel's attention." He stroked her cheek, gave her a kiss, then said, "Remember what I said. Weapons are all around you."

Bunny nodded to appease him—as if she could be bothered to remember something so useless. Right now, all she wanted to remember was why she'd left a voicemail with Wreak and Havoc.

Using her Heavenly-access portal, she reappeared in her Pink Palace, her place of work. The thought of work made Bunny chuckle. Why work when she had all the money she wanted?

No more carte blanche. Oh. Right. That was why she'd summoned Wreak and Havoc.

Bunny found the Redheads' shared minions waiting on her front porch. "We have an emergency, boys."

Quickly, Bunny explained about Satan's conniption fit and how she'd taken away all of Bunny's funds. Throwing her arms in the air in imitation, Bunny fumed. "How can she expect me to work without money? Doesn't she know War is expensive?"

"Um, Bunny," Wreak said, "when you say 'war,' are you talking about actual campaigns or yourself?"

Bunny perched her fists on her hips. "Of course I meant me! Now what are you two going to do about this disaster?"

"What can we do, Mistress of Destruction?" Havoc asked.

"It's not like we can hack Satan's bank account," Wreak said with a faraway gaze. He hummed. "Or could we?"

"We *could*," Havoc said, "but that's not the point. If Satan catches us, there'd be Hell to pay. Or have you forgotten what it was like before, in the Pit?"

Wreak scratched his chin thoughtfully. "Maybe we could put Bunny on a budget?"

All three of them laughed.

"No, really," Bunny said, "what are *we* going to do?"

"We?" Wreak shook his head. "Oh, you mean what are *we* going to do," he said, indicating himself and Havoc with a waggle of his finger.

"Exactly," Bunny said. "Now hop to it!"

As Wreak and Havoc headed for the door, they murmured between themselves. But Bunny caught one of them saying, "We may *have* to put her on a budget."

Ha, Bunny thought. *I'd go on a diet first.*

Sara Lee stepped through the iron gates to the Main Concourse of Wrigley Field. She inhaled the delectable scents of yeasty beer, fried food and sugar. And, unfortunately, mold—a problem with many old places. But the food smells dominated.

October was both National Pizza Month and National Dessert Month. She should honor that. But which to eat first? Decisions,

decisions. Better to eat dessert first, just in case. After all, Hell probably had frozen over. The Cubs were in the World Series.

Wreak and Havoc somehow got Sara Lee a seat in left field, behind the Cubs dugout, for the deciding Game 7. She wore extra-stretchy leggings, her favorite high-heeled black boots and the Cubs jersey that Oscar had bought her years ago. At that time, it had hung on her then-much-smaller frame. Now it fit all too well.

Oscar had been a huge Cubs fan. He always rooted for the underdog—although historically, famine wasn't kind to underdogs. He and Sara Lee had gone to several Cubs games over the years. She felt like she owed it to him to see them play in the World Series. And now she wouldn't feel bad about eating a hotdog when Oscar couldn't—though she'd gladly give up every bite of food if Oscar could be with her again.

You should get back to work, you lazy bitch.

That voice sounded like Satan. Sara Lee could do with fewer voices in her head—though not as few as Bunny had. Maybe this was how Joan of Arc had felt.

Or maybe not. Sara Lee wasn't exactly a saint.

After loading up with a hot fudge sundae in a real batter's helmet (none of those mini-helmets for her!), an extra-large Giordano's pizza with everything on it, a hotdog with ketchup and mustard and an ice-cold Green Line beer so big it would give a Spring Breaker pause, Sara Lee staggered toward Section 115.

The usher at the entrance said, "Ticket?"

She handed him the pizza box, set the hotdog, sundae and beer on top of it, and dug inside her purse. As she handed the man the stub, he asked, "Is that hotdog kosher?"

She did a double-take. "Jesus? I thought you were over your mid-afterlife crisis."

"Oh, I pretty much am."

"Then why are you here, dressed like an usher?"

He grinned. "You don't think the Cubs got here on their own, do you?"

"Isn't it unfair to help one team over the others?"

"Just evening the scales." Jesus leaned in confidentially. "Satan's been helping the other team. That musical 'Damned Yankees'? Based on a true story."

"Figures."

Jesus showed Sara Lee to her seat and helped her get

nested with her food.

"You know, I'm really glad to see you *here*," he said.

"Me too. This is my first vacation since Oscar and the other Horsemen fell into oblivion."

"Gotta get back to work," Jesus said, tipping his ball cap. "Try not to make yourself sick."

Sara Lee had arrived early, wanting to savor the pre-game environment—and the ballpark food. She took a heaping spoonful of her sundae. As the delightful contrast of cold ice cream and hot fudge played across her tongue, she turned her attention to the field. The Cubs were hosting some sort of children's pre-game event. A boy in a batting helmet stood at home plate, bat cocked and ready. A man standing beside a pitching machine pushed a button. The machine belched out a ball. The boy swung and missed.

Cute idea—as long as no kid gets beaned. Even as a former lawyer, Sara Lee couldn't help but consider potential liability issues. It was a sickness.

The bleachers on the buildings surrounding Wrigley Field teamed with partying fans. She turned her gaze to the old-fashioned, manual scoreboard. The first time she and Oscar had come to Wrigley, they took a tour and got to see inside—

Something whooshed past her ear. After a meaty thunk behind her, someone screamed.

Sara Lee turned to see a spectator lying on the stairs, blood pouring from his cracked skull. Nearby, an adorable, blonde-haired girl raised a bloody ball in triumph.

"I got it!" she cried.

"That's great, sweetie," the child's father said, his gaze on his phone. "Now go wash it off."

Sara Lee instinctively reached for her purse to get a business card, then remembered she didn't practice law anymore. Jesus trotted down the stairs and touched the downed fan. He immediately revived, his skull healed. Jesus helped him to his feet.

Another ball whooshed past Sara Lee and struck a fan two rows back whose gaze was likewise glued to his phone. Blood spurted from the man's nose. Crying out in dismay, he wiped the screen with his sleeve. The little blonde girl raced after the second bloody ball. Smart kid. World Series balls would fetch good money on eBay.

Sara Lee turned back to the field. The pitching machine

was aimed squarely her way. Another ball shot toward her. Sara Lee dove behind the seats in front of her. Peeking over the top, she saw the ball strike a beer vendor in the wrist. He screamed in pain and dropped his tray of filled cups, sending a waterfall of foamy beer down the steps. Sara Lee sighed. What a waste.

Jesus rushed to the vendor's aid.

The man running the pitching machine pushed against it, but it didn't budge. Another ball streaked toward Sara Lee. She ducked. Groaning in resignation, she dumped the ice cream from the batting helmet, wiped it out with a crumpled napkin, then put it on her head. Better safe than brain dead—or obliviated.

Ball after ball rained down on Section 115. People dropped like target ducks at a carnival. Jesus squinted out onto the field. After a wave of his hand, the ball machine squealed and bucked. Black smoke poured out of it, then it shuddered and died.

"Thanks!" Sara Lee said. "Though you could have done that *before* I dumped my sundae."

"I'll buy you another," Jesus said, frowning at the defunct ball machine.

"Oh, no need. I have pizza—" The box at Sara Lee's feet lay crushed. Her spirits followed. She must have landed on it when she ducked for cover. Cheese glued the cardboard lid shut. Her beer had overturned and mixed with the rapidly melting ice cream. Sara Lee could have cried.

But the ballpark had no shortage of food. And thanks to Wreak and Havoc's hacking of Donald Trump's bank accounts, Sara Lee had no shortage of funds. As Jesus worked at healing the wounded, she headed back to the concession stands.

She'd no sooner settled in with a fresh pizza when someone sat in the seat beside hers. After a few moments, she felt the weight of a stare. She turned to find a twenty-something man smiling at her. He wore an expensive suit and blood-red silk tie and matching pocket square. He sat with perfect posture, even in the uncomfortable folding seat.

Sara Lee blinked hard. "Jimmy Dean?"

Oscar's younger brother inclined his head. Oscar had had the same regal bearing when he and Sara Lee first met. But after much work, she'd surgically removed the stick from his butt.

"What are you doing here?" he asked. "I never thought to see a familiar face."

Not that familiar. Oscar and Jimmy Dean had fallen out over something or other right before the wedding, and Oscar pretty much cut his brother out of his life. The rest of their family must have backed Jimmy Dean, for Oscar cut them out too. Sara Lee had tried to get Oscar to mend fences, but the cause of his estrangement to his family was the one thing he refused to talk about. Given how screwed up her own family was, Sara Lee hadn't pushed.

"I couldn't resist seeing the Cubs in the World Series," Sara Lee said.

Jimmy Dean stared out across the field. "Oscar brought me here the last time the Cubs won the World Series."

"In 1908?" Sara Lee shook her head. "Sometimes it's hard to remember that you and Oscar have had such long lives—afterlives."

A wistful smile played across his lips. "Yes, we used to go everywhere together."

Sara Lee's heart ached. Losing Oscar must have hurt Jimmy Dean as much as it had her, maybe more, since they'd parted on bad terms. "He'd love that we're both here, Jimmy Dean."

"Please, call me JD," he said with a pained expression.

"Sorry. Oscar always referred to you as Jimmy Dean." She took a swig of her new Green Line beer. It was ice-cold and hoppy, just the way she liked it.

"And I suppose you never called your brother by a name that annoyed him?" JD asked.

Sara Lee snorted beer through her nose. His expression bland, JD handed her a napkin, and she mopped it off her face.

"Oh, I had tons of pet names for Duncan Hines Malloy," she said. "Cake Man, Fudgie, Dough Boy—"

JD raised an eyebrow, his blue eyes sparkling. "Isn't that casting stones?"

"I was lots thinner then," Sara Lee said, surprised she didn't feel offended. Maybe it was because his expressions were so like Oscar's. Physically, the brothers hadn't looked much alike. Oscar was skeletally thin and kept his mouse-brown hair in a buzz cut, while JD had an athletic build and wavy dark brown hair. Oscar's eyes were pale blue and JD's were an intense sapphire. Not that looks mattered much to Sara Lee. She'd loved Oscar for his intelligence, personality and wit. Fortunately, he'd felt the same way about her. In an anti-fat society, it had been refreshing.

"Well, looky here."

At the sound of Satan's voice, Sara Lee and JD froze.

"If it isn't the picture of familial harmony. I just might puke." Satan stood at the end of the row. She sported an A-Rod jersey and a Yankees ball cap. Behind her, in matching garb and carrying foam fingers with the middle finger raised, stood the Librarian from Hell, along with Joy—the widow of the Anti-Christ—Mike from Tech Support, and Sara Lee's former assistant Little Debbie.

"Ah, now the pitching machine incident makes sense," Sara Lee said drily. "As does your 'kind' offer of vacation."

"I wouldn't have to stoop to such methods if *someone* would do their job," Satan said with a meaningful glare.

Sara Lee sighed in resignation. "So what's stopping you from killing me now?"

Satan rolled her eyes. "God sent me a missive." In a squeaky voice, she said, "'I don't like to interfere, but ... I really don't like it when *you* interfere. So stop it!' He never lets me have any fun." Satan's glare shifted to JD. "You two look awfully cozy."

JD flushed. "I told you, I won't be coerced ... into rooting for the Yankees—unlike these flunkies."

"Hey, we're not flunkies," Little Debbie protested.

The Librarian smirked. "Nooo. Just because we pretty much do whatever Satan wants doesn't make us flunkies. Oh, wait. It does."

"At last," Satan said. "Someone who understands their place in the scheme of things." She swept a hand to indicate JD's suit. "Who are you supposed to be—the freaking Commissioner of Baseball? Buy a jersey—a Yankee's jersey—and get on the right team." She slapped him on the back hard enough to rock him. "Enjoy the game—while you can. Just remember, if you keep this crap up, there'll be Hell to pay."

Satan stomped off, her entourage following.

"Too bad the Cubs don't stand a chance," JD said, his expression bland, as though Satan's threats didn't concern him. "It's unfortunate that Satan is backing the Yankees."

Sara Lee offered JD a slice of pizza. "Have faith."

"I have complete faith in Satan." JD pinned her with a challenging stare. "Where do you place your faith, *Famine*?"

She rejected the idea of telling him about Jesus. "Hey, the Cubs made it this far." She offered the pizza again.

"True," JD said, taking the slice. "Anything *might* happen."

"So, is it cliché to spend part of our honeymoon at Niagara Falls?" Zoe shouted to be heard over the water's roar.

"Probably, but for once it would be nice to experience an iconic world wonder without having to work."

"We do have an inordinate number of pickups here, don't we?" Zoe considered, then shook her head. "And that's a cheery thought. Let's not let work ruin our vacation. It really is pretty here."

"Especially without broken barrels on the rocks." Jake leaned out over the rail. "Yep, right about ... there ... that's the spot."

Zoe glanced over the rail but didn't lean the way Jake did. She was deathly—and yes, she recognized the irony—afraid of heights. She admitted it to Jake during their courtship, though she'd deny it to anyone else. She'd look across the picturesque Falls but never, ever *down.*

"Um, gee, Jake, I'm sure it's great and all, but don't we need to be heading toward the boat?"

"What? Oh, yeah, right. The *Maid of the Mist* tour," Jake sounded uncertain. "We're doing the tourist thing, aren't we?"

"According to the guidebooks, it is the best way to see the Falls, and I thought you liked boats."

"About as much as you like heights." Jake shuddered. "But if you really want to ... let's go."

"There are other things we can do." She pulled him away from the rail and linked her arm through his just as a scream brought a flock of tourists rushing to the railing. Zoe counted far too high before hearing the splash over the roar of the Falls. "We could take a nice walk through the botanical gardens. Or check out old Fort Niagara. Seventeenth century history. Could be fun."

"Have I mentioned lately that you have strange taste in fun?" He pulled her closer to him as they left the leering crowd behind.

"I love history too, and though it was before your ... time, I thought you might enjoy it."

Jake grinned. "Oh, I've been to the fort before. Several times. It was a working military installation for a long time—lots of people stationed here. It was kind of sad when they turned it into a museum."

"I hadn't thought of it that way. So you don't want to go?"

"Oh, I want to go. I want to see how accurate they made the museum. It's always fun to play *Where's Waldo* with history." He guided her through the late-blooming autumn flower beds lining the sidewalks. "Let's go. We can mess with the tour guides."

"Now who has strange ideas of fun?" Zoe asked.

Zoe and Jake sailed through the ticket booth after dodging EMTs swarming the Falls. They encountered no lines.

"Guess we hit it at a *dead* time," she said attempting to wiggle her eyebrows.

"Really? Death puns? You?" Jake's voice deadpan. "Too easy."

"Come on, honey, vacation. Let me have a sense of humor." Zoe pulled him along, walking backward.

"Yeah, but at least make an *effort*." Looking around, Jake clucked his tongue and shook his head in clear disappointment. "No. No. No."

Zoe turned to see a bunch of actors dressed in what looked to her like British uniforms from 1812. "What's wrong?"

"I was. This isn't *Where's Waldo*; it's a Hidden Objects puzzle. You know, find the ten errors in the pictures? So many random little inaccuracies make all of this … sad."

"Cut them a little slack for modern textiles and such, Jake. Besides, they're working off books and pictures. They don't have your … scope of knowledge and … experience…" She let the sentence falter as his expression shifted to hurt.

"Thanks for not coming out and saying I'm old." His tone dripped with sarcasm.

"You know what I mean, honey. I love your attention to detail." She knew she dug her hole deeper, but couldn't seem to stop.

"Let's change the subject," he said as they passed a unit in firing formation. A shot rang out from a reenactor's Baker rifle. Zoe felt a puff of air and a sting on her ear. A chunk flew out of the post downwind of her. Zoe whipped around, slapping a hand to her ear, as Jake dragged her to the ground.

"What just happened?" Zoe struggled to her feet.

"I think we were shot at." When no other shots fired, Jake stumbled upright and helped Zoe regain her balance.

"Don't be ridiculous. No one would shoot at tourists."

Jake, checking out the post, pointed at the hole. "That's a bullet hole. It barely missed you. Us."

Before his words fully registered, a museum official scurried up, in full obsequious *please don't sue us* mode. The middle-aged suit stumbled over his apologies.

"Rest assured, ma'am, what just happened here was purely an accident."

Zoe blinked at the obsequious middle-manager. Confusion burned away as his words registered. "*Excuse me?*"

"Let it go, dear," Jake said, laying a gentle hand on her arm. "He doesn't know."

Fortunately the manager missed the exchange and plunged ahead. "An investigation is underway. The cast member is already being disciplined for the unconscionable breach of safety protocols."

Zoe glanced over to where a twenty-something actor huddled on the ground, surrounded by other actors and guys in Security emblazoned Day-Glo shirts. The young man's freaked out expression tore at her. He seemed to be crying a little as guards battered him with questions.

"But it wasn't even supposed to be loaded!" As terror sank in, the boy looked even younger than he probably was. "And I didn't *mean* ... it just went off! I swear. I wouldn't shoot at anyone for *real!*"

The manager pulled Zoe along. "Come with me, please. Let's get you get out of this ... place and into someplace ... quieter."

"And without confessions going on, would be my guess." Jake muttered so only Zoe could hear. She snorted back a laugh, turning it into a cough.

"I'm sure it was a freak accident," she said. "It didn't come anywhere near me."

"Um, Zoe, your ear's *bleeding.*" Jake grabbed her shoulders and stared in horror at the side of her head.

Zoe shrugged off his grip to touch her ear. Her fingers came back with a red smear. "Oh, it's a scratch. I'm fine."

"It not *fine!* It's bleeding on *Earth.*" Jake's tone sounded a bit strangled. "You're *vulnerable.* You have to be more careful."

Two hours and a pile of fine print paperwork later, Zoe and Jake left Fort Niagara with writer's cramp and some gift shop swag. Zoe turned the coffee mug in her hand while they walked.

"Hey, it's one of those changeable mugs. When it's cold, the soldiers are British. When hot is added, the soldiers change to

American."

"Funny." Jake stretched his fingers. "I haven't used a pen that much since Willie and I collected all those fairy tales."

"I guess when an organization perceives litigation, they get very, very comprehensive." Zoe sighed.

"Okay, so which of the Horsewomen put *that* into play? You? Plague? Wasn't Famine a lawyer in her other life?"

"It may have been one of those joint things we came up with over drinks at the Sulfur Well. I don't remember because ... drinks. It's effective though."

"I'll bet. Come on. Let's go find something for dinner. Maybe take that walk around the botanical gardens."

"Or we could just go back to the hotel—"

Zoe felt herself lurching along behind Jake as he pulled her back toward the hotel, the boat ride and botanical gardens completely forgotten.

An hour or so later, they finally came up for air and electrolyte replenishment. Zoe reminded herself of the *other* agenda for this trip.

"We have to figure out where to find any of my remaining relatives," Zoe said after the room service waiter left their tray.

"I've done some research into that." Jake pulled a tablet out of the quiver of the Cupid-carved night stand of their satin and bedazzle covered honeymoon suite.

"A tablet? Really?"

"How else did you expect to Skype with Bambi? And yes, I know about the app. Remember the one I used on our first date? Besides, the genealogy sites all have apps, and this is way more portable than a laptop, and easier to read than a smart phone."

"Good point." Zoe bit into her heart-shaped hamburger and let the juicy goodness dribble down her chin. Food did taste better on Earth, and for a brief moment, she truly felt for Sarah Lee and hoped Famine enjoyed her time on Earth. Zoe shook her head to focus on Jake. "So? What did you find?"

"There are three different family lines you could be related to. They're scattered across the country, but fortunately, they all seem to be having reunions this month." Jake shifted on the satin bedspread and nearly slid off the kitschy, heart-shaped bed. Zoe grabbed his plate while he saved the tablet.

"Yeah, amazing coincidence that." Zoe didn't bother to contain her sarcasm. "Wonder who nudged *that* one along—

God or Satan? Not that it matters. We might as well get to it. When's the first one?"

"Not until after we stop in New York."

Chapter Three

Bunny sorted through her email—many important advertisements for sales, many more unimportant messages from the Pentagon or U.N. marked "urgent." All the Pentagon ever wanted was a "go ahead" for an assault, terms for peace and money for weaponry and vehicles. The U.N. always wanted money to fund a study. Like she cared about any of it.

Someone knocked at the rear door.

Ignoring the insistent pounding as more of Hell's constant, annoying background noise, Bunny deleted the nuisance messages in her inbox. "Sorry, boys, War is broke." If they wanted new "toys," they'd have to pony up the cash themselves—or hold a bake sale or maybe a garage sale.

The portal leading to Ares's training grounds gave off a faint hum, something Bunny had never noticed, but then, she'd never been sitting in her Pink Palace when someone arrived from there before. Semyaza, wearing his usual leather jacket with holes for his large, black, bat-like wings, strode forth.

"You didn't answer your door," he said.

"Hello to you too," Bunny replied.

"Why didn't you answer?"

"Because I wasn't expecting anyone," Bunny said. "And you know how annoying those door-to-door salesmen are."

"What door-to-door salesmen?" Semyaza asked.

"All those idiotic demons and imps prattling on about something or other. Who listens?"

Semyaza raised his gaze upwards, shook his head, then muttered, "Lord, is there any chance I can redeem myself and get out of here?" Then he exhaled loudly and muttered, "I didn't think so." To Bunny, he said, "Those idiotic demons and imps were messengers from Satan, probably reminding you of meetings you're always missing."

"What meetings?"

"War councils, reports to Satan on Earth's relevant current events, and you're supposed to greet *your* officers every time one of them ends up down here."

Bunny dismissed all that with a wave. "For a minute I thought you were serious. Have I missed a training session?"

"Several, but who cares? I'm here because *Satan is sending a message*. She wants to remind you that you have an actual vacation on Earth and, and I quote, 'I'll be damned if any of those screw-ups doesn't take advantage of my rare and uncharacteristic generosity.'"

"What's the point in going to Earth if I'm out of money?"

"You're asking the wrong person," Semyaza said. "I don't see the point in the whole planet or its ape-descended inhabitants. Frankly, I'm disappointed you girls didn't pull off the Apocalypse early. If you'll take a little friendly advice ... take the vacation." He whipped around, flinging his wings, and stomped out in a classic fallen angel huff.

About then, her phone played the song "War," Wreak's and Havoc's ringtone.

The moment she answered, they started yammering. "We have a budget for you," they chimed. "So will you answer your front door?"

As Bunny headed to the door, she wondered if she'd missed their knocking during Semyaza's lecture or if she was starting to ignore knocking on principle.

As soon as she opened the door, she said, "I hope you remembered a generous allowance for shoes ... and gowns ... and salon days ... and grooming bills for my horse Devastation and the Poodles of War. Oh, and for jewelry ... and gym expenses. I can't cut Candace's salary just because Satan is cheap." As Bunny smoothed her hands along her firm thighs, she added, "That girl is worth every penny."

"I notice you didn't mention *our* salaries," Wreak said.

"Cuts have to be made somewhere," Bunny said. "But I figure you still have money coming from the other three Redheads."

"Yeah," Havoc drawled out, "but Zoe makes us jump through all sorts of red-tape hoops for a paycheck, Butterflye is always saying the 'check's in the mail,' and Sara Lee just laughs at our bill and says, 'I'll let you boys know when you've earned it.' You were the only one who paid whatever we asked, no questions, no audits, no complaints."

"Still, you boys should be able to manage on just three million a month."

Wreak and Havoc looked at each other.

"Right," Wreak said. "As if *they've* ever paid a million for our services."

"Hey, does that mean I've been over-paying?" Bunny parked her fists on her hips.

"No one else has us cleaning out stables or picking up dog poop," Wreak said.

"Anyway, Mistress of Destruction," Havoc said, "we have a budget that might be workable."

"Can't I just have a garage sale?" If the Pentagon could do it, why not her?

"I know I'll regret this," Wreak said, "but what would you sell?"

"Follow me." Bunny led them through four hallways in her fifty-two room mansion before reaching a locked door. She took the key from atop the door frame and opened the door with a flourish. "Voila! The junk room."

Bunny strolled inside while Wreak and Havoc stumbled in like awe-struck zombies. Paintings covered the walls. Those that wouldn't fit were stacked in a corner. A dozen marble and bronze statues stood evenly spaced throughout the room. Busts rested on pedestals. Vases from China filled one corner. In another, a bunch of old musical instruments sat on shelves.

"Junk room?" Wreak said.

"What else would you call it?" Bunny asked, drawing a line through the dust on a gilded picture frame.

"A treasure trove, maybe," Havoc said.

Bunny snorted. "Treasure is gold and jewelry. This"—she waved at all the stuff—"is old souvenir crap that Ares collected."

Wreak headed for a stack of paintings, while Havoc circled a statue of a frowning woman standing with her arms crossed and her foot with the toe raised liked she was tapping it.

"I don't believe it," Havoc said. "It actually exists!"

"What exists?" Wreak asked, digging through the paintings.

"It's Rodan's woman, called *The Motivator*. She was supposed to be displayed behind *The Thinker*. You know ... behind every great man, that sort of thing. I thought it was just legend."

Wreak reached the back of the stack. "She's got at least three lost Van Goghs, a couple of Cezannes, a Rembrandt, a Manet, three Warhols and a da Vinci in just this stack!" Wreak flapped his arms. "I haven't even started on what's hanging."

"See?" Bunny said. "A bunch of foreign crap."

Wreak grabbed the top painting. "Why would you hang *Dogs*

Playing Poker in your living room when you have Van Gogh's *Le Pigeon Aux Petits Pois*?"

Bunny arched her brows and let out a low chuckle. "Pigeons? Does anything in that collection of badly drawn squares look like pigeons? Besides, how cool would it be if dogs could play poker? I've tried to teach the Poodles of War, but they just chew on the cards and pee on the chips."

"I like *Dogs Playing Poker*," Havoc said. "It's the Jesus on black velvet that I question."

"It glows in the dark," Bunny said. "And his eyes follow you."

Wreak, like a poodle with a bone, shook the Van Gogh he still held. "But *this* is a masterpiece!"

Bunny scoffed. "I can draw better than that, but I don't pretend my scribbles are works of art."

"So it's an acquired taste," Wreak said. He picked up another painting. "Here's a da Vinci I've never heard of—*Portrait of God*."

"Whoa," Havoc said, drawing closer as if approaching a fire. "That looks just like Him—though admittedly I've only ever seen Him once in a parade."

"He's in the Macy's Thanksgiving Parade *every* year," Bunny said. "He's the star." She squinted at the painting. "That doesn't look anything like God. Granted, the guy in the painting's got a beard, but where's the belly like a bowlful of jelly? What happened to the twinkle in His blue eyes and the rosy cheeks? And why would anyone paint God in a bath towel?"

"That's a toga," Wreak said. "Surely you recognize that. You did marry an ancient Greek."

"To be fair," Havoc interjected, "Bunny didn't know Ares in the olden days."

"Ares never wore a dress—except that one Halloween. He usually wore tight leather pants." Bunny sighed. Ares had cut such a dashing figure.

Wreak squinted upwards and mused, "It's eerie, but sometimes I'd swear I see Ares around Hell, skulking about the really shady parts."

"I didn't know Hell had any trees," Bunny said.

"Not that kind of shady," Wreak said.

Bunny shrugged. Canopies and awnings didn't provide the deep, cooling shade of a tree. Maybe she should talk to Satan about doing some landscaping. A few trees and flowers might improve Hell's New Jersey-like reputation.

"I know what you mean," Havoc said. "I thought I saw him too."

"Hmm?" Bunny searched her memory for the thread of conversation but found only images of her favorite shoes with matching feather boas. Ooh ... she should wear the open-toed fuchsia pair with the fuchsia and gold boa...

"I was saying I thought I'd seen Ares too," Havoc said.

That was the thread of conversation? Bunny shrugged. "You must've seen Mars, Ares's identical twin brother."

"Ares had a twin?" Wreak groaned. "Just what the world needs—another Ares."

Havoc waved Wreak quiet. "One moment, Divine Mistress. I thought Ares was Greek and Mars was Roman? How can they be twins?"

"Simple," Bunny answered, "Ares took after his mother."

"It doesn't work like that," Wreak said.

"It does too," Bunny said. "I don't know how many times I've heard that someone took after his mother or father."

"But if they're *identical* twins..." Wreak stared expectantly at Bunny. Then he sighed in surrender, suddenly reminding her of the French prime minister. "Never mind."

"What's important," Havoc said, "is now we can figure a new budget, if you're willing to sell some of this."

"You think it's worth a few hundred dollars?" Bunny asked.

"Oh, Mistress, it's worth a bit more than that," Havoc said.

"A few thousand dollars? Enough I could stay someplace nice while I'm vacationing on Earth?"

"Easily," Havoc assured her. "Tell us where you want to go, and we'll arrange everything."

"My sister lives in San Jose. She works at the yeti institute in Mountain View. Which is weird, because I was in a movie called *Bride of the Yeti* and that was set in Alaska, not California."

Wreak and Havoc stared at each other a moment, their eyes growing wider by the second.

Finally, Wreak blurted, "You mean the S.E.T.I. Institute?"

"Seti—yeti—whatever. She's some sort of astrologer."

"You mean astronomer?" Wreak said.

"Same thing," Bunny said. "They're what you call sameoldnames."

"I think you mean synonyms," Wreak said, "and no they're not. An astrologer claims to chart your destiny by the stars, while an astronomer seeks the answers to life, the universe and everything by studying the stars."

Bunny shrugged. "Like I said, same thing."

Havoc had wandered to the rack of instruments, many in old leather cases. Gingerly, he opened a case and shrieked, "It's a Stradivarius!"

"It's a fiddle," Bunny said.

"This *violin* is a work of art," Havoc exclaimed.

"It would be more useful if it were an actual fiddle," Bunny said.

Havoc lifted the violin from the case and examined it as though holding a baby. "It's named Rosebud."

Wreak smirked. "That would be a better use of the name 'Rosebud' as a dying breath than for than a sled."

"Really?" Bunny blinked. "Your last words were for a sled named Rosebud? Did you know Orson Wells made a movie about your life?"

"Those weren't my last words," Wreak said. "As I recall, I said something like 'No, you idiot, don't cross *those* wires.' Then I found myself here." He cocked his head and rubbed his chin. "I wonder whatever happened to Lucky?"

"His name was Lucky?" Havoc said.

"Yeah, on afterthought, it wasn't the best nickname."

"My last words were 'Crap. I'm going to Hell for this.'" Havoc grinned. "On the plus side, I could've ended up in a much worse circle."

"At least you had last words," Bunny said. "I was just standing on the set when all of a sudden a heavy lighting cam light fell on me. I didn't even realize I was dead until Ares explained it to me, then swept me off my feet." She sighed. "Why aren't men romantic like that anymore?"

"I'd play the violin for you, but I wouldn't want to risk damaging the strings." Havoc gently cradled the instrument in its case. "You just leave everything to us."

"Yes," Wreak said, rubbing his palms. "*Leave everything* to us."

"I meant," Havoc said sternly, "that we'll get you a nice hotel in San Jose. And we'll set you up with a laptop so you can Skype with us if you need anything else."

"You can Skype with Earth?" Bunny asked.

"We got you online accounts with all your favorite shopping places," Wreak said. "Skyping is a piece of cake. We hijacked a few satellite signals and piggybacked onto Satan's crossroad connections that let her make deals for souls."

"Great. While I'm gone, muck out Devastation's stall every morning, keep his hooves polished and his coat and mane brushed. Give my poodles walkies every evening *precisely* at five and clean up after them. This place may be Hell, but that doesn't mean it can't have clean streets. And don't forget their daily treats. Oh, on Saturdays they get a pedicure."

Wreak grabbed the yellow-hued doodle by Van Gogh. "Fine, but it's gonna cost you this."

Havoc clutched Rosebud to his chest. "And this."

"Whatever," Bunny said, waving her hands at the piles of junk. "Sell whatever you can. I'll expect a hotel that *I consider nice*—not what you two think passes for nice—and a limo."

Sara Lee's taxi pulled up to an Art Deco hotel housing the restaurant JD had chosen, "Chez $$$$$," one of the hottest and most expensive restaurants in Chicago. At least the name had truth in advertising. Two uniformed doormen waited at the bronze and crystal doors.

JD paid the driver, then climbed out of the cab. Sara Lee opened her door and started to slide out. Her red satin gown trimmed with rhinestones fit even snugger than usual after celebrating the Cubs' glorious World Series championship with every sort of chocolate imaginable.

"Wait, wait!" JD called. "I'm coming."

Sara Lee blinked in confusion, then realized he wanted to help her out of the taxi. She didn't mind; she simply didn't expect it. In the early eighties, when Sara Lee started practicing law, some women had acted offended when men held a door or helped them in and out of cars, while others got offended when they *didn't* do those things. She couldn't blame men for being confused. But good manners never offended her.

Sara Lee took JD's proffered hand and tried to rise gracefully. The Iron Underwear cut off her breath, and she flopped back onto the seat.

"Whoops!" She gave a nervous laugh.

JD offered his hand again. Sara Lee scooted closer to the open door. Her slitted skirt slid upward, exposing too much thigh. Hastily, she pulled the skirt into a decent position.

"Hurry up, girlie, or I'll have to charge you for standing," the cabbie said.

"The problem is that I'm *not* standing," Sara Lee said.

The cabbie chuckled. "You got me there."

Trying not to grunt, and failing miserably, Sara Lee struggled to her feet amid a dreaded ripping sound.

She glanced down. The seam above the slit had torn all the way to her hip. The bottom of her beige body briefer showed.

"Oh, hell," she muttered. Fighting a blush, Sara Lee dug in her suitcase-sized handbag, past the yarn ball and knitting needles Candace had given her, the blackjack she carried for personal defense, the most recent Jim Butcher novel and a baggy holding the dusty remains of some breath mints she'd accidentally touched the last time she was on Earth. Finally she found the bag of safety pins she kept for this sort of emergency. Once, while still married to Oscar, she'd had to pin an entire side of her gown when she'd breathed too deeply after beating the Burger Grande eating challenge—a three pound burger with five kinds of cheese, half a pound of bacon and a pound of fries in thirty minutes. Fitted clothing was not for the faint of heart—or the hefty of appetite.

Mercifully, JD said nothing while she pinned the skirt. When she finished, she found him staring at the hazy glow above the rooftops. Half of Chicago was in flames from revels and riots. It reminded Sara Lee of Hell—or Detroit.

"These people are crazy," Sara Lee said, grateful he didn't comment on her fashion "fail."

"You should have seen Rome burn," JD said, his eyes glowing with reflected light. "Nero really knew how to throw a party. Damned good lyre player too."

"I thought he played the fiddle while Rome burned," Sara Lee said.

"A misconception held by those ignorant of history," JD said. "The fiddle didn't exist in 64 AD."

"Ignorant, huh?" Sara Lee grinned. She'd forgotten how "aristocratic" Oscar's family was. She'd never put much stock in birthrights. After all, she'd started life in a trailer, and she'd done pretty well for herself.

JD bowed his head. "I didn't mean to imply—"

"No, you pretty much said it outright." She chuckled. Between working at a big New York law firm and the first few years she'd spent with Oscar, Sara Lee had a pretty high tolerance for arrogance. "I admit, I didn't spend enough time studying history in school. But I loved hearing Oscar talk about it. He really brought it to life, maybe because he *did* live it. You must have seen some amazing things too."

"Most definitely." JD offered his arm. "The Crusades, mustard gas drifting over the trenches in World War I, the sacking of Troy. Oh, and the Inquisition was quite amusing. But I never should have bet on Nazi Germany. I lost my best mare to Oscar." JD gave Sara Lee an oblique look. "Of course, it's *your* horse now."

"That pathetic bone-bag was your *best*?"

"She wasn't like that until Famine rode her."

"Ah." Sara Lee had renamed the skeletal horse Anorexia. She was convinced the horse stayed bone-thin just to mock her.

After they were seated, JD excused himself, presumably to go to the restroom, not that he would ever announce anything so crass. As if aristocrats never had to go.

A sommelier in a white dinner jacket brought the leather-bound wine list. Sara Lee looked up to thank him and blinked hard.

"Jesus?"

He inclined his head, his hair tied in a neat ponytail.

"What are you doing here?" she asked.

"I find that walking a mile in another man's shoes helps me to better understand him," he said.

"Uh-huh. I think you're following me around." She eyed him for telltale signs, but Jesus had a helluva poker face.

He smiled. "Why would I do that?"

"To lead me from temptation?" She waved toward the restaurant's entrance. "By the way, the fire out there? Not my doing."

"Yes, so far, your vacation visit has been far less damaging to the world than some of your work visits," Jesus said.

"Try to start the apocalypse one time and no one ever lets you forget it," Sara Lee muttered.

"Well, I'm glad to see you're still *here*," Jesus said.

"I told you I have vacation until the end of the month," Sara Lee said. "Why would I leave early?"

Jesus laughed. "I'll check back in a few minutes."

As Sara Lee looked over the pages of red vintages, she practically bounced in her seat. It had been so long since she'd had a really great bottle of wine. JD soon returned. When she glanced up, he sat watching her with an expression she found hard to read. Oscar had been like that when she'd first met him—pleasant, charming, but always holding part of himself in reserve. Sara Lee had never been good at that. After a few months, she'd finally cracked Oscar's protective shell. Mostly.

She flashed JD a smile, then returned to perusing the wine list. "Ooh, they have Rocket Science!"

"Excuse me?"

"It's a fantastic red blend," she said. "And the bottles always have these cute paragraphs that tie in with the name. The winemaker holds a contest every year—"

JD reached across the table and gently extracted the wine list from Sara Lee's grasp. He glanced at the entry, then said, "I think we can do better."

"No, really, it's—"

"Trust me."

"Okaaay." Some men, especially the old-fashioned ones, needed to be the expert. She didn't care which wine he picked, because whichever it was, the wine wouldn't turn to dust in her mouth.

Jesus returned to the table. He winked at Sara Lee and put a finger to his lips. She guessed he didn't want to discuss his mid-afterlife crisis with JD. Jesus needn't have worried. Aristocrats took little notice of servants, beyond giving them orders.

"I'd like a bottle of the Jean-Louis Chave Cuvee Cathelin Hermitage," JD said, with perfect French pronunciation.

Sara Lee had studied Spanish. French words had too many letters, and that extra accent mark. And what the hell was up with that squiggle under the C?

Before Jesus could take the wine list, Sara Lee intercepted it. She looked at the price three times before her brain agreed to process what her eyes saw. "Seven *thousand* dollars?"

JD flushed. "It's of no consequence."

"Sorry," Sara Lee said, handing Jesus the book. He inclined his head and walked away. "It's just ... seven *thousand* dollars? Satan must pay you a whole lot more than she does me."

"I would prefer not to discuss money," JD said.

"Oh, right. Sorry." That was another aristocrat thing. Talking about their conspicuous consumption embarrassed them. "So, should we move on to discussing politics or religion?"

He chuckled.

"Or maybe ... you could tell me what happened between you and Oscar?" she asked.

A look of surprise broke through JD's cool veneer. "He never told you?"

"No. He said he didn't want to discuss it."

"Then perhaps it's best left in the past."

Sara Lee nodded, though she'd really hoped to clear up the one mystery Oscar had left her with.

After Jesus brought menus and a basket of French rolls, Sara Lee said, "Tonight's my last night in Chicago. I'm heading to Kansas City tomorrow."

JD raised an eyebrow. "On purpose?"

"Hey, it's home," she said. "I ... thought I might drop in on my brother. I haven't seen him since I died." Guilt poked at her, but she squashed it like a bug. It wasn't like she planned to *force* Duncan to take the job.

"That should be quite the shock," JD said. "What spurred you to visit him now?"

Sara Lee hesitated, then decided there was no harm in telling him about the family loophole.

As she explained, the enigmatic look returned to JD's face. "I notice that since acquiring Oscar's job, you've done little besides try to get rid of it. Did you hold it in such low regard when you were married to him?"

"Oh, no!" Sara Lee said. "I admired Oscar for putting so much effort and creativity into his work. Hell, he started the whole 'thin is in' movement in the seventies and convinced people to starve *themselves*. But he was good at being Famine. I've only ever been good at arguing. That's why I became a lawyer."

JD's blue eyes sparkled in amusement. "You know what Shakespeare said about lawyers."

"'First thing we do, let's kill all the lawyers.'" Not that she hadn't heard that line a thousand times.

"Perfectly quoted," JD said.

"I may not have studied much history, but I was a Shakespeare nerd in college."

"You hide it well," he teased.

Sara Lee gave him a playful kick under the table. "Oscar said you were a brat."

Jesus returned. "I'm sorry, sir, but we're out of the wine you requested. If you'll permit me, I can select one I think you'll like just as well."

Gaze on his menu, JD nodded. Jesus turned to a serving

cart and touched a carafe of water. It turned a beautiful ruby red.

As Jesus poured a taste, Sara Lee covered a grin.

JD sipped, then his eyes widened. "Very good, thank you."

Jesus wiggled his eyebrows at Sara Lee. "Can I get you more bread?"

"Not just yet," she said, shaking with unvoiced laughter.

After Jesus poured the wine and left, JD raised his glass in a toast. "To Shakespeare."

"And killing lawyers?" Sara Lee clinked glasses with his. JD winced, then so did she. Clinking glasses was very "middle class." Hastily, she sipped the wine. It danced across her tongue in a parade of delicious flavors—berries, pepper, smoke and others that led to a faint vanilla finish. "Wow. That's the best wine I've ever tasted. You were right about being able to do better."

JD's hard-to-read look returned. "I'm certain we can do better about a great many things."

Bunny's limo pulled up in front of a nondescript building, the sort of bland structure in which ordinary people conducted business. Bunny had always conducted business at her mansion, the other person's mansion or in a four-star restaurant at a four-star hotel, and once poolside at an exclusive resort in Palm Springs.

So this was the Setter Institute. They should have a dog on their sign, pointing the way. As Bunny opened the glass doors, sadly lacking a doorman, she pitied her half-sister's life. Being War could well be an improvement.

A uniformed man wearing a badge stopped Bunny. "Name, please?"

"Bunny Louise Baker." She waited for a reaction. After all, her name was as recognizable as Marilyn Monroe's or Ginger Grant's.

"I don't see you on the list. Who are you here to see?" the guard asked.

For a second, Bunny blinked. Was it possible this man had never heard of her? Wearing a disappointed frown, Bunny said, "I'm here to see my sister, Kitty Hawkins."

The guard eyed her closely. "You're a bit young to be her sister."

Bunny's cheeks warmed from the compliment. "Thank you,

but I'm her older sister, actually."

"Not possible." The guard sat back, his finger poised over an intercom button.

Bunny pursed her lips. She was sure she'd been born first. After all, Bunny came from her mother's first marriage. She was twenty-eight, and her sister, born in 1959, was twelve. No—that was her age when Bunny had died in 1972. Bunny stayed twenty-eight forever now. But Kitty would be... Bunny scrunched her forehead for the math. It was now the year two thousand and something ... fourteen ... fifteen ... twenty? Bunny never kept close tabs on the year. It wasn't like she needed to keep up with current events. By now, Kitty had to be really old, like a hundred or something.

"Okay, you're right. Kitty is my older sister now," Bunny finally said.

The guard grunted, then called a receptionist. After hanging up, he said, "Kitty Hawkins doesn't have a sister. Whoever you are, you'll have to leave."

"Oh, I understand the confusion." For a change, Bunny really meant it. Actually understanding something someone else didn't felt weird—but a good weird. "I'm her dead sister."

"I'm going to have to ask you to leave."

"Call her back. Tell her my name this time."

"Your name won't change the fact she doesn't have a sister. If she does have a dead sister, it obviously isn't you."

Bunny shuddered with rising anger. "Don't make me Stomp." Her War Stomp could level the building and make the guard's head explode. It was an awesome ability—one she would hate to give up. But having a pension would be loads better than a stupid job without an unlimited expense account. "Listen, bud, I'm Bunny ... *the* Bunny ... *War!* Get my sister on the phone."

Something must've clicked in the guard's head, for he jumped to his feet. Bunny smiled, expecting an escort. Instead, he flipped the safety off his gun. "What do you mean by *War?* Put all weapons on the counter. Now! While I call Homeland Security."

Bunny scoffed—like Homeland Security would be any help. "Do I look like I'm carrying any weapons?" She stretched her arms. Her tequila sunrise sequined gown sparkled under the otherwise unflattering florescent lighting. "I ask you, *where* would I hide a weapon?"

"Strapped to your thigh or ankle," the guard answered

without missing a beat.

Bunny raised the hem of her evening gown to her lower calf, revealing her pink diamond-studded stilettos. "Be serious."

The phone rang. Never taking his eyes off of Bunny, the guard answered, "Redhead. Ditzy. Wearing an evening dress with a winged helmet. Yeah. Yeah. Oh, yeah. Okay. I'll bring her up." To Bunny, he said, "It turns out you *are* Dr. Hawkins's dead sister."

"Who's Dr. Hawkins?"

"Your sister," the guard answered deadpan.

"My sister's name is Kitty Hawkins ... oh, wait. I get it. But she's not a doctor. She's an astrologer, or something."

The guard rolled his eyes. "Follow me."

When the elevator doors opened upstairs, a secretary met them. She led Bunny to a room filled with computers and clicking, noisy machines. An old woman looked up through glasses. Grey streaked her blonde hair, but she had the family green eyes.

"I'm glad I missed old age," Bunny said.

"I'm only *fifty-five*," Kitty snapped.

"Then old will be really bad," Bunny said sympathetically.

Kitty sighed. "Why are you here?"

Now that she was here, Bunny realized she should've thought about what to say. A second later, she remembered the reason for her visit—to sell her sister on the idea of becoming War. The best way to sell an idea was to give it a big pitch. If only there was something big about war.

"Well?" Kitty asked, her expression a mixture of bored and stern. "Don't know what to say or did you forget?"

It was both, but Kitty didn't have to remind Bunny of her poor memory. Bunny squinted at her. "It's sad how old you got ... but I guess it can't be helped—or so I hear."

"I believe we've gone over that. If that's all you wanted, you could've mailed me a card."

"No. That's not why I'm here." Bunny drew a deep breath, straining her beaded gown, which felt tighter across her nice rack. As she exhaled, inspiration struck. "I've got the best job in Hell. And it comes with a beautiful pink stallion, and a pack of precious toy poodles—they used to be Rottweilers, but now they're poodles, so really you could have any dog you wanted."

"You're telling me this because...?"

"Just wait, this job comes with thousands of strong,

handsome men in uniform. You're still single, right?" Even as Kitty nodded somewhat unhappily, Bunny barreled through her spiel. "You'll have access to Heaven as well, because you'd be God's secret agent as to the goings on in Hell. Wait, that's a secret. Forget I mentioned it."

"Why do I care, Bunny? Get to the point."

"Wait. Don't decide now. There's still more. You can travel to Earth pretty much whenever you please, since there's always some stupid war going on. You can even dictate with a parasol, if you're interested in hosting a peace party. Now how much would you pay—I mean, doesn't that sound great?"

"Dictate with a parasol?" Kitty repeated.

"Parasol, parabola, prototype." Bunny shrugged. "It's some big word that starts with p. I think it has something to do with sending out an advance copy."

Kitty scratched her greying blonde head, muttering, "Dictate with a parasol... Oh, you mean dictate protocol."

"See? You'd be great at this job."

"What do you mean *I'd* be great at this job?" Kitty's tone rang sourly of suspicion.

Bunny grabbed Kitty's forearms. "How'd you *love* to be War? It's the job opportunity of a lifetime—or an afterlifetime. Just think of all the things you could do, all the power you'd wield." Bunny's head spun from a dozen conflicting thoughts.

She hated her job, even though the job rarely interfered with Bunny's afterlife. Sure, without the job, she'd have a pension, but no trips to Earth. Plus, she'd have no more training, though she couldn't decide if that was a good point or bad one. Maybe she could make do without Semyaza. Except he gave her great makeup tips. She'd miss Michael too, since he wouldn't make time out of his own training schedule to see her. But she'd go to Heaven—or so God had said. There, she'd see more of Adam and could spend more time in "Bunny's Hoppy Acres," her heavenly sanctuary for all dead animals.

Just when losing the job seemed to offer the best arguments, Bunny remembered everything being a Horsewoman had to offer. Heaven was a really, really nice place to visit—but it didn't have Gucci shoe boutiques or Hollywood premiers. As War, Bunny got Heaven *and* Earth. So what if she also got Hell? She had a nice mansion, and Wreak and Havoc had rigged her place with every convenience. Plus, she had a better air conditioning system than Satan.

She decided to keep the job, even without an unlimited expense account.

Before Bunny could speak, Kitty shook her head and repeated a resounding, "No, no, no. You couldn't pay me to be War."

"Actually, it's not paying at all right now," Bunny said.

"I don't want the job," Kitty reiterated. "*This* is the job I want."

"Doing horoscopes for dogs?" Remembering that she didn't want to talk her sister into the job, Bunny added, "But if you're happy..."

"Why don't you offer the job to our brother? He's about to retire from the Navy. I'm sure he'd jump at the opportunity."

Bunny shook her head. "I'd never ask Teddy. War's a woman's job. Men have already made such a mess of it, and we both know who always cleans up after a man's mess."

"Then I suggest you take out an ad in the employment section of the newspaper."

"Can't. The job has to be passed to a relative."

"That's tough then. We have some cousins, but there's been a family feud and we haven't talked to them in over ten years."

"Oh, well," Bunny said, suppressing a smile. "So, do you know the horoscope for poodles? Are my dogs having a good day?"

"I don't do dog horoscopes—and I won't ask why you think I do. I'll just show you what I do."

Kitty led Bunny to a bank of humming and clicking machines with computer screens and printouts of all sorts.

"These machines pick up signals from outer space," Kitty explained.

"Really? So that's where those strange television channels come from. I'd wondered about that. I knew there weren't that many stations on Earth."

"What are you babbling about?" Kitty asked.

"You should know. You're broadcasting the signals."

Kitty sighed heavily. "We aren't picking up TV signals from outer space."

"Are you sure? Have you seen some of the programs aired?"

"I'm positive!"

Bunny perched her hands on her hips. "Then what other kind of signals are there?"

"The sort that proves there's life out there—somewhere *not* on Earth!" Kitty's voice kept raising.

"Wouldn't alien television shows prove that?"

Kitty made a fist. "Yes," she snapped reluctantly. "*If* we were picking up television signals. But we aren't."

"What are you picking up? Phone calls? Because I'm pretty sure that's illegal."

Now Kitty had two balled fists. "We don't know what we're looking for. We're looking for *any kind of signal.*"

"Then it *could* be alien television shows," Bunny said.

"Arrrgh." Kitty paced in a tight circle.

"What do you have against alien programming?" Bunny asked.

"Nothing. I would *love* to pick up an alien show. But we're focused on finding a communication signal."

Bunny nodded sagely—as that seemed the right reaction to Kitty's meltdown. "Maybe they want royalties for the alien programs you're broadcasting on cable."

"For the last time!" Kitty said.

A man with as much hair as bigfoot jumped up from a tiny cubby hole and screamed. "We got something!"

Kitty's head snapped around, almost loosening her too-tight bun. "Are you sure?"

"It's not a pulsar. It's a bona fide signal. There's some repetition and regularity, but it has ... rhythm." He shrugged with the last word.

"Play it," Kitty demanded.

He fiddled with the mouse, clicking on boxes on the computer screen. Then some beeping blared from the cheap speakers.

The sound went "do whop do whop whop, do whop do whaaaaa, do whop do diddle-de-whop, do whop whop whop a-do."

"It's incredible," Kitty murmured.

"It's proof," the man with the ponytail and beard said.

"It's Gabriel," Bunny said.

They both stared at Bunny.

"The archangel Gabriel," Bunny explained. "I recognize the tune. Michael took me to listen to one of Gabriel's jam sessions with the Epistles."

Kitty arched a brow. "Do you mean the apostles?"

"No. It wasn't Peter, Paul or Luke. It was their wives—the Epistles."

Kitty rolled her eyes. "The wives of apostles are not called epistles."

Bunny scrunched her nose at her sister—who'd always assumed she was stupid. "I know that. The Epistles is the name of their group. The wives of apostles are called apostlettes—or apostrophes or something."

"Whatever," Kitty said through clenched teeth. "Are you sure about the signal?"

Bunny nodded. "Gabriel likes to play on frequencies picked up by some group called Setty. I never heard of them, so I assumed they play rap."

"*We are S.E.T.I.*" Kitty spelled every letter with emphasis.

"I didn't know you were a musician."

"We are *not* musicians," Kitty snapped. "We look for extraterrestrial signals. Now you tell us the first real clue we've gotten is from an archangel's jam session?"

"He messes with Earth," Bunny said. "Archangels are always saying they don't like humans and that we infest the Earth, but they must like us or they wouldn't play games with us."

"Bunny, I think you should go," Kitty said, her voice tired.

Back in the limo, her mission essentially complete, Bunny contacted Wreak and Havoc by Skype—after three attempts to guess the computer password. Who thought "War" would be a good password? Probably Wreak. He had the weirdest notions of what would be easy to remember.

Within moments, Wreak's and Havoc's faces bobbed on the laptop screen.

"Did you forget where your hotel is?" Wreak asked.

"Did you need something?" Havoc asked with more emphasis.

"Isn't that what I asked?" Wreak said.

"No. You implied our wonderful, kind and generous Mistress of War couldn't remember something as simple as the name of her hotel."

Bunny frowned. Maybe Havoc had set the password. No matter. "Boys, boys, boys. I don't have time for squabbling. My mission with Kitty is a bust. She won't take the job." Try as she might, Bunny didn't feel like putting on a sad face. Then she remembered she was an actress and gave it "Pout Number 3."

Wreak and Havoc exchanged big grins.

"That's marvelous news," Havoc exclaimed.

"Yeah," Wreak chimed in. "Now we won't have to train a new War."

"What does that mean?" Bunny snapped.

"It's just Wreak's insensitive way of saying he'd miss you," Havoc said.

"Yeah ... it's *her* I'd miss." Under his breath, Wreak added, "Not her bank account at all." But Bunny could lip read.

"I miss my bank account too," she said. "Which reminds me, did you get me enough money from selling Ares's old junk to rent me a nice place in Beverly Hills? Since Kitty isn't interested in the job or in seeing me, I figured I'll spend the rest of my vacation in Hollywood, where I might find a movie role. I used to make $20,000 dollars per film! Since most of them wrapped up shooting in about ten days, that's $200 a day!"

Wreak started to speak when Havoc clapped his hand across Wreak's mouth. "We'll find you someplace real nice," Havoc said. "Do you have a favorite motel?"

Bunny let out a long breath. "The Beverly Hills *Hotel* is nice, but I hate public places. It's hard to relax by the pool with strangers around. I'd rather have my own private mansion."

"We can rent you a mansion for the month," Havoc said. "Give me a second." He turned away from the screen. In the background, Bunny heard typing and clicking.

His mouth again free, Wreak blurted out, "Ten times two hundred is two thousand, not twenty thousand!"

"Smarty-pants, I was calculating in my agent's fee and taxes." Really, she hadn't, but that sounded like the smart thing to say.

Before Wreak could snipe back, Havoc pushed his way in front of the screen, saying, "I found a lovely mansion near Rodeo Drive."

"What's it gonna cost?" Wreak asked.

"For the month, three-hundred thousand dollars," Havoc answered.

Bunny laughed. "Hollywood doesn't pay actors that much."

Wreak rolled his eyes.

"Don't worry, Mistress," Havoc said. "You can afford the mansion. We found a good buyer for one of the Monets."

Bunny's eyes widened. "Wherever did you find someone stupid enough to pay that kind of money for a blurry painting?"

"At loot.com," Havoc answered.

"Okay, then. Just give me the address. No, wait, give it to my chauffeur."

"You're taking a limo to Los Angeles? All the way from

Mountain View?" Havoc asked.

"How'd you know I was still in Mountain View?" Bunny asked.

"We have a GPS chip in your laptop," Wreak said. "You realize there are cheaper ways to travel than by limo."

"You found one gullible buyer," Bunny said. "Find another."

"She's fine," Havoc said sharply to Wreak. "Let her take the limo if she wants."

"And I'll need a staff to take care of the mansion," Bunny said.

"I thought you didn't want people around," Wreak said.

"Staff aren't people," Bunny explained. "Now, hop to it!"

"Sometimes I forget how entertaining humanity can be," Zoe said as Jake led her through teeming throngs surging through the Javits Center in Midtown Manhattan. A group of men in Japanese school girl outfits flounced past. "Especially in what they choose to wear."

"It *is* New York Comic Con, dear." Jake guided her around a unit of Stormtroopers surrounding a Slave Leia posing for pictures.

"Oh, I'm not talking about the costumes, though I guess even the ones *not* dressed as characters are still in to some kind of 'costume' to fit in." Zoe watched a mousy-haired young man in blue plaid pants and a brown-striped, button-down shirt fastened all the way up pick through boxes of comic books.

"Will there be social commentary the entire time we're here?"

Zoe grinned. "No. I'm sure there will be a bit of snark and some fan girl squeeage. And shopping. I should find some souvenirs for Bambi. You want to try to find something for Reaper?"

"Why me?"

"I think *brother* trumps *minion*. You'd know what he likes more than I would."

"True, but *you'd* know what would annoy him more, if we went gag gift."

"This is what makes us a beautiful team, Jake. You're devious on a whole other level. I'll keep an eye out. So what do we do now?"

"There's a Famous Bad Guy panel starting in an hour or so. We could head over there and get in line."

"There are lines?" Zoe asked, surprised.

"For the more popular guests and topics, very long lines. But we can try. I know you like the bad guys."

"In movies. Only in movies. Let's go check out this panel."

Due to random encounters of Ewoks, anime characters and the random cult film actor along the way, it took awhile before they got to the panel room. They reached the room just as the doors opened. The crowds seemed to melt away, leaving a wide swath for Zoe and Jake to sail through.

"Wow. That was easier than you led me to believe," Zoe said.

"Because that wasn't normal."

"What? Why?"

Jake pulled her into a hug. "Oh, honey, even on vacation you're still Death. There's an ... aura about you. Power."

"Is that a pretty way of saying people are scared of me, even if they don't know why?" Zoe let a slow, satisfied smile grow as they settled into seats three rows back from the stage. "And this is good. Close enough to see everything without risking neck spasms."

"Thought you'd be okay with this." Jake scanned the room with a distracted air.

She studied him for a moment. "You okay?"

"What? Oh, yeah, just thinking. Nothing important."

"Let me guess. The last time you were here, it was a particularly weird call?"

"You could say that. One of those guys from a cable TV science show set up a controlled explosion based on an internet video. Fortunately for him, it was a shaped charge. The cable guy lost his eyebrows, but the first row? Well, melted latex and spandex leaves behind a *unique* odor. It stays with you. Hey, the panel's starting."

Mark Sheppard, Tom Hiddleston, Ralph Fiennes, Julian Richings and Burn Gorman slipped into seats along the raised stage to the enthusiastic welcome of the audience. The intensity level rose when the moderator, Robert Carlyle, stepped behind the podium with a chilling yet heartfelt, "Hello, dearies."

The panel started out with signature lines, evil laughs and random ways to thwart heroes before going to questions. Zoe was in fan-girl heaven. She giggled like the teenager she hadn't been for far longer than most people at the convention around them.

"That was so much fun. Even if they did add that guy who's

been playing Death on that TV show as a villain."

"Well, not everyone is as versed in the office as we are," Jake said as they scooted through a little-used door to avoid the crowds flowing out of the hall.

"Okay, I'm completely turned around," Zoe said, frowning at the near-empty corridor. "Which way do we go?"

Jake seemed uncertain, but pointed left. "Let's try that way."

They headed down the corridor and nearly ran over Tom Hiddleston as he exited the men's room. All three stopped short. Hiddleston glanced around furtively, as if looking for his escorts or security.

For a second, Zoe couldn't form words. She gripped Jake's arm, squeezing unconsciously. Before she knew what she was doing, she sank in a semblance of a curtsy/bow hybrid move—even though the Norse gods weren't part of her hierarchy.

"There's no need for that." Hiddleston's silky British accent flowed over her like warm water. "I'm just an actor."

"Of course you are. All the better to blend in. I get it."

"No. Really. I appreciate the ... enthusiasm and sentiment, but I am an actor playing a part."

Zoe nodded. "Right. Right. And a very good actor you are too. I wish you all the best."

"Thank you?"

"Mr. Hiddleston! There you are. I'm sorry we were separated. You're needed for your signing." The volunteer skittered up, eyeing Zoe and Jake nervously.

The popular actor nearly leaped toward his staff handler. "Yes, that's right. So sorry. Obligations, you know. Must run. Lovely to meet you."

"I should find out from Bambi what his longevity looks like. We may need to extend that." Zoe spoke mostly to herself as she watched the actor scurry away.

Jake studied his shoes. "You don't really believe he's the Norse god, Loki, do you?"

"No."

"Good."

"Not completely anyway. He's from the bloodline—that much is obvious. A lot of them gravitate to the performing arts."

Jake narrowed his eyes at the retreating actor. "Really?"

"I'm surprised you didn't know that. It's one of the first things I looked up when I got access."

"I guess I had other things to look into," Jake said. "Come

on. Let's check out the Exhibit Hall. I hear the classic cartoon display is amazing."

Zoe let Jake lead her away. She glanced back over her shoulder, but Loki—in whatever guise he used now—was nowhere to be seen. Soon they were swallowed by the crowd swarming the Exhibit Hall.

The classic cartoon display claimed a major chunk of real estate in the center of the hall. Zoe stepped into the homage to Warner Bros., Hanna-Barbera and Disney and felt her heart soar. Though many of the franchises aired after she died, Zoe had watched them with Orcas. He used cartoons to relax after particularly hard cleanups. She didn't get it then. She understood now. In the cartoons, the damage was rarely permanent, and characters rarely died.

The exhibit had everything, including a grand piano suspended over a dish of seed in the center of a target on the floor. She bounced over to the edge of the area to get a closer look. Jake tried to stop her with a hand on her arm.

"Be careful."

"What? Why?" Zoe rolled her eyes to the piano. "Don't you think with a hundred thousand people here, they secured that thing every way possible? Besides it's probably balsa wood or papier-mâché."

Jake's face scrunched into a doubtful expression. "I don't…"

An ominous groan, followed by a series of loud pops, froze Zoe in place. Suddenly the ropes and wires gave way. She couldn't tear her eyes from the black lacquered mass coming at her—and it *was* coming straight *at* her. How was she that close? Surely the ropes—

Her thought shattered as she was yanked backward off her feet to land in an ungraceful heap of limbs too numerous to be just hers. She registered screaming. The part of her brain still functioning felt relived *her* voice wasn't making those awful screeching sounds.

She slowly turned her head. Jake was saying something to her. She focused on his lips.

"Are you okay, Zoe?"

"I think so." She shifted her weight to get to her feet but the floor seemed squishy. It moved … and groaned. She squirmed away only to be pulled to her feet by mismatched hands. One hand belonged to Jake, the other … did not. She tracked the long, lean fingers up to Tom Hiddleston's face.

"Loki…"

"Tom. Please. *Please*. I was signing just there for an animated film and saw the piano. I had to help."

"Thank you." Zoe tried to keep her voice—and frankly the rest of her—from shaking. She didn't want to admit how freaked out the close call made her. The fan-girl inside rushed to the fore.

"I'm just glad you're all right," the actor said.

"We should repay your kindness. Dinner or something."

Hiddleston waved her off. "Your thanks is enough."

"Tom! Over here!" Hiddleston and Zoe both turned to the shouting male voice.

Flashbulbs nearly blinded her, reminding her of the crowds of witnesses, almost all with phones and cameras. A swarm of matching-shirted convention staffers closed ranks on the area. Zoe saw a familiar shimmer across the debris and gripped Jake's arm.

"Calvary's here. Someone wasn't as lucky."

Zoe and Jake sidled around the debris to see a pair of stripped leggings and red shoes sticking out from the shards of piano and wire.

Zoe shook her head. "Okay, so you were right. The piano was real. And, wow, bad day to wear a *Wizard of Oz* costume."

Jake gave her a sharp look. She shrugged. "You know Reaper's going to say something like that. I just got there first."

"Too soon, especially considering how close that came to being you. And honey, you're on *vacation* on *Earth*. If that's you, *that* is you only worse, because it's oblivion." Jake pointed to the shoes and the soul being collected by one of their minions while Reaper made notes on a tablet.

Reaper headed over to them. "So who wanted the Wicked Witch of the East dead?"

"No one. Wrong place wrong time. It just fell," Zoe said.

"Yeah, no. That support system was helped. There are strategic cuts along the ropes and wires. Not an accident," Reaper said. "Sucks to be her."

"Yeah, if it was meant for the witch," Jake muttered.

"What's that supposed to mean?" Reaper asked, eyeing them carefully. "Zoe, do you have *birdseed* in your hair?"

Before Zoe or Jake could respond, concerned staffers rushed them. "Ma'am? Sir? We're with the convention. Can we have a word please?"

Zoe and Jake were hustled off the convention floor and once more cocooned in legalese and concerned butt-covering reassurances before Zoe even registered the use of the dreaded "ma'am." They were deposited in soft chairs in a backstage area and plied with food and bottled water. Hollywood-coiffed strangers glared until assistants and handlers whispered in their ears.

"Hiddleston gets all the breaks," Zoe heard one of them say before being back into her own drama.

She leaned over to Jake and muttered, "I think I'm done with Comic Con for this trip."

"Right there with you, Zoe."

Chapter Four

Butterflye stared at the table. She'd never seen so many pieces of flatware, china and stemware at one place setting. She ran her fingertips along the lip of the crystal water glass and it hummed. Or was it the white wine glass or the brandy snifter or the sherry stemware? She sat beside _Squalor of the Sea's_ commanding officer, a squat man with a graying beard who only looked debonair because of his dress white uniform.

Ralph, clad in a ruffled green baby bonnet and a shirt that read, "Last Clean T-shirt," sat in a booster seat at Butterflye's right. He snatched a dinner roll off the captain's bread plate. Butterflye smiled at the captain as she stealthily slapped her pet on his maxillary palp.

The captain, whose name contained no vowels, leaned forward and asked Butterflye a question in his Latvian accent. She giggled and nodded, though she had no clue what he said.

In the dining room below the captain's table sat a man who looked like he wore a weasel hairpiece. Nearby, four men in black suits and wearing earpieces and black-framed sunglasses stood at attention along the wall. Trump yelled, "I was supposed to have dinner with the captain tonight."

His server responded, "Not tonight, sir. Now sit down and enjoy your Spam®."

"Wine, madam?" the captain's personal server, Raul, asked Butterflye. He held up a bottle of Riesling.

She nodded. Raul had the most piercing blue eyes and wavy blonde hair. She smiled broadly at the eye candy serving her drink, then reluctantly returned her attention to the captain. "Where does one go to school to become the captain of his own ship?"

"University of Phoenix," she extracted from his response. "Two-year online course."

He leered at Butterflye and placed his hand over hers. "I thought a Mr. Gump was dining with us." He glanced at the other guests around his table. "However, I'm fortunate to be the only man tonight."

Across from Butterflye sat Mrs. Levington-Sprout, the wife of a software billionaire, and her two teenage daughters, making it one estrogen-charged table. Mrs. Sprout smiled at Butterflye. "So, Mrs. Plague what do you do?"

Butterflye started to remind the woman that her name was hyphenated, but decided to keep a low profile. "Just call me Butterflye. I'm in charge of healthcare for my company." The server placed a bowl of foamy green soup in front of her. Butterflye looked up at him. He had a big nose and mustache and wore black plastic framed glasses. "What is this?"

"Asparagus soup."

"I didn't order this. I told the other server I wanted shrimp cocktail."

He returned the bowl to his tray. "I'm sorry. He wrote down soup."

Mrs. Sprout raised her hand. "Don't waste it. I'll try it."

"Very good, ma'am." He set it in front of her.

The eldest daughter picked up her silver-plated soup spoon. "Mummy, may I please taste it?"

Mrs. Levington-Sprout pushed the bowl toward her daughter. "Of course, Honoria."

Both daughters tried the soup. "It's a little salty," Honoria said.

A disturbance broke out in the dining room below. Ralph scurried out of the swinging kitchen doors, followed by a chef wielding a cleaver. Ralph wielded a drumstick.

"Come back here, you vermin," the cook yelled.

Butterflye glanced at the empty toddler seat next to her. She covered her face with her hands. *When did he slip away?*

Butterflye was still waiting for her shrimp—and Ralph's return—when her cell phone belted out the first four vocal bars of her one-and-only rock hit, "Hell's Bells." At the sound of Butterflye's singing voice, the captain cupped his hands over his ears and screamed.

"Oh, no." Butterflye fumbled around in her over-packed handbag. She finally found her phone and moved the slider to silence the device. Her recorded singing stopped, but a moment too late to save *Squalor's* commanding officer, who leaped off of the balcony headfirst into a bowl of minestrone. His hand struck the tines of a fork, sending it flying end over end. It sank into the neck of one of the black-suited men, who clutched his bleeding throat as he collapsed to the floor.

"Waiter, what's the captain doing in my soup?" Trump demanded.

The server eyed the bowl. "Looks like the nose dive." He pushed the captain off of the table and collected the pieces of the broken dish. "Would you like more soup, sir?"

Still staring at the scene below, Plague heard a female voice through the phone speaker. "Butterflye. Pick up. It's Sister Angelica."

Butterflye punched Facetime on her phone. "I told you never to call me here."

Angelica, who was blessed with an extraordinarily prominent nose, sat so close to the camera she appeared to be nothing but an enormous honker with beady eyes and a receding forehead.

Butterflye heard Wreak and Havoc giggling in the background. She smiled at her dinner companions and stood up. "Sorry. I don't want to be rude. I'll be back."

Havoc pushed Angelica out of the camera view. He rubbed his hands together and cackled. "Wreak and I played with Helvetica's reservations website and upgraded your cabin."

"*You* changed my cabin assignment?"

"Oh, yeah."

Wreak pushed him out of the way. "We also got you a premium liquor package. Think of us—and Donald Trump—whenever you enjoy your 18-year-old scotch."

Sister Angelica manhandled both minions away from the phone and moved closer to the screen, appearing to be simply one huge talking proboscis with flaring nostrils.

"So, Sister, what's so important? You can sign my signature on the scotch requisition forms as well as I can."

With trembling hands, Angelica lit a quarter-inch cigarette butt. It fizzled. "I need a smoke."

"You usually keep your pack in your right habit pocket, under your crucifix hankie."

"I've already smoked them. Since nicotine was originally used as an insecticide, Satan banned it from your domain. It's smoke-free down here!" Angelica pulled back from the screen and slapped a third nicotine patch on the inside of her saggy arm. "You've got to do something. It's hell here."

"Sis, I hate to tell you this, but you live in Hell."

"It gets worse. Because alcohol also functions as a germicide, it's been banned too."

Butterflye stared blankly into the phone screen. "No scotch? We've got to repeal this."

"I think it's got something to do with LDS," the nun said.

"You mean LSD?" Butterflye corrected.

Sister Angelica shook her head. "No, I'm sure they were LDS."

"LDS? Sister, Mormons aren't that bad."

"The word is, they must have influenced Satan."

"Damn them."

"Too late, Boss. They're all down here. Hey, Wreak has some more news for you."

Wreak reclaimed the screen. "I was researching your genealogy, looking for a relative. Man, those Mormons really know their stuff. Anyway, before you croaked, did you know a guy name Latimer?" A black-and-white photo of a dignified man driving a Rolls Royse replaced Wreak's face on the screen.

"Yeah. I dated him just before I met Osmodeus. I think Dr. Latimer owned a hospital. Ironic, isn't it?"

"Since you died without family, Loopy Latimer bought all the junk from your estate."

Butterflye looked over the balcony rail and watched some waiters wheel the captain and the black-suited man away on gurneys. "And you're telling me this, why?"

"Apparently he was obsessed with you—"

"Creepy obsessed—" Havoc yelled.

Wreak pushed into view of the screen. "Your boyfriend—"

"He wasn't my boyfriend."

"Your stalker also owned several medical research companies. According to an article in the journal, *Mom Genes*, Latimer's grandson, a human geneticist, succeeded in making a clone of you in 1976." The wacko's image was replaced by a woman's photo. It was like looking at a photo Butterflye didn't remember having taken. Instead of long flowing red hair, she had short tightly permed hair in the same auburn shade. "Meet Marley Jones."

"Get ... me ... off ... this ... ship," Butterflye whispered. "I have to meet her."

"Butterflye, without your powers we'd have to hire a helicopter to get you two together. It would be a real hassle. With Satan's spies everywhere, your boss would find out in a nanosecond. So—"

Havoc once again monopolized the camera. "When we got

word you were being shanghaied by Satan, we arranged for Miss Marley Jones to"—he made quote signs with his fingers—"'win' a cruise. She lives in Houston and thinks she won the Bailey's Buttermilk contest. Your clone is *with you* on *Squalor of the Sea.*"

"That's great. I'll just casually finish dinner, then try to locate her."

Havoc disappeared from the screen a moment after Sister Angelica's right cross connected with his cheek.

"I'll text her itinerary to you," the sister said.

Butterflye stashed her phone back in her purse and returned to the table. Ralph again sat in the booster seat and was helping himself to the captain's lobster tail. Across from him, the entire Levington-Sprout family had assumed room temperature. Mom's lifeless head lay submerged in the partially consumed bowl of asparagus soup, her spoon still in her hand. One daughter slumped in her chair, and the other lay face down on the carpet.

Butterflye dabbed the corners of her mouth with her napkin. "Hmm. Maybe I'll just get room service from now on."

Sara Lee left the secured area at KCI airport and entered the main concourse. Around her, fellow travelers hugged waiting family members, exchanging smiles and exclamations. Sara Lee shuddered. No doubt all that happy-to-see-you crap would disappear when they got home to their usual sniping and back-biting ways.

Thankfully, no one would be meeting her—

To her left, a uniformed chauffeur with a neatly trimmed beard and ponytail held up a cardboard sign that read "Sara Lee Mayer." He smiled and waved.

Sara Lee changed course toward him. "Hey, Jesus. We've got to stop meeting like this."

"I'd rather hoped we wouldn't meet," he said, a hint of disappointment in his expression.

Sara Lee sidestepped him. "No one asked you to pick me up, not that I don't appreciate the gesture."

Jesus hustled to catch up with her, then dropped the sign into a recycling bin. "I *meant* I hoped not to see you *here.*"

"Ah, *here.* So you know about the loophole."

"Your own brother?" Jesus said in exasperation.

"It's not like I plan to put a gun to his head," Sara Lee said defensively. "Mostly because I don't have one. But he might *want* the job. What's the harm in asking?"

Jesus looked at her askance. "You're better than this."

Sara Lee snorted.

"You've come so far," Jesus persisted. "I'd hate to see you backslide."

"I've already been judged," Sara Lee said. "What's my incentive?"

"Virtue is its own reward?" Jesus said hopefully.

"Riiiight."

Ignoring her own rusty conscience, Sara Lee headed toward the baggage claim. Jesus heaved a sigh, then followed.

"By the way," Sara Lee said, as they waited, "good job with the Cubs. I couldn't talk to you about it at the restaurant, but I saw Satan after the game. She fuming so much, she covered half the stadium in a green sulfuric fog."

"It's good for her to lose sometimes," Jesus said. "No offense to Dad, but I think he lets her get away with too much."

"You'll get no argument from me."

Jesus helped Sara Lee wrangle her five matching suitcases outside into the crisp autumn breeze. Sara Lee was glad she'd chosen to wear a blinged-up sweater, jeans and her black leather boots with buttons up the sides.

"I always traveled light," Jesus said.

"I like having stuff when I want it," she said. "I'm pretty high-maintenance."

"No, really?"

Sara Lee gave him a playful shove. "If you want someone without much luggage, you should follow Bunny around. She just buys everything she needs."

"Bunny's a little *too* high-maintenance. Besides, Dad always handles her." Jesus stopped by a bright yellow, cockroach-sized car nestled among Lincoln sedans and limousines. "This is it."

"A Smart Car?" Sara Lee said, grimacing. "In *yellow*?"

"It's good for the environment," Jesus said. "And yellow is easy to find."

"That thing has the horsepower of a lawnmower." Sara Lee surveyed the glove-box-sized hatch. "And no way my luggage fits."

"Have faith. Compared to multiplying loaves and fishes and turning water to wine, this is nothing." After helping her squeeze into the narrow passenger seat, Jesus returned to the luggage.

He must have done a "Son of God" thing, because somehow he got all the bags in the car.

Jesus slid into the driver's seat, hunching over the steering wheel to fit. From his uniform pocket, he pulled out a small figurine with a suction cup and stuck it to the dashboard.

"A plastic Jesus?" Sara Lee said in disbelief.

"I love that song—you know, 'I don't care if it rains or freezes, as long as I've got my plastic Jesus riding on the dashboard of my car.' I love the idea of me surfing the highways on people's dashboards, keeping them safe."

"Personally, I like the little bobbing-head Scotty dogs."

"Just for you." Jesus reached into another pocket and pulled out a little black dog with a bobbing head, exactly like the one Sara Lee had as a child, and set it on the dashboard in front of her. Add a pine tree-shaped air freshener and a shiny crystal bauble hanging from the rearview mirror and it would look like her mom's car always did.

"Thanks," she said.

"Now all we need are some tunes."

As Jesus reached for the radio tuner, Sara Lee said, "Please, no rap music."

"I'm way past that phase," Jesus said. "I'm into polka music now. Polish is the best, but German's not bad."

"I like Weird Al's polkas," she said.

"Doesn't everyone?"

He drove them out of the airport and onto the interstate. The car rode closer to the ground than a skateboard. Other cars, towering over them, sped by, horns honking. Sara Lee gripped the armrest hard enough to crush the foam. By the time they reached her brother Duncan's house, she was one giant knotted muscle.

Jesus pried Sara Lee free from the car, then handed her a key fob.

"What's this for?" she asked suspiciously.

"You need transportation," Jesus said.

"That"—she pointed at the yellow Smart Car—"is *not* transportation. It's a form-fitting coffin with wheels. Anyway, what about you?"

"I don't actually need a car to get around," Jesus reminded her. "This way, I make sure you don't drive some gas-guzzling SUV."

"Can I keep the Scotty dog—and the plastic Jesus?" Sara

Lee asked.

"Sure."

"Thanks. I'll need all the divine help I can get." Sara Lee glanced at the house, then back to Jesus. He had vanished.

Duncan's stone-faced house was practically a mansion, two stories with a rounded turret on the left side. The expansive yard of Kentucky bluegrass and extensive landscaping must cost a fortune to maintain. Not bad for a little shit from the trailer park. "Duncan Hines Malloy, you've done good."

Sara Lee strode to the stoop, reached for the doorbell, then jerked her hand back as though the button were a hot coal. What should she say to her brother? What *could* she say?

She drew a steeling breath and pressed the doorbell, which played Leonard Skynnard's "Gimme Three Steps."

"Okaay." Sara Lee bounced on her heels while she waited.

Finally, the door opened. It took several moments to recognize her little brother in the middle-aged man framed by the doorway. As a teen, Duncan had been a chubby nerd. Now, he was lean and muscular, his salt-and-pepper hair well-groomed. He wore pressed khakis and a polo shirt with "Dr. Malloy" embroidered on the pocket. The cartoonishly stunned look on his face was priceless.

"Hey, Bundt Cake," she said with forced cheerfulness.

"Sara Lee?" he whispered.

"In the recorporialized flesh." She pasted on a bright smile.

"You're ... you're..." Duncan blinked hard and shook his head sharply. "You're *fat!*"

Sara Lee's smile faded. "Thanks for noticing."

"What are you ... *how* are you...?"

"Invite me in and I'll explain," she said. "These heels are killing me."

"This isn't like a vampire thing, is it?" he asked, his gray eyes narrowed in suspicion.

Sara Lee huffed and pushed past him. "You need to learn the difference between fiction and reality."

"You're *really* dead. What am I supposed to think?"

"That 'there are more things in Heaven and Earth, Horatio, than are dreamt of in your philosophy.'"

He chuckled. "Still a Shakespeare nerd, huh? You know what he said about lawyers."

"Why is *that* the line everyone remembers?" Sara Lee demanded.

"Because it's such a great idea." Duncan closed the door and led her through a marble-tiled entry hall, past a formal living room to a gourmet kitchen. The Viking cooktop, Sub-zero refrigerator/freezer and tons of counter space made Sara Lee long to make a fancy meal. She'd always loved to cook, but cooking in the tiny kitchen of her New York apartment had been more acrobatic than fun. She sat at the round kitchen table.

Duncan, his entire body clenched in anger, sat across from her. "So what the hell happened to you, and what the hell are you doing here?"

"Funny you should mention Hell." Sara Lee took a deep breath and told Duncan about meeting and falling in love with Oscar, and about the shock of learning he was *the* Famine of the Four Horsemen of the Apocalypse.

"The only way we could be together was for me to die," Sara Lee said. "Oscar was willing to wait, but I—"

"How could you do that?" Duncan exploded, slapping the table. "You knew how much Dad's suicide screwed us all up. How could you do that to Mom and me?"

Sara Lee met his furious gaze with an icy stare. "I didn't think it would affect you much. Every bit of communication between us was instigated by me. When I sent you plane tickets to visit me in New York, you cashed them in. I really, literally did not think either of you cared."

"I was a teenager. Of course, I was self-involved. And you know Mom was afraid of flying. But yes, your suicide 'affected' me. It took fifteen years of therapy to get my shit together after you died."

"I died for love—jeez, why was Oscar the only one who ever appreciated that?"

"Because he's the only one who benefitted," Duncan said. "I looked up to you—a successful New York lawyer with a cool apartment, who took vacations to exotic places."

"By myself. I was a huge success *by myself.* Then I met someone I loved being with, who I wanted to be with forever, and I had the chance to do it, so I took it." Her sudden anger faded to bitterness. "*That* didn't work out so well."

"He ditched you when you got fat?"

Sara Lee huffed. "No, Oscar did not ditch me. He fell into oblivion." She explained about the ice fishing incident and the rules about vacation on Earth.

"So you're not a corpse," Duncan said.

"What's left of my body is still in the urn"—she flashed him a mock-annoyed look—"behind the dead mower *in your garage.*"

His lip curled. "Did you expect me to build you a shrine?"

"No, I get it. Anyway, I'm a recorporialized soul. Everyone in Hell is. But for this October, I'm as human as you are."

A wicked glint entered Duncan's eyes. "So if I killed you right now..."

"Yep. Oblivion for me too."

"Why risk it?" Duncan asked, serious again. "And why come here?"

"Maybe I just wanted to see my stupid little brother again," Sara Lee said.

He folded his arms. "Just like that. After all these years."

"Time doesn't have the same meaning after you die." Sara Lee scooted onto the seat next to his, pulled his arms apart and clasped his hand. "I would have come to see you if I'd thought it would help."

"So why now?" he repeated, breaking free.

Sara Lee considered telling Duncan the truth, but figured he wouldn't be receptive to hearing it at the moment. "I heard Mom died a few years ago. We're all each other has left. This is the first vacation Satan has given me since Oscar died, and I want to spend it with you."

He opened his mouth, then closed it into a thin line and stared into space.

Sara Lee passed a hand across his vision. "Earth to Dough Boy."

He sighed. "I hate those stupid nicknames."

"I know," Sara Lee said, grinning.

"Look, I need time to process all this," Duncan said. "Call me tomorrow?"

"Sure."

He grabbed a notepad from the counter, jotted down the number, then walked her to the door.

She squeezed into the Smart Car and headed for the highway. JD had recommended a five-star hotel on the Country Club Plaza, Sara Lee's favorite place in Kansas City, with its graceful domes, colorful Spanish tiles and numerous fountains.

Not long after she merged onto the interstate, movement in the corner of her eye drew her attention. A semi-truck entering the highway accelerated toward her. Sara Lee glanced left. A pickup prevented her from changing lanes. She stomped on the accelerator.

Nothing happened.

"Damned squirrel-powered engine!"

The semi tapped the rear bumper. The Smart Car flew forward, then shimmied. Sara Lee turned into the skid and straightened the car's course. As the truck accelerated again, she steered onto the shoulder and hit the brakes. The semi roared by, then tried to turn. It slid into the next lane, crushing a Nissan Leaf, a Chevy Volt and a Toyota Prius. So far, "green" cars weren't impressing Sara Lee. The GMC Yukon, however, had simply been knocked aside.

Brakes screeching, the truck careened to the opposite shoulder and dented the guard rail. On the back of the trailer was a "How is my driving?" sticker.

Sara Lee rolled down the window and shouted, "This isn't funny, Satan!" Satan probably figured God couldn't do much more to her for disobeying His orders. It wasn't like Satan hadn't done it before.

Still breathing hard, Sara Lee patted the plastic Jesus on the head. "Thanks."

Good thing she'd taken that Dale Earnhardt race car driving course at Disney World. Which reminded her—the Food and Wine Festival was going on at EPCOT.

Beautiful, overhanging trees lined the street on which the limo carried Bunny. The road wound uphill to a gated estate, Rosewood Manor. Bunny let out an excited squeal as she clutched the key. It felt like 1969 again, when she'd bought her first mansion, after her film *The Thing from Outer Space* became a blockbuster—playing at midnight showings everywhere.

Inside, a marbled entrance with rose quartz pillars and facing, curved staircases greeted her. A crystal chandelier hung over a mosaic on the tiled floor.

Bunny gasped. Suddenly, she thought it was too bad Kitty didn't want to be War. Bunny could enjoy retirement here. Then she remembered, she'd have to retire in Heaven. Oh, well.

As she strolled toward French doors draped in white lace, they swung open into a sitting room. Automatic doors in a house. Pure genius. The boys thought of everything.

She tossed her purse at a credenza. The purse arced in

mid-air, clearly coming up short, but its trajectory altered and the purse landed on the polished wooden surface. *My aim's getting better. Who knew I could manage a hook shot?*

Wanting to soak up the luxury as she relived her glory days, Bunny sank into an overstuffed chair. Although a recliner wouldn't fit the decor, it would be nice. Bunny raised her feet anyway and murmured, "A footrest would be nice."

A fringed ottoman scooted across the room and stopped beneath Bunny's raised feet.

Bunny sat straighter, gripping the chair arms. "No way! Voice-activated furniture? Wow! If I had money, I'd give those boys a bonus!"

The chauffeur had hauled in Bunny's luggage, then left. Seeing the blushing pink, faux-leather computer case next to her guava pink suitcases, Bunny hopped to her feet. Her stilettos clicked against the stone tile.

She opened the laptop, thought for a minute before remembering the silly password—War—then Skyped Wreak and Havoc.

"Boys! The mansion is perfect!" Bunny squealed. "You've really outdone yourselves!"

"Whoa, Mistress," Havoc said, popping his jaw and rubbing his ears, "can you take it down a notch?"

"Take what down?" she asked.

"Never mind," Havoc said, "I'll adjust the volume."

"You'll have to do that yourself," Bunny said. "I can't be bothered popping into Hell just to fix your computer. Besides, I thought you boys were supposed to be so computer savvy."

Wreak started to say something when Havoc interrupted, "Just let it go." Staring at her, he continued, "Mistress, is that the reason for your call?"

"I called for two reasons, actually. First, where's my staff? They should've been lined up in the foyer to greet me and introduce themselves. And B, this place has remote-controlled furniture! Stuff comes when you say something. I think it's voice-controlled ... or ooh, maybe there's tiny robots under the furniture, or some sort of powerful magnet—"

"She's babbling like you do sometimes," Havoc said, looking sideways at Wreak.

"Not funny," Wreak said. "The day I sound like Bunny, shoot me."

"Okay. Just remember you asked me to." Havoc let out a

malicious chuckle.

Bunny wrinkled her nose in confusion. "What would be the point? He's already dead. He'd only recorporealize."

"Yes," Havoc said, "but he would go through the excruciating pain of it ... and while he's between states, I'd get a few moments of peace and sanity."

Bunny cocked her head, wondering if that was all Satan ever wanted. She certainly killed and re-killed tormented souls over and over. She'd threatened to do worse to the Redheads often enough. Bunny shook her head. It was pointless. After death there was no more death ... unless someone died a second time while on vacation.

Bunny gasped. "I'm on *vacation!*"

"Yes, Mistress?" the boys chimed.

"I just realized, I need to be careful. No ice fishing for me!" *As if.*

"Mistress," Havoc said, snapping his fingers, "about your staff ... we can't get any. No one will work at the mansion because ... well, because ... you see, it's ... oh, it's kinda—"

"It's *haunted,*" Wreak blurted. "Get to the point faster. You always beat around the bush. And you say *I* sound like Bunny."

"What's that supposed to mean?" Bunny asked.

"It means you take the scenic route when you're telling a story," Wreak snapped.

"Hush," Havoc said. "Miss Bunny paints a lovely picture when she's relating a story."

"That's because I'm an actress. We artistic types are naturally poetic." Bunny sighed inwardly, while smiling wistfully outwardly. Adam was naturally poetic. If he weren't a cowboy, he'd have made a fine actor. The way he read poetry, he could've done Shakespeare—the guy who wrote such famous plays as *Phantom of the Opera* and *Peter Pan.*

Then Wreak's words sank into Bunny's head. She leaned in closer to stare into the boys' screen-lit eyes. "What do you mean by haunted? Are you telling me there's a man with a hook or the boogeyman living in my closets?"

"Technically, those wouldn't be hauntings," Havoc said gently.

"Those would be horror movies," Wreak said, not so gently.

"You have a ghost, according to all accounts," Havoc explained. "No one has ever seen the ghost, but unexplained things keep happening. Scary things. We'll find you another place, Mistress."

"In the meanwhile," Wreak said, "don't antagonize the spirit."

"You're crazy. Nothing scary has happened. Everything here just works on automatic. It's very cool, and I love it here." Bunny folded her arms to show that she meant business. "Besides, who needs a staff when the furniture comes when you call? Even my purse knows to land on the credenza and not the floor."

The boys rolled their eyes.

"You could be in danger," Havoc said. "Remember, you are on vacation."

"It's remote controlled," Bunny maintained. "There's no such thing as ghosts. You know how Type A Zoe is, and her motto— 'No man left behind.'"

Havoc tsked. "That's not *her* motto—it's actually one of yours—or more specifically, it comes from the Marines."

Bunny shrugged. "No matter. Zoe hates open cases. She'd never forget a soul, and it'd be Reaper's hide if *he* ever did." She waved off the conversation. "I need to contact my agent and see if I can get some work. Someone has to make me money. I sure can't live off the few bucks you'll get for Ares's old junk. Some vacation."

"But Mistress," Havoc said.

"Try to focus," Wreak said.

Amid their babble, Bunny shut the laptop. She needed her phone, which was in her purse, all the way across the room. The boys were crazy. This place wasn't haunted. There were no chains rattling, no ghostly moans, no inexplicable pounding. Hadn't the boys ever heard of *A Christmas Story*, the tale of the ghost Bob Marley and his lame son Charley, who eventually won a chocolate factory?

Bunny held out her hand and said, "Purse, come to me."

The purse floated to her waiting palm.

"See. Remote control." Bunny grinned. For once, she was smarter than the boys.

"Actually," a disembodied voice said, "it's me."

A ghostly pale figure of a man appeared and bowed politely.

"Who are you?" she asked.

"No one you would recognize by my real name. But I'm well-known as D.B. Cooper."

"Dee Bee? Are you a foreigner? I've never heard of a foreign ghost. I thought ghosts had to return to their homeland. Or is that vampires?"

"D.B. isn't a name, it's initials," the ghost interrupted. "It's what people call me. And I'm not a foreigner."

Bunny perched her hands on her hips. "What's with everyone going by nicknames? First Adam wants to be called Pernell and now you." She leaned forward. "Wait, were you a cowboy?"

"Not exactly," he said. "Let's just say I was an entrepreneur, a visionary, a man ahead of his time."

"Now it makes sense. I'm sure Reaper will find you when it actually *is* your time."

"I beg your pardon?" D.B. said.

"You said you were ahead of your time. I know how that feels. I died before my time too. Luckily, Ares was there to collect me—or I might've ended up a ghost too."

"I see what your companions on the computer meant. No matter. I like you. There's something genuine about you."

"It's really me, all right," Bunny said. "I'm not one of those celebrity look-alikes or impersonators."

"You're a celebrity?" The ghost studied her closely. "You do look familiar, but you can't be who you look like. She died years ago. Plus, if she'd lived, she'd be in her sixties or seventies by now."

"I'm Bunny Louise Baker, star of film and television," Bunny said, lifting her head. She had every right to be proud. Her impressive film career included the starring role in *Madame Curie Defeats the Martians.*

"Get out of town! I'm a big fan! I've seen every movie you made! Up until my death, that is." The ghost hovered closer. "Did you fake your death? Because your plastic surgery is amazing!"

"Hey! I haven't had plastic surgery!" Bunny folded her arms with a huff.

"Then how are you still alive and looking twenty-two?"

Bunny brightened. "I'm twenty-eight ... but I moisturize." Then she shrugged. "I stopped aging when I died."

"You're the most solid-looking spook I've ever seen."

"I've been recorporealized. Right now, I'm on vacation, so I'm actually alive ... again. I'm War—one of the Four Horsewomen." Bunny quickly explained, over the next hour and a half, about her fellow Redheads and their husbands' demises. She finished with, "Anyway, not everyone has heard of the Four Horsemen, so I wouldn't expect people to know they had wives."

"Pretty much everyone has heard of the Horsemen," D.B. said. "But you're right—I had no idea they were married."

"Ares kept his work and home life separate, something I appreciated. I mean, who cares about what happens during a war? It's always the same old thing."

"So, now *you're* War, and you have no interest in war. Interesting."

"Oh, it's not interesting. Lately, I have more important things on my mind." Bunny sat on the white sofa with turquoise and gold throw pillows. She propped her elbows on her knees and rested her chin on her palms. "I've lost my expense account, so I have to find a way to make some money."

She grabbed the remote and turned on the television. A news broadcast filled the large, flat screen. A woman with plastic-looking hair and an even more plastic expression droned on.

"The president has signed a bill giving the Pentagon ten billion dollars for the latest drone technology."

Bunny turned off the television. She glared at the ghost. "Can you believe it? I'm broke and they're spending all that money to start a band."

"A band?"

"That newscaster just said they wanted to learn modern drum techniques."

"*Drone technology*," D.B. said. "You know—remote-controlled planes that target the enemy."

"And bombard them with drum music?" Bunny cocked her head. Maybe some of her more innovative thinking had rubbed off on the war department.

"There's no drums involved—although the planes make a sort of droning noise."

Bunny flung herself backwards on the sofa. "They've got ten billion and I'm on a budget. I'd like to see *them* operate on a budget."

"Uh, Bunny, they *do* operate on a budget. Most people and organizations on the planet have to budget."

"Even the government?" Bunny asked.

"Well, they *should*, but they don't have the hang of it."

Bunny tapped her chin. "Maybe I should get my job declared a government position. Then I wouldn't have to live on a budget either."

"It doesn't work that way," D.B. said.

"Have you ever been War? I didn't think so." Bunny pushed to her feet and paced. "For now, I need a way to make a quick buck." She spun around. "Do you know anything about scoring a lot of cash fast and easy?"

The ghost shifted uncomfortably on cloudy feet. "I may know something ... not that it worked out all that well for me. Though I did get a good laugh when I heard the FBI finally closed the case against me awhile back, after getting no new evidence for so many years."

"Whatever. I'll think of something else." Bunny snapped her fingers. "I'll make another movie! Hollywood is always paying actresses loads of money. I'll bet they're paying more now than when I was alive." She felt like her insides had lit up like a light bulb—or at least a glow-stick. Then she paused. This brilliant new idea sounded familiar. Shrugging off the feeling of déjà vu, she said, "I might even make fifty thousand dollars."

Bunny pulled her smart phone from her purse and searched the directory for her old agent. Even as it dawned on her that he'd be an old man, she found his listing.

A receptionist answered her call. "Tommy Sangers's office, how may I help you?"

"I'm a client of Tommy's, Bunny Louise Baker."

"One moment please." After a moment, she said, "I can't find your listing."

"I was a client up until 1972," Bunny explained, "then I sort of retired."

"You must've been Tommy Sangers, *Sr.'s* client. This is the office of Tommy Sangers, Jr. I'm afraid his father has passed away. One moment, and I'll see if Mr. Sangers can see you."

"Don't bother if he's dead," Bunny said. "He won't still have his old contacts."

"I was referring to his son," the receptionist said.

Muzak played through the receiver.

Finally, Bunny heard, "Mr. Sangers can see you next week."

"I don't have that much time. I need to see him *today*. Perhaps you should remind him that I'm War."

"War?" the woman on the phone said.

Bunny launched into her "brief" explanation.

Twenty seconds in, the receptionist interrupted, "I don't have time for your life's story. Can you give me a reason why Mr. Sangers should see you in ten words or less?"

Bunny considered a threat involving her Warstomp, but

wasn't sure she could explain that in ten words or less. She settled for saying, "Remind him I starred in *For the Love of War*."

More Muzak.

A young man's voice came on the line. "Miss Baker, I'm Tommy Sangers, and I believe I have the perfect project for you. As luck would have it, last week I received a script in the mail titled *Return of the Space Thingy*. It's a sequel to the film you did, *The Thing from Outer Space*, and reprises your role. You're perfect for the part."

Bunny squealed. Her mother, Birdy, had always said Bunny was the luckiest girl alive. Certainly, good things seemed to happen to her.

The drive through rural towns and farmland of the Smoky Mountains actually made a nice change after the mad rush of New York and Comic Con. Zoe leaned back in the rental car seat and sighed as she let herself relax for one of the few times since she inherited her job.

The wind whipped through her hair. They'd sprung extra for the black Mustang convertible. What better way to experience the autumn countryside than with the top down? Zoe stretched her arms overhead like on a roller coaster. She loved this feeling, but a quick glance at Jake indicated a possible fly in the honeymoon ointment.

"What're you thinking about?" Zoe asked.

"Whether or not there are actually coincidences."

"You're still worried about that?" Zoe twisted in her seat to study his profile as he drove. She'd never thought to ask how or when he'd learned the skill, but sure enjoyed the ride. "Come on, honey, accidents happen. That's all they were."

"Yeah, well, I come from more … cynical stock, and I'm your husband. It's my job to worry."

"And I love you for it, but until we see something more concrete, let's just crank some tunes and enjoy the scenery." She reached for the radio and laughed maniacally as AC/DC's "Highway to Hell" blasted from the speakers. Jake responded by stepping on the accelerator.

"Oh, and a bathroom stop wouldn't be unwelcome."

Jake looked at the dashboard. "We could use some gas anyway. Keep an eye out for a good place."

Twenty miles later, they pulled into a new-looking Tres Zoom convenience store and gas station. "Pick up some snacks and drinks while you're in there," Jake said.

"Aye, aye, Captain." Zoe threw an insolent salute and sauntered inside.

She felt drawn to the short-order kitchen section of the store. Pre-packaged processed snacks didn't call to her, but the bathrooms were about to start screaming in her head.

"Can I he'p ya, honey?" A big-haired matron bustled through the store. Her strong country twang blurred the words into near incomprehensibility.

"Just trying to make a decision. What's good?"

"Welp, the catfish is fresh." The words seemed to ooze from the woman with more syllables than necessary. "Grew the onions for the onion rings my own self and the batter's from my Granny, God rest her soul."

"I'll take an order of onion rings."

"Try the tea, too. It's just brewed. Sweet and pine. Just there."

As much as Zoe wanted to know what "pine" tea was, she had pressing concerns. "Will do. But first, the facilities?"

"Ladies is 'round the corner."

Zoe scurried to the restroom to take care of business. She thought she heard the door open and the woman greet a new customer. In moments, she emerged, feeling much lighter and happier. She scanned the racks and shelves on the way back to the tea urns, but only really noticed a baseball cap floating just above them.

"Yer rings're done, honey. Bagging them up now."

"Thank you." Zoe studied the urns. One had "Sweet" scrawled across it in Magic Marker. The other was blank but for condensation. Zoe grabbed two larger Styrofoam cups and filled them from the blank urn.

Zoe paid and gathered up the drinks and the paper bag already stained with grease.

The woman said, "You come back, now."

Zoe nodded and left the store without looking at the other customer. She headed back toward the car. Jake had finished pumping gas and passed her on his way inside.

"I'll be right back," he said.

Zoe settled the food and drinks in the car and leaned on the quarter panel to wait for Jake. Just as he stepped out, a figure in the hat she'd noticed inside pushed past Jake, nearly knocking him down. Before she could do anything, the woman burst out.

"Hey, mister! You left your burrito or whatever in the microwave! And you didn't pay for it!"

She swung toward the guy ... at least she thought it was a guy hurrying away in loose jeans, t-shirt and flannel shirt. Something clicked in Zoe's head, something familiar—

"Jake! Move!" she shouted.

Jake grabbed the larger woman's arm to propel her toward the car. The convenience store exploded behind them. Jake and the woman were thrown halfway to the gas pumps.

Zoe dove to the ground as waves of heat drove the breath from her lungs. The pressure from the explosion drove asphalt into her palms and cheek. The roar died down to crackling flames. "Jake!"

"We're okay."

Jake staggered to his feet, helping the woman up as he did. They had a few cuts, scrapes and bruises. They looked shaken but generally unharmed. Sirens already bore down on them.

"Are microwaves supposed to do that?" The woman sounded dazed.

"Not in my experience," Zoe said. "But I don't know about yours."

"Did you see where the man went?" The woman sounded stronger. "I think he might've done something to it."

"And that's what you need to tell the authorities ... Rose." Zoe finally realized the woman had her name stitched on her uniform the whole time. They sat her on the curb as far from the building as possible and high-tailed it out of the area.

"Okay," Zoe said after a couple of miles. "Maybe it's not a coincidence."

"Not a time I want to be right. Are we going to talk about it?"

"Not on an empty stomach." Zoe dug into the grease-laden bag.

"What did you get us?"

"Onion rings and 'pine' tea."

"Love onion rings, but I don't know what pine tea is."

Zoe shrugged, trying not to be scared out of her mind. "Me neither, but the lady back there was really nice about it."

Jake saluted her without taking his eyes off the road. "Here's to the nice ones."

"I'll drink to that." They both took pulls off the straws. Zoe scrunched up her face. "Oh, it's ordinary unsweet tea."

"Are you sure she said, 'pine'? Could it have been 'plain'?" Jake asked.

"She did have a very distinct and thick accent." She took another pull of the tea. "So what do we do now?"

Jake stared out the windshield with a stern, determined look. "We go to the first family reunion. If we can find the relative right away, we can spend the rest of the time trying to figure out who's trying to kill you."

"You really think...?"

"I do now, don't you? How did you know to warn me?"

Zoe grinned in spite of herself. "Don't you remember *Grosse Pointe Blank*? It's one of the best movies *ever*. And that was a scene from it. I feel sorry for the lady though. She seemed lovely."

"You could always reward her."

"You're right." Zoe pulled out her phone and called Bambi.

"Hiya, Boss, did you buy me anything?" Bambi sounded chipper.

"Maybe, but that's not why I'm calling. I need you to check something for me. A convenience store just blew up in Tennessee. There was a woman working there, only name I have is Rose."

"Okay." Zoe heard Bambi tapping away. "Got it. Rose Elliot. She's not—"

"No. She made it. We were there. She's ... let's add a couple of years to her span. She'll need it to get back on her feet after today."

"Any particular reason?"

"Just chalk it up to buying time."

"You got it, Boss."

Zoe hung up her phone, grabbed an onion ring from the bag and bit into it. It was still warm, despite having been in the bag for a while. The onions were soft with still a bit of crunch and coated in a light, well-peppered batter. "These are to die for, Jake. Now, let's go find a relative."

Chapter Five

"You're sure I'm related to these people, Jake?" Zoe couldn't help the trepidatious tremble in her voice. They were deep in Midwest hillbilly country, in that no-man's land between Arkansas and the Mississippi border.

"It's just a family, and yes, a branch of your family. How bad can it be?"

She wanted to laugh at Jake's sudden, inexplicable optimism, but knew he was trying to reassure her. "You're kidding, right? First warning sign. The 'nice' hotel in the closest town is a Motel Six. And second? I see fire. Which probably leads to beer."

"Beer?" Jake perked up at that. Though he didn't drink all that much or often, his German heritage seemed genetically wired to respond to beer.

"Down, boy. It's the American redneck versions—Coors, Bud and Miller."

Jake waved the words off dismissively. "That's not *beer.*"

"It is to them, and unless you want a brawl on your hands, I'd keep that opinion to yourself. Now, how are we identifying ourselves to these people?"

"You're a cousin."

"That doesn't narrow it down much. In this part of the country, some of these folks are multi-level cousins and know it."

Jake held up a hand. "Let me finish. When you were alive, you had a cousin Clara."

"I remember her. When we were kids, people thought we were sisters, we looked enough alike."

"And that's what we'll use. Clara had a daughter, Karen. Karen split with the family when she was a teenager. She had kids. You're one of them."

"And if any of those kids are here?"

"From what I've learned from some of your living-challenged relatives, the family never reconciled. Your Aunt Mildred has kept tabs on her family through the generations. Clara's still alive, but frail enough she can't travel and hasn't had contact with any of them in decades. Heartbreaking, really."

"Social commentary aside, which branch are we dealing with here?"

"The Mow family. Your Scottish roots. Did you know the Mow clan motto is 'An interest after Death'?"

Zoe had to laugh. "Little do they know, right? Let's go see if we get lucky the first time out."

Jake parked the car near a group of SUVs and pickup trucks. The sound of raucous laughter and musical instruments drifted toward them.

"Do I hear … *banjos*?" Jake asked as they made their way to the giant tent in the middle of the open field.

"Probably, and some fiddles and guitars, but we don't have to run just yet. Wait and see if there's any shooting first."

Jake shot her a startled look. "Is that a possibility?"

Zoe laughed once more—with only a hint of hysteria. "Oh, honey, you have *no* idea. Let's make the best of this. I want more civilization in my American Road Trip."

As Zoe and Jake entered the tent, they got more than a few stink-eyes, though it was hard to tell through the dynastic-ally awesome facial hair—most of which was on the men folk. As their presence registered, the music stuttered and stalled.

"Can I he'p you?" The genteel, male country drawl held a faint note of threat. "This is a private event."

Zoe looked up—and up—at the very tall, very large man with a neatly trimmed, but still impressive beard. He wore a designer polo shirt and khaki shorts. His twang was refined, cultured and used to getting its way. Zoe smelled "lawyer."

She smiled at him and let all the twangs she'd heard for the last few days slightly color her speech. "I'm so sorry to show up like this, but Mama made me promise on her deathbed that I'd do my best to reconnect with the family. She was tore up over the rift, but didn't know how to make it right."

"And what family is that, exactly?" the man's voice rumbled deep from his facial hair.

"I'm Clara's granddaughter, Zoe. She and Mama had a huge fallin' out…" As Zoe spun the tale, the expressions around her softened.

"She is the spittin' image of Auntie Clara." A dainty woman stepped up beside the hulk of a man. Her head barely reached his biceps. She put her hand on his arm. "Let the lady sit,

Charlie Ray."

"Now, Lyndie—"

"This ain't one of your court cases, Charlie Ray." Lyndie stamped her designer boot-flip-flop combo shoe. "It's a *family* reunion, so let these good kinfolk come in and get to know the family."

The big man actually backed down from the bouffant-haired, aging beauty queen. Lyndie grabbed Zoe's hand and dragged her into the tent and introduced her around as music and conversations resumed.

"You hungry, honey?" Lyndie asked after an interminable parade of introductions. "What a silly question. Of course, you'll eat. Ruby Jean, get Zoe and her handsome hubby some barbecue. You two sit right down here, now, and Ruby Jean will fix you right up."

Zoe sat obediently on the folding picnic bench with Jake sliding in beside her. The whole scene had a catered feel, probably Lyndie and Charlie Ray, and that weirded Zoe out more than the facial hair and bluegrass music. She gripped Jake's hand under the table. "Don't leave me."

"I was going to say the same thing to you."

Plates overloaded with smoked meats covered in blood-red sauce, along with beans, potato salad and coleslaw, appeared in front of them.

"Let me get y'all something to drink. There's also about four kinds of pie and cobbler. You just help yourselves." Lyndie didn't wait for them to answer. She sailed off, barking orders to relatives in her sugary drawl.

"So? What do you think?" Jake asked quietly.

"I think I should've worn yoga pants instead of jeans. Even if I only eat half of this, I'll need the stretching. And there'll be hell to pay with Candace when we get home." Zoe dug into the potato salad.

"That not what I meant. The mission," Jake said around brisket.

Zoe resisted the urge to unbutton her jeans before tucking back into her plate. "One, it's not a 'mission.' We're not spies … much. And two, we just got here. Give it some time—and cobbler. I *love* cobbler."

"As much as me?" Jake's puppy dog expression made her both melt and giggle.

She patted his face. "Cobbler is forever, and it's a different kind of love. But for now, we eat, drink and get to know people. See if anyone clicks as someone who can take my place."

"No one can take your place."

"Awwww, you're cute. Now eat your brisket."

The awkward beginning to the meeting of the clan broke when a cherubic little girl with ringlets and a frilly dress bounced up to the table and asked gravely, "Are you really related to us?"

"Yes, I am." Zoe matched her seriousness.

"Good, 'cuz you're pretty. We need more pretty girls 'sides me."

"Reba Sue Mow, what did you just say to Miss Zoe?" Lyndie glared at the child.

"Nuthin'."

Zoe winked at Reba. "Sorry you got middle-named for that."

"I'm used to it. Always more fun when I earn it." Reba dashed off to play with the other children.

Zoe's exchange with the girl broke the ice with the adults. Before she knew it, she was whisked out onto a temporary dance floor and swung by multiple partners. She caught various glimpses of Jake with pie and wondered how he'd managed to avoid the Hoedown Hell she was in.

She staggered away from the dancing to collapse on a bench, trying her best to catch her breath. Jake appeared at her side with a Solo cup and helped fend off would-be dancers. She snatched the cup from his hand and drained it without caring what was in it.

"Good thing that's not the moonshine I've been offered six times while you were doe-si-doeing," Jake said with a laugh.

"We'll compare notes on who had it worse when you're helping me bandage blisters later. I was not prepared for this."

Jake shuddered as he glanced around to make sure no one was listening. "I don't think anyone's prepared for *this*. So you know, I'm ready to go when you are. This place is ... odd, and so are the people. Let's keep one of them as the last resort."

"That's ... disturbing. Let's start saying our goodbyes and get going." Zoe heaved herself to her aching feet.

"Y'all aren't leavin' already?" Lyndie stepped in front of Zoe and Jake as they tried to make a quiet and graceful exit.

"Yeah, well, I just ... it's been a long day..." Zoe tried to slip past, but Lyndie seemed to magically be in their way.

"Nonsense. You can't leave yet. The fun's just getting

started." Lyndie linked arms with them both and turned them back into the tent.

Zoe caught a glimpse of a couple in a shadowed corner of the tent, ardently making out. "Um, is *that* part of the fun?"

Lyndie followed her gaze. Her face lit up. "Oh! Look at that. Willie and Wanda finally got together. Charlie Ray, who wins that bet?"

Charlie Ray appeared out of nowhere. "Well, I believe that would be their mama."

Zoe swallowed hard and reached for Jake's hand. "Is 'mama' now considered both singular and plural?"

"Oh, no, they just have the one."

Jake's hold on Zoe's hand tightened hard enough to shift the bones. She winced. "Is one of them adopted?"

"Heaven's no. She always said they were close in the womb and just needed time to get back to that. Everyone here is biological, with a handful of 'in laws,' but we've known everyone for generations."

"I guess *Sister Wives* means something different here." Zoe tried to keep her tone light when she was simply burying her rising panic. She started seeing lecherous gleams in several sets of eyes and the growing number of occupied shadows.

"We don't truck with those multiple marriage things. We have standards." Charlie Ray actually puffed up in pride at that.

"Of course, my apologies, what was that, Jake? Oh right, our reservations. We really should be going. Thank you so much for having us. It's been enlightening to reconnect with family after all this time. We'll connect online. Stay in touch."

Zoe and Jake backed away during her speech, noticing the family members inching closer to them with hopeful hunger in their eyes, making her skin crawl.

They made it out of the tent. Zoe swallowed and said, "Don't run. I'm not sure turning our backs is a good idea either."

Once in the car, Zoe hit the door locks as Jake cranked the key. "Okay, darling, drive very fast. There's no way I'm handing over my domain to a relative who doesn't believe in family trees that *fork*."

A sea of hungry humans crowded around the hostess's desk at the entrance to the ship's dining room. As Butterflye moved to the front of the line, her phone signaled the arrival of another text message. "MJ dinner assignment: 1st seating, table 333. Good luk."

Butterflye squeezed to the front of the line. She tested her spiel on herself. "'Marley Jones? Do you know anything about cloning?' Yeah. Like she'll buy that."

While the hostess ushered a family to their table, Butterflye pushed to the vacant desk. She ran her index finger along the maître d's floor plan, until pinpointing table 333 on the lower floor of the cavernous dining room. In the background, a piano chimed out, "What a Wonderful World."

"Hi, Marley," Butterflye whispered to herself. "I'm your twin. We were separated at birth... Nope."

She slipped through the door and hugged the portside wall until she found her clone's table, in a corner with no view except the ladies bathroom door. "How about, 'Hi Marley. You don't know me, but we're sisters'?"

MJ sat with her back to Butterflye.

"Marley Jones?" Butterflye said to the woman with wavy shoulder-length hair the same hue as her own.

Marley turned around. "Yes?"

Both Redheads gasped. It was like looking in a mirror. Butterflye's rehearsed words escaped her. Instead, she stared and said, "Uhhhh..."

Marley Jones stood up. They were identical, almost. Marley had a fifteen-pound advantage on Butterflye that translated into a rounder face and a more robust figure. Marley Jones's interpretation of Butterflye's waist-length copper blonde tresses was a tightly permed shoulder-length do. Even on casual night, Butterflye donned her beaded blue evening gown, while Marley Jones wore a pink tank top with a burgundy "MJ" printed on the left boob. *How Laverne and Shirley.* They looked each other up and down, and back up again, stopping to study blue eyes to blue eyes.

"Wow," Marley said. "Doppelganger, man."

"I can't believe you talked me into this," Duncan muttered for the thousandth time since he and Sara Lee left Kansas City for Orlando.

"Oh, come on," Sara Lee said, nudging his ribs as they climbed the jetway toward the terminal. "Disney World is awesome. You just have to approach it like a child."

"I didn't mean going to Disney," he said. "I meant going

*any*where with my corpse sister."

"I told you—I'm not a corpse."

"Yeah, yeah, you're a recorporialized whatever. Is recorporialized even a word?"

"It is in Hell," she said. "So what happens with all of your patients while you're gone?"

"A pediatric dentist friend of mine is covering for me," Duncan said. "I've done it for him often enough. I've got the bite scars to prove it."

After retrieving their bags, they went to the rental car counter and got the biggest SUV Sara Lee could find. *Sorry, Jesus, but if Satan's coming at me with semi-trucks, I want a fighting chance.*

Before they pulled out of the lot, Sara Lee dug the Scotty dog and the plastic Jesus out of her purse and suction-cupped them onto the dashboard.

Duncan did a double-take. "A plastic Jesus? Seriously?"

"There are no atheists in Hell holes, little man," she said.

"Isn't it a bit late for faith?"

Sara Lee shrugged. "Jesus has been vague on that point."

"*You* know Jesus," he said with an incredulous stare.

"Sure. I'm Famine. I work for his dad—and, unfortunately, for Satan."

"So what's Jesus like?"

"He's ... nice. Really nice. And even when he doesn't like what I'm doing, he always lets me know in a nice way. God, on the other hand—"

Duncan's eyes bulged. "You've met *God*?"

"I told you—He's my boss. God appears to people in the way they best relate to Him. Zoe experiences God as a mind-blowing presence. Bunny sees Him as Santa Claus."

Duncan shook his head. "You're pulling my leg."

"I'm speaking the gospel truth, Chocolate Chunks," she said.

He glared at her. "Is Hell as bad as the Church says?"

"For most people, it's what you've heard," Sara Lee said, scanning the tollway for runaway semis or missing segments of bridges. So far, so good. "Torture, torment, fiery pits. But for those with higher-ranking jobs, it's not so bad. Oscar's place—well, mine now—is a little bungalow with a view of the Lake of Fire. Very romantic. The house is smallish, but three times the size of my New York apartment—and no roaches. They all live with Butterflye—she's Plague. Bunny—War—has a sweet mansion. But there's a lot more money in war than famine."

"You seem pretty matter-of-fact about having a job that involves starving people."

"Hell kind of desensitizes you," Sara Lee said. "Anyway, the world's overpopulated. And it's not like I'm very good at my job." Or *any* good.

"I'm surprised you haven't been replaced."

"God and Satan can't simply replace any of us. There are rules."

She'd wondered how to bring up the topic of loopholes, and now Duncan had given her an opening. She explained about the marriage contract. "I found a loophole that said if we could marry men acceptable to both God and Satan, then those men could assume the mantle of the Horsemen."

Duncan chuckled. "Look at you, with a mantle of office. In Hell." He cocked his head. "Have you thought about remarrying?"

Nathan's handsome face flashed in Sara Lee's mind—his mischievous blue eyes, that seductive smile...

"I'll take that dreamy look as a 'yes,'" Duncan said.

"Yeah, well, he has a kid, so him dying to be with me was a deal-breaker."

"Oh, sure, you worry about someone else's kid," Duncan muttered.

"She's *five*," Sara Lee said. "And her mother died in a car crash right after she was born. Anyway, after Nathan, I'm not ready to try love again."

"There's always a marriage of convenience."

"That didn't work out so well for Butterflye," Sara Lee said. "It led to the divorce of inconvenience. It was ugly, even by Hell's standards."

"So are there any other ways you could get rid of your job?"

This was almost too easy. But to her surprise, she couldn't bring herself to tell Duncan about the blood relative clause just yet. He'd think the only reason she was spending time with him was to get him to agree to take her job.

Isn't it? Jesus's voice said in her head.

Hush. She thunked the plastic Jesus on the back of the head. She hated it when he was right, if only partly.

They reached the Animal Kingdom Lodge, where Wreak and Havoc had obtained two Savanna View rooms, courtesy of Trump's credit card. They entered the lobby decorated with bamboo and with couches covered in bright African patterns. A man playing bongo drums called for children to join in on various drums that lay beside him—a special torture that Satan had adopted in Hell for people without children.

"You're gonna love this place," Sara Lee said. "Animals walk right by your balcony."

"What kind of animals?" Duncan asked warily.

"Ostriches, giraffes," she said. "No predators."

Duncan's grin made him look younger. "Giraffes? That's cool."

They checked in and left their bags for the bellmen to bring. Duncan's room was two doors down from hers. Sara Lee suggested they settle in, then meet for a late lunch. Paradiso 37 had the best margaritas—and this amazing spicy, cheese-coated corn.

On entering her room, decorated in African patterns of glaring orange, red, purple and yellow, she headed to the balcony. She slid open the glass door. The only animal currently in sight was some African version of a longhorn cow.

Maybe she should get a burger for lunch.

She checked the bathroom. "Only four towels? That won't do." Sara Lee took the sign requesting that she consider the environment and reuse her linens, stuffed it in a drawer, then called Housekeeping for six more towels. Like washing a few towels would destroy the rainforest. The "green" that hotels liked was the money they saved by convincing people to reuse their linens.

Someone knocked on the door. Sara Lee grabbed her purse so she could dig out a tip. After she opened the door, the bellman wheeled in a cart piled with her suitcases. As Sara Lee turned from closing the door, a tan blur streaked from the balcony and slammed the bellman onto his back. A lioness rested on his chest, pinning him with her softball-sized paws. She wore the same happy, open-mouthed expression as playful house cats right before they shredded their owners' hands. The bellman dragged in a breath, then screamed for help.

As the lioness slashed her paw across his throat, Sara Lee ducked into the bathroom and slammed the door. The bellman's screams quickly died.

"This is too much, Satan!" Sara Lee dug in her purse again and found her phone. She tapped the Skype app.

Havoc's welcome face appeared on her screen. "Hello,

Mistress," he said. "How's your room?"

"Kind of crowded," she said. "And I think I'll be charged a pet deposit."

The lioness roared and batted at the door.

"Was that a lion's roar?" Havoc asked.

"Lioness."

"Ooh, they're the real hunters in the pride. Not good."

Someone knocked at the room door.

"Help!" Sara Lee shouted.

The door creaked open. "What the...?" came a woman's voice. The lioness growled.

"Good kitty," the woman said, her voice high with fear. "Good—" She screamed, then fell silent.

Sara Lee cracked the door. The lioness sat licking blood off her paw. Her gaze snapped toward the bathroom and Sara Lee slammed the door.

"What should I do?" she asked Havoc.

"What tools do you have available?" Wreak asked from off camera.

"Uh, four towels, the free little shampoo and soap, a roll of toilet paper and the contents of my purse."

"Which are?"

A thud shook the bathroom door, followed by a throaty growl.

Sara Lee set her purse on the counter and started pulling things out. "Blackjack, knitting needles."

"Do you have any tuna in there?" Havoc asked.

"Seriously?" Sara Lee said.

"If you smack the cat hard enough on the nose with the blackjack, it *should* decide you're not worth the trouble," Wreak said.

She huffed. "I'm not Schwarzenegger." Another thud shook the door, and wood cracked. "This door won't last much longer."

She set aside the paperback, the dusted mints and bag of safety pins.

The top half of the door buckled inward. The lioness scrabbled at the jagged wood.

"You could stab her with a knitting needle and hope you hit a vein," Wreak said.

"Hope is not a plan, Wreak." Heart pounding, Sara Lee reached inside her purse again. Her hand landed on something soft. The ball of yarn Candace had given her. She pulled it out.

"Kitty want the ball?" she asked in a singsong voice.

The lioness tilted her head, a growl vibrating in her throat. Sara Lee waggled the ball in front of the big cat's amber eyes. "Go fetch."

She lobbed the ball over the lioness's head. The yarn landed past the bed and rolled out onto the balcony, trailing an end behind. The lioness's focus locked onto the rolling ball. She crouched, then sprang after it. The ball slid between the balcony railings and tumbled toward the ground. In a graceful leap, the lioness cleared the balcony. Still gripping her phone, Sara Lee wrestled the damaged bathroom door open, jumped over the dead bellman and ran to slide the balcony door closed. Below, the lioness contentedly mauled the yarn ball.

"Good work, Mistress," Havoc said.

"Blasted cats," Wreak muttered.

"Thanks, guys," Sara Lee said, her voice breathless. "I'll get back to you later."

She surveyed the damage. The bellman and housekeeper lay with their throats torn out. Sara Lee took the dropped pile of towels and threw them over the blood pooled on the carpet.

"Drat," she said. "Now I need more towels." Like anyone would use blood-soaked towels, rainforest be damned.

Reaper appeared in her room, phone in hand. "Two, heaven-bound," he said into the speaker. He looked from the screen at the bloody mess, then at Sara Lee. "What happened here?"

"It's all part of the circle of life, Reaper."

Chapter Six

The first day on the set was always the most exciting—except for the time when a cam light fell on Bunny, killing her. But that sort of excitement only happened once in a lifetime.

A young woman in a black and white-striped shirt with a red flower in her hair rushed towards Bunny. She carried a clipboard with yellow pages—script changes, by their looks.

The woman smiled. "Ooh la la. C'est la vie. Pommes frites et crème brûlée."

Bunny stared at her quizzically. No one told her this was a foreign film. "I'm sorry, but I didn't understand a word you said."

"Ooh la la. La plume de ma tante," the strange woman said. "Ooh la la, Mimi."

"You have to speak English," Bunny said. "I never picked up any Spanish."

"She *is* speaking English," a thirty-something man with a trim black beard and moustache said.

Bunny wrinkled her nose, then peered at the woman. Louder, she said, "Try speaking louder. What's your name?"

"Ooh la la, Mimi," the woman said with emphasis.

Bunny shrugged, her words of wisdom having fallen on deaf ears.

"Her name is Mimi," the man said. "She's your assistant."

Her head cocked, Bunny asked, "Who are you?"

The man thrust out his neatly manicured hand. "I'm Wil Wheaton, your co-star."

Bunny assessed him before shaking his hand. Wil was her love-interest in the film. He had dark hair, which she favored, and he was nice looking, though not as tall as she preferred. Oh well, she'd just wear lower heels. "I'm Bunny."

"I know. As soon as I heard you'd be doing this film, I contacted my agent for the job. I'm a fan of your old films." He wagged his head and sucked air through his teeth. "Not so much a fan of your current work though."

Bunny blinked. She hadn't made a movie since her death,

and no one counted reality television as work—in the professional sense. This was the only current work she'd had in decades.

"If you don't like *this* film, why are you doing it?"

"I wasn't referring to this film," Wil replied. "I mean your work as War. I'm a peace-lover, myself."

Bunny swished her hands in the air. "Don't blame me for anything. Ares made a huge mess of things, and I don't clean up after other people." An idea lit in Bunny's mind. "Oooh, I wonder if there are maids who could clean up the Meddling East?"

"You mean the Middle East?" Wil said.

"That's what I said." Bunny focused on the babbling woman. "Settle down Fifi, and tell me whatever you're trying to say, calmly."

"C'est *Mimi!*" An exasperated look crossed her heart-shaped face. "Ooh la la. Frère Jacques, Frère Jacques, dormez-vous? Aloutte, gentille Aloutte, Aloutte je te plumerai."

Bunny sighed in defeat. "Are those script notes for me?"

The woman nodded. As she pulled a couple of pages from the clipboard, she said, "Ooh la la. Dulce du leche."

Bunny scanned the pages. A new scene had been added.

"That must be the giant stingodile scene," Wil said.

"What's a stingodile?" Bunny asked.

"A mutant stingray-crocodile mix the Space Thingy creates with his blend-o-ray gun."

"This movie must have a *big* budget. It'll make … thousands of dollars at the box office."

"You're half right," Wil said. "It'll probably make *thousands* of dollars, but it'll be in DVD sales."

"I love intellectual films," Bunny said. "Science is really important—or at least that's what Wreak says."

"You do realize this is science *fiction*," Wil said.

"Of course. Fictioning is that process where Texas tea is taken out of the ground."

Wil furrowed his forehead. After a moment, he said, "I think you mean fracking, but that has nothing to do with our movie."

"Sure it does. The Space Thingy is made of oil, so naturally, he'd come to Earth to take our natural resources."

"According to the script, the Space Thingy is made of shale." Wil raised both eyebrows. "Actually, Bunny, you're close enough. However, the creature is here to rob Fort Knox of our nation's gold. Don't ask me why. I quit trying to figure out SyFy Channel movies years ago."

"Well," Bunny said, "what is gold, if not our natural resource? The world can't run without it."

"Technically, we've been off the gold standard for decades, but I take your point."

"Ooh la la. In vino veritas. Veni, vidi, vici." Mimi flapped her clipboard in the direction of the stars' trailers.

"You're due in wardrobe," Wil said.

"It'd be much easier if she'd just say that," Bunny said.

"She did, and *in English*," Wil muttered.

Bunny followed Mimi to a silver trailer sporting a gold star. At least Bunny's name had been written in English. Then she thought how lucky it was that her co-star was multi-ethnic—or multi-something-or-other. Speaking another language must be confusing. Foreigners had different words for everything!

Bunny found her costumes hanging on a rack, each labeled with the date and sequence used in filming. One garment lay on the love seat, a pair of cut-off shorts and an orange halter top. Bunny groaned at the tacky outfit. Green and black sequin trim made the halter more tacky—something she never would've thought sequins could do. In a sequined-flash, she remembered what she hated about acting: wearing tasteless clothes. Yet all great artists had to suffer for their work.

With reverence, Bunny peeled off her clinging, plunge-neckline, lilac gown with the organdy ruffles gracing the back of her neck and shoulders. In its place, she donned the offensive costume. The shoes that went with it were not a pair of suitably matched cork or rope heels, but worn out, generic sneakers! Bunny's feet would never forgive her.

On some level, she knew she shouldn't be concerned about clothing ... but then again, a woman's appearance spoke volumes about her self-image and showed consideration for those who had to look at her.

After waiting five long minutes, Bunny poked her head out of the trailer and announced, "I'm ready for hair and makeup."

Wil, who sat in the shade with a soda, waved. "We do our own. Budget cuts."

Bunny closed her eyes. Since she'd been gone from Earth, Hollywood had gone to Hell in a golf cart. At least *she* had gone to Hell astride a magnificent steed.

Bunny headed back inside. In another few minutes—twenty-five of them—she emerged, her hair and face done perfectly. "Voila!" Bunny announced.

Her use of Italian seemed to summon Mimi. Quickly, the brunette babbled, "Ooh la la. Danke schoen, mein Führer. Ach, du lieber." She flapped her arms. "Schnell, schnell, sayonara."

The production manager approached, staring at Bunny. "Why aren't you made up?" Flipping through a handful of pages, he said, "This is the attack of the stingodile scene. You're supposed to look like you've been through a fight."

Bunny perched her fists on her hips. "I *am* War. I know how I should look in a battle, and believe me, this isn't it."

"No, it isn't. Use the dirt-smudge makeup at your mirror and muss your hair!" He stormed off.

Wil strolled up, his hair too short to muss, but dirt and fake cuts covered his face. "Do you need help? I've gotten pretty good at doing makeup for SyFy movies."

"It would be appreciated." Back in the trailer, Bunny asked, "Have you done a lot of films?"

"I've done a few," Wil said. "I've been acting since I was a kid. Maybe you saw me on *Star Trek: the Next Generation*?"

"Captain Kirk had a son?" Bunny recalled her reality dating show. Had she married Captain Kirk, Wil would've been her stepson, which would make the upcoming romance scene awkward.

"No, he didn't. No one in the show was descended from the original characters."

"Then how can it be the next generation? I may not know a lot of science, but I know how a generation works. And living in Hell, I know how regeneration works too. People get killed and re-killed all the time. They 'poof,' then recorporealize. I've been told it's a slow and painful experience."

"Has it ever happened to you?"

Bunny shook her head. "I'm one of the Four Horsewomen. No one torments us. Well, that's not entirely true. Sara Lee says Satan torments her with her weight—and the fact she can't eat anything outside of her domain. Butterflye says everyone on the job torments her. Poor dear. And Zoe is tormented when Reaper brings her decaf coffee by mistake."

"Doesn't anyone torment you?"

"Not really. Training with weapons is boring. Like I would do any actual fighting myself. That's what the Army is for."

"There you go. You're finished," Wil announced.

Bunny looked in the mirror at her disheveled self. She hadn't even noticed him working. She squinted at the dirt on her cheeks and forehead. Her hair looked like she'd ridden in a convertible through a tornado. Speechless, she made a face. After all, if you couldn't say anything nice, it was best to say nothing at all. So she settled for a half-smile and a shrug.

A knock at the trailer door and a yelled command gave them five minutes to appear on the set.

Wil handed Bunny her script. "Don't worry. There's not much dialogue—thank God."

"God edited our script?"

"No, He didn't. Not even Jesus could save this script."

"Yes, he could," Bunny said. "Jesus saves everything. You should see his collection of crosses. He says it's kind of morbid to keep them, but they have sentimental value."

"I'll take your word on that."

Wil led Bunny to the backlot. Cameras and lights hung from booms and lines. Wonderful, yet not entirely comfortable, canvas chairs sat in rows with names on the back. Bunny found hers up front, near the director's. A familiar, thrilling chill tickled her spine. How she'd missed being an actress!

"Take your places, people!" the director shouted.

Mimi dragged Bunny toward a taped X, her blathering words tripping over themselves. "Ooh la la, ooh la la! Cinqo de Mayo. La cucaracha. Adios, muchacho."

A partially curved wall of concrete blocks with a surrounding window formed the backdrop.

"Okay," the director said, once Bunny and Wil stood on their marks, "you're in the lighthouse when you look to the horizon. Take it from there." Louder, he called for the clapboard man.

"Scene 17, take 1!" The clapboard snapped, making a loud thwack.

Bunny stared at Wil. Wil stared at Bunny. After a couple of minutes, the director called, "Cut!"

"You have the first line," Wil said.

"I was getting into character," Bunny explained.

"Do that in your trailer," the director snapped.

At a nod from the director, the clapboard man shouted, "Scene 17, take 2!" Thwack!

Bunny lurched onto her tippy toes and pointed out the window. "Look! Do you see that strange, not at all Earthly-looking lump rising out of the ocean?"

"Cut!" The director jumped to his feet. "You're pointing the wrong way."

"How am I supposed to know where to point?" Bunny asked.

"You might've pointed towards the green screen," he said, exasperation tinging his voice. He snapped his fingers at the clapboard man.

"Scene 17, take 3!" Thwack!

Bunny pointed at the blank screen that didn't look anything like the ocean. "Look! What is that earthy lump rising out of the ocean?"

"Cut! Cut! Cut!" The director stormed their direction. "I don't expect to get everything in one take, but I would like to get a whole scene. Bunny, that's not the line. The creature rising out of the ocean is not at all Earthly. You called it an earthy lump—which would make it a pile of dirt."

"Sorry. I only got the script this morning."

"A good actor never makes excuses."

Turning his head aside, Wil muttered, "A good director gives his actors a chance to learn the script." He patted Bunny's arm. "I'll try to help. I know it's been awhile since you've acted—not that I mean you look old by any means."

Of course he didn't mean that. Bunny took care of herself.

"Scene 17, take 4!" *Thwack!*

Bunny pointed at the screen. "Look!"

"I see it," Wil jumped in. "It's some sort of unearthly lump, rising out of the sea. Whatever could it be?"

"Cut!" The director loomed into Wil's face. "No ad-libs. Stick to the script!"

As soon as the director turned around, Wil muttered, "I hate when directors write the script. They think every word is sacred."

"Scene 17, take 5!" Thwack! Thwack! Thwack!

Three hours later, the clapboard man, his shoulders sagging, clapped the board again, his shout worn down to a hoarse cough. "Scene 17, take 45!"

Wil winked at Bunny. "We'll get it this time."

Bunny jumped to her toes, pointing. "Look! Do you see that strange, not at all Earthly-looking lump rising out of the ocean?"

"Yes, I do. It is some strange, not at all Earthly lump." Wil staggered. "Oh, the horrors!" He pointed frantically at the screen. "It has a crocodile's head and a stingray's flippers and stinger!

It's … it's … a stingodile!"

"How could such a thing exist?" Bunny asked, clapping her palms to her cheeks. She shook her head wildly, opening her green eyes as wide as possible.

Wil assumed an authoritative stance. Rubbing his beard, he said, "It's my theory the Space Thingy has some sort of mutating, creature-blending ray gun—a blend-o-ray gun, if you will. He must be using it to create monsters to destroy the Earth."

"Why would he do that?" Bunny asked, glad her dialogue covered the important topics. Without *her* character, the audience wouldn't know what was happening.

"Again, I am just theorizing, but I would say the Space Thingy is out for revenge since we sent him packing the last time he visited Earth. Or have you forgotten how we reverse-engineered his rocket and launched him towards the sun?" Wil sighed heavily and wrung his hands. "Unfortunately, it appears that this sort of creature can survive the sun's heat."

"Maybe he's made of asbestos," Bunny said, wondering what asbestos was and whether it would survive Hell's heat any better than some of her gowns had—most especially ones with bits of ostrich or marabou feathers.

"It's coming! I'll protect you, Amy!" With that, Wil lunged for Bunny, wrapping his arms around her.

"Who's Amy?" Bunny asked quietly.

In her ear, Wil whispered, "You are."

Together they huddled and trembled. Then the set started to shake. A wall cracked, then split in two, crumbling to either side of Wil and Bunny. A fissure opened in the floor. Overhead, lights started swinging, along with sandbag weights.

Wil, glancing upward, said nervously, "I don't think that's supposed to happen."

"If it wasn't supposed to happen, it wouldn't," Bunny said calmly. "I'm sure our director is quite competent."

"Based on what?" Wil asked.

A sandbag shot toward the floor and struck a hapless cameraman. As the sandbag exploded, so did the man's head. The cameraman's dead body fell from his chair, the thud barely audible over the chaos.

"I'm sure *that* wasn't supposed to happen," Wil said. "We don't have the budget for those kind of effects. That's our cue to vamoose!" He grabbed Bunny's hand and dragged her as he ran.

Overhead, the metal bracket holding a cam light broke. The light whistled as it fell. Wil kept running. The light crashed behind them, crushing an errand boy trying to get into pictures.

"That was close," Bunny said. "And really familiar."

A man with swarthy skin and a goatee stood off to one side. He wore black leather with a breastplate. He reminded her of someone, but there was no time to ponder that.

Wil and Bunny raced through the studio. Sandbags and lights rained down, barely missing them. Most struck the floor harmlessly, but three hit fleeing people, killing the donut girl, an extra and the clapboard man.

Meanwhile, Mimi ran in circles. "Ooh la la! Ooh la la! Merde! Scheiss!"

His face beet-red, the director shouted, "Cut! Cut! Cut!"

A cameraman shouted back, "Who's filming?" Then he ducked under a catering table.

Wil pointed. "He's got a good idea!"

When they reached a food-laden table, Wil lifted the tablecloth for Bunny to crawl under first.

Once every sandbag and light had fallen, the chaos stopped. Wil peeked out from under the table, then announced, "It's safe."

As Bunny crawled out of hiding, she spied the familiar-looking man. She would've sworn she'd seen his face not just before, but every day before. He looked just like ... *Ares!* Yet Ares had gone to oblivion. After a mental reboot, it struck her—he was Mars, Ares's twin brother.

Bunny smiled. How nice of her brother-in-law to watch her film—just like Ares used to do, only she hadn't known about it. Ares had been shy. Maybe Mars was shy too.

Bunny waved to her brother-in-law.

Mars scowled, then ran behind a cart pulling scenery. By the time the moving wall of plants and furniture had passed, Mars was nowhere to be seen. Oh, well. He probably figured he shouldn't be on the set of a closed shoot.

Wil climbed to his feet. "That was scary." Wryly, he added, "Too bad the film won't be."

"Accidents happen," Bunny said. "No one's to blame."

"I just witnessed five people *dying*," Wil said. "Not cheesy, computer-graphics deaths, but really *die*."

Bunny batted her lashes. "What do you think happened to

me? So don't think I can't relate. It's just that I know where they're going. If they were good people, then they really are in a better place. If not, oh, well. That's what Hell is for."

"Wow. You really take death nonchalantly." Wil rubbed his temples. "I need to lie down." He glanced at the ruined set. "It'll be awhile before we resume shooting anyway."

As Bunny opened her mouth to speak, another familiar figure caught her eye. She waved goodbye to Wil, who staggered toward his trailer, then she headed toward Reaper.

"Are you here to watch me film?" Bunny asked. "Because there's been an accident, and we won't be shooting for at least an hour."

Reaper raised one eyebrow. "I'm here because seven people died."

"Seven? I only saw five." Bunny rolled her palms upwards. "But I guess you know your business. If anyone is kicking and screaming that he doesn't want to go, you might check his pulse."

That earned Bunny a glare. "I can tell the dead from the living, thank you."

"Do you like working with the dead?" Bunny asked.

"Eh. There's moments." Reaper grinned wickedly. "The ones who go to Heaven are boring, but the wicked are pretty amusing when they see the gates of Hell." His eyes glazed over in rapture. "They usually mutter stuff like: 'I don't believe in Hell.'" Reaper laughed. "It's hysterical!"

"It sounds depressing, but I'm glad you enjoy it. Of course, that wasn't how it was for me when I died." Bunny clasped her hands to her heart. "Ares took me to a beautiful green, grassy mound. From there, a portal led to his mansion." There just wasn't romance like that anymore. Adam tried, and he was very sweet and attentive, but where were the heroics? Ares had come to her rescue—granted it had been *after* her death—but it was the thought that counted.

Reaper grunted. "You didn't enter Hell through any of the proper checkpoints. That should've gotten you thrown out, but you married Ares." He shook his head. "Why, remains a mystery. Ares was such a—" Reaper growled, then shook it off. "Did you know you were supposed to go to Heaven?"

Bunny nodded. "God told me. He tells me everything."

"*Everything*? Really?"

"Oh, sure. We're buddies. I'd invite Him to parties, but He

never goes to Hell." Bunny snapped her fingers. "Parties! I forgot. It's October. Halloween." She frowned. She wouldn't be back from vacation until Halloween. She'd just have to work around it. "Say, Reaper, what is the day after Halloween?"

"November first?"

"No. The holiday. Isn't it something to do with the dead?"

"November first is All Saints Day. I think you mean the second—which is All Souls Day, or Dia de los Muertos."

"I don't know why you're babbling in French, but All Souls Day will work. I'll host my Halloween party then."

"It won't be a Halloween party ... oh, never mind."

Bunny ignored Reaper's negativism. How did Zoe work with him all day long? "I've gotta start sending invitations."

Back in her trailer, Bunny Skyped with Wreak and Havoc regarding her plans. "So, I need you to set up an eVite. I'll get you the list later." Thinking about the mess in the studio, she added, "It looks like I have a little free time."

The Magic Kingdom was truly magical, the complete opposite of Hell. Unless you happened to be the mother of four screaming brats standing by the balloon man and watching a recently-acquired Lightning McQueen balloon sail away. Or the cast member, her Disney-patented smile strained, explaining to outraged parents that the height rules were, in fact, for the safety of their child and were not a plot to ruin their family vacation.

Sara Lee and Oscar had always been laid back about vacation. After all, the point was to relax and have fun. She'd never understood why people worked themselves into a lather when things unavoidably went awry. Sure, if something could be fixed, she'd ask someone to fix it. But self-ruining your vacation seemed kind of like putting *yourself* in Hell.

Duncan looked around with game enthusiasm, clearly trying to get in the spirit. He wore cargo shorts and a Micky Mouse shirt. "You were right about how cool the view at the hotel is. A giraffe came right by and peeked in my room. What did you see?"

"Oh, just one of those Ankole longhorn cows," she said. "And a couple of vultures later on." The vultures had cleaned up the remains after the lioness had her fill of Ankole cow.

"Well, I'm sure you'll see something better than that soon," Duncan said. "I saw employees leaving food around to encourage the animals to come near the hotel."

Whatever Satan used to draw in the lioness had really pissed that cat off. The Disney cleaning staff was as good as their reputation, however. Not a speck of blood remained on the carpet in her room.

A man in a Goofy costume waved as he loped by. Sara Lee wondered if that was Jesus. But he really seemed more of the Pluto type.

The Magic Kingdom was laid out like a big wheel. Disney studies showed most people defaulted to heading right, so Sara Lee and Duncan went left. Disney had made a science of crowd behavior, down to predicting with pinpoint accuracy which parks would be busy and which would have lighter crowds on any given day. After Satan "borrowed" their algorithms to predict which people would be most easily tempted into damnation, it had upped her returns sharply.

They bypassed the kiddie rides in Adventure Land and got in line for *Pirates of the Caribbean*. There was something quintessentially Disney about a ride that spawned a movie that spawned a redecoration of the ride to match the movie. Small wonder Satan copied their marketing strategies. Funny how something that promoted innocent fun could be twisted to such diabolical purposes.

Or maybe it wasn't funny at all.

Their "going left" strategy worked and within five minutes they settled into their boat. Sara Lee and Duncan had the back seat. Immediately ahead of them sat a couple with a ten-year-old boy, while three teenage girls occupied the front. The girls bent over their phones, giggling and paying no attention to the wonderful artistic details around them.

The boat set off with an ominous ghostly voice warning, "Dead men tell no tales." Actually, people in Hell always wanted to tell their stories and whine about how unfairly they'd been treated.

The giggling girls started to annoy Sara Lee. But she took deep breaths and looked around at a beach scene with pirate and mermaid skeletons and a cute animatronic crab snapping its claws. The boat drifted into darkness, then took a short dive down a "waterfall." The girls screamed like they were taking the fifty-foot plunge on Splash Mountain. When the boat emerged into a scene depicting a pirate ship raid on a walled town, the girls had vanished from the boat.

Stupid twits. Leaving the boat would get them ejected from the park. Better for everyone else, though—

A phone screen glowed on the front seat. Weird that one of the girls left her phone. Sara Lee had thought the things were welded to most teenagers' hands these days.

The cannon on the pirate ship boomed. A cannon ball streaked toward the boat. It splashed down inches away, spraying them with water.

"That was close," Duncan said.

"Don't worry. Disney has this stuff down to a science," Sara Lee said, though she didn't remember getting wet last time she'd ridden *Pirates*.

The boat passed several more rooms and entered a scene where the pirates had captured the town and were selling captive women as "brides." When a chant of "we wants the redhead" arose, Sara Lee smiled. Oscar had always leaned close and whispered that he, too, wanted the redhead.

In the next scene, the pirates had set the town ablaze. Fake fire flared in windows and "embers" glowed on the ground. The faint smell of smoke hung in the air. Amidst the destruction, pirates celebrated with jugs of rum.

"Now this is my kind of party," Sara Lee said.

Duncan shook his head. "You worry me."

A fireball sailed from a window and flew over their boat. Screams from behind pierced Sara Lee's eardrums. Turning, she saw that the boat behind them had been set ablaze. Maybe Disney had redone the ride again to make it spookier. Though dummies with blackening flesh and hoarse screams seemed overly gruesome for the most child-oriented park in Disney World.

When another fireball whooshed past Sara Lee's cheek in a streak of searing heat, she realized the obvious and pulled Duncan down. They crouched at the bottom of the boat while the boy in the seat ahead clapped in delight.

"What's going on?" Duncan asked.

"Satan's trying to send me to oblivion," Sara Lee whispered in his ear.

"Then who would be Famine?"

"I don't think she cares, as long as it's not me."

"Shouldn't you go into hiding or something?"

"There's no point. We're microchipped—Satan's way of making sure she can find us fast if we spend more than our allotted time on Earth. Well, all of us except Bunny. Knowing where Bunny is just pisses Satan off, and if Satan really wanted to know, she could follow the credit card charges. So anyway, we might as well have a good time."

He shook his head. "You really do roll with things."

"I'm on vacation. I *am* going to have fun if it kills me—figuratively speaking. I hope."

Without further incident, they made it to the end of the ride, a treasure room where Captain Jack Sparrow sang, "Yo, ho, yo ho, a pirate's life for me."

After the family climbed out, Sara Lee reached over and picked up the abandoned phone. Behind a selfie of the three girls, someone in a latex pirate mask brandishing a wicked hook had photo-bombed them. *How rude! Even for Satan.*

"That was ... bracing," Duncan said as they rode the "rolling gangplank" up to street level.

Sara Lee patted his back. "Welcome to my world."

After getting drenched on Splash Mountain and spin-dried on Big Thunder Mountain Railroad, they headed for Fantasyland. As Sara Lee surveyed the crowds at various rides, she spotted JD standing near Princess Aurora, who was signing autographs. Despite the heat—and the locale—JD wore a charcoal suit that seemed custom made for him—which it probably was.

Clearly JD had followed Sara Lee here. Maybe he was little sweet on her. Or maybe he was after that marriage of inconvenience thing so he could have Oscar's job.

Might as well find out. She steered Duncan through the gauntlet of ankle-bruising strollers toward JD, who seemed to be searching the crowd for someone.

Maybe me? Sara Lee wasn't sure how she felt about the possibility of JD having an interest in her. He was Oscar's brother. It felt kind of weird—not quite in an Arkansas way, but close.

She stopped a few feet from him. "Hello there."

JD turned. He covered his brief startled look with a smile. "I wanted to surprise you."

"How did you even know where I was?" she asked.

"My valet plays poker with Wreak and Havoc," he said.

Sara Lee whistled. "Brave."

Duncan cleared his throat.

"Oh, sorry, bro." Sara Lee made introductions.

Duncan looked JD up and down. "So you're also..."

"Recorporialized," JD said, "though I'm not sure that's a real word."

"All words were made up at some point," Sara Lee said.

"Do you want to join us?" Duncan asked, for which Sara Lee felt grateful. If she could find a way for JD to get the job instead of Duncan, she was all in favor of it. And spending time with JD gave her the best shot of seeing whether something could work with between them—if that was his intention.

"Sara Lee was about to put me in a hammerlock and make me ride 'It's a Small World,'" Duncan said.

JD made a face. "The most puerile ride at Disney World?"

"Have you ever ridden it?" Sara Lee asked, her gaze challenging him.

"No," JD admitted.

"You're not allowed to mock it until you've suffered through it," she said. "It's a Disney rite of passage, something you only do once—like walking thorough the Swiss Family Robinson Tree House or eating Dole Whip."

"I liked Dole Whip," Duncan said.

"Anything sweet would taste good to you," Sara Lee said. "You've been on a diet since 1995."

Ten minutes of the same sunny, sappy song performed in a dozen languages by too-cute, spinning puppets had Sara Lee considering the virtues of oblivion. But watching JD and Duncan enjoy mocking the ride made it worthwhile. And no one tried to kill her. Maybe that was another of Satan's torments—that Sara Lee should have to endure the entire ride before the mercy killing. Best to watch for trouble at the end.

When the boat reached the dock without incident, JD and Duncan climbed out. Before JD could turn to help Sara Lee, a cast member with a trim beard offered his hand. His name tag said "Jesus" and listed his hometown as "Nazareth."

"Hi, Jesus," Sara Lee said.

"Most people here use the Spanish pronunciation." His gaze darted to JD, who stood laughing with Duncan out of the way of people exiting the boat. "It really is a small world," Jesus said.

"I think JD might have a little thing for me," Sara Lee said, hauling herself up with much help from Jesus.

"And would you happen to have a little thing for him?"

A blush heated her cheeks. "I'm not sure."

"Well, take it slowly," Jesus said, wiggling his eyebrows. She smirked. "Yes, Dad."

Butterflye, wearing a silver snakeskin tankini, entered the spa. Ralph waddled unsteadily behind her on two legs, wearing a pink bonnet and a t-shirt that read, "I'm with Stupid." The arrow pointed down.

At the back of the room, Butterflye spied three occupied hot tubs with steam rising from the churning water. Fortunately, a faux-marble fiberglass tub tucked in the opposite corner sat vacant. As she walked through the spa, she deeply inhaled the air and smiled. "This artificial rose arrangement doesn't smell like rot."

She took a few more steps, stopped, closed her eyes and took in the spicy eucalyptus fragrance from a scent diffuser. "Oh, wow! That doesn't smell like gangrene."

As Butterflye passed the designated smoking section, the room's bouquet changed. "Hmm. That smells like Sister Angelica."

She hurried past the occupied tubs and stopped at the vacant Jacuzzi. This one smelled like vast quantities of chlorine. "Aww. This nice ethanol/isopropyl blend smells like … bacteria dying, my favorite scent, next to scotch."

Flowery prints washed in soothing hues covered the walls. The shelves above Butterflye's tub offered a skincare collection, as well as overpriced spa products and an antique, chrome lady's electric shaver embellished with rhinestones. She eyed the shaver. *Strange ambiance for a spa.* But it didn't matter. She had seized the only available hot tub, and baby, she was going to enjoy it.

She tested the water temperature with the tip of her toe. "Ah, perfect." About a hundred and fifty degrees lower than at home. She eased her body into the water and slid onto the seat high enough to keep her head above the water's surface. She leaned back, closed her eyes and lost herself in the sensation of water bubbling up around her. It felt as if angels were caressing her skin with their feathers; hopefully Satan wouldn't find out.

A few minutes later, she opened her eyes long enough to spot Marley Jones near the spa entrance. Butterflye waved to her clone.

Marley ambled down the row of tubs to the one holding her

other self. "Got room for one more?"

"Sure. Plenty of room."

"I'd have been down here earlier, but I had to stop for a smoke." Her eyes were red and her pupils dilated.

"That stuff will kill you," Butterflye said.

"Yeah, well, so will too much water." Marley looked closer at Ralph, who snoozed on the fiberglass ledge. "I didn't know you had a kid. What's his name?"

"This is Ralph."

Ralph woke up for a moment and cocked his head in Marley's direction. She scrambled back, almost falling into the neighboring hot tub. She straightened, closed her eyes and repeated, "It's a hallucination, a residual effect from PCP."

Ralph twerked his abdomen and resumed his nap.

"Don't take this wrong, Butterflye, but, wow, that's an ugly kid." She mumbled under her breath, "I'm related to her. Geeze, note to self: get tubes tied."

"Ralph and I aren't actually related," Butterflye said. "He belonged to Osmodeus, my late husband."

As Marley dropped into the pool, droplets sprayed into the air and a wake of chlorinated water swept over Butterflye's head. For a smoker, Marley's skin smelled more like Cheech Marin than the acrid Sister Angelica. The clone wore a too-small, green bikini with the letters MJ displayed prominently on the left boob.

Butterflye nodded at the bathing suit top. "Do you have your initials on all your clothes?"

"Those aren't my initials."

Pointing at Marley's boob, Butterflye said, "Everything I've seen you wear has 'MJ' on it."

"Huh?" Marley stared down at the initials. "Wow. I've never noticed that before. 'MJ' stands for my company, Mary Jane. What a coincidence."

"What does your company do?"

The clone smiled proudly. "I design environmentally responsible apparel from renewable sources."

Feeling a little ashamed for her destructive course in life, Butterflye shrugged. "That's very noble."

"Yeah. My clothes are made from hemp."

"Really?"

"Yeah." Marley rubbed the fabric covering her boobs. "The fibers are tetrahydrocannabinol-enhanced—to make them softer and more durable."

"Of course. I'm sure THC makes everything more durable," Butterflye said sarcastically.

"Don't get the wrong idea. I don't sell or advocate the use of drugs—"

Butterflye nodded. *Liar.*

"—but the shirts come in kilo and half-kilo sizes."

"A whole kilo?" Butterflye tried to hide her smile. *This broad's a pot dealer! She'll make a perfect Plague!*

"Hey, it takes a lot of hemp to make a shirt. Instead of coming on a coat hanger, you buy them already rolled up."

"Okay. How's business, Marley?"

"Call me MJ—it *was* great. Note the emphasis on the word *was.* Ten years ago, Mary Jane went public at thirty dollars a share." MJ sighed deeply. "Now, we're down to three dollars."

"Sounds like one of my investments. What happened?"

The clone cringed. "Legalized marijuana. Since Colorado voters approved recreational pot, I haven't had a single order from the Centennial State. Had to shut down all of my boutiques in Denver. And now Alaska, Washington and Oregon have followed suit.

"I'm competing with street dealers *and* the legal pot shops. Our largest market was in California, but now medical marijuana there is killing me. Anyone with a hangnail can get a script. Medi Mary Jane is now legal in twenty-five states. Head shops all over the country have stopped carrying our product. And in Texas and Arizona, drug lords are crossing the river with loaded mules."

"I feel so sorry for those people."

"No, I mean mules with four hooves and long ears." MJ illustrated jackass ears with her hands. "They walk across the Red River into Texas with a thousand pounds on their back. Now pot bags are a dime a dozen, almost. Nobody needs to smoke a THC-enhanced t-shirt to get high any longer. Not that I advocate the use of illegal substances. My apparel has gone the way of buggy whips and floppy discs.

"Street dealers are getting squeezed too. They're starting to threaten me, 'cuz I'm pinching their declining business. My plant in Clear Lake burned to the ground last month. I read in the paper that the engineers at NASA had the munchies for a week. No one's died yet, but the insurance deductible on the plant really hit my bottom line. If I could find a buyer, I'd unload the entire operation in a heartbeat."

"Really?" Butterflye smiled. This lady definitely had Plague potential.

"What do you do?" MJ asked.

"I run a health agency."

"I wanted to be a doctor," MJ said wistfully. "I got thrown out of pre-med when I accidentally released a flesh-eating bacteria from the biology lab." She grimaced. "That was nasty."

"Really?" Butterflye smiled more broadly, then furrowed her eyebrows to simulate a sympathetic expression. "I wouldn't let one little incident discourage me from something I wanted to do. Well, I would, but you shouldn't."

"It wasn't just one incident. The truth is, if I went into medicine, there'd be a mounting death toll."

"What if you had a chance to—"

"Uh-oh. Looks like we have company," MJ interrupted Butterflye as a party of four approached their tub.

"Durka durk ha," a Frenchman said to his lady.

"Oui oui." She giggled and pointed to Butterflye's hot tub. "Durk durka ha?"

Ignoring the two Butterflyes, all four intruders climbed into the tub. The woman, who had the fur density of a Sasquatch, moved her piliferous legs way too close to Butterflye's face.

Butterflye turned away from Ms. Squatch's pelage. "Hey, lady, you need to take a trip to Brazil. They can help you with that little matting problem."

Mrs. Squatch giggled. "Desculpe. Desculpe. Mover-se sobre." She bumped Butterflye, knocking her into the water. By the time Butterflye resurfaced, Mrs. Sasquatch had happily settled into the Redhead's bench.

The female yeti said something to Butterflye in French. The best translation Butterflye could muster was, "We live in a grapefruit seed."

Butterflye responded angrily with either, "Grapefruits make wonderful pool tables," or "I visited Grapefruit a little over a century ago."

After her attempt to tell off the intruders, the newcomers spoke only among themselves, oblivious to their hosts. The air around the hot tub took on the aroma of the unbathed, or more accurately, Bigfoot's evolutionary cousin, skunk ape. No telling what kind of bacteria was being introduced into the water. The bleached blonde pulled her curly locks up around the crown of her head, and in the process exposed her morbidly unshaven pits and the putrid fragrance residing therein.

Butterflye quickly turned away again, but it was too late. The image of the underarm hair would invade her REM dreams for the rest of eternity. Butterflye climbed out of the tub and stepped away, leaving a trail of watery footprints on the deck.

MJ followed her cell donor out of the tub. "What has been seen cannot be unseen. I'll be in therapy for years. Again!"

"Let's go somewhere more pleasant, like the waste treatment system," Butterflye said.

MJ sniffed the air. "Oh, yeah."

Butterflye and MJ had only taken a few steps when the shelf next to their Jacuzzi collapsed, spilling its contents into the hot tub. The cosmetics boxes floated, but the electric shaver sparked, buzzed and sank to the tub floor. All four French bathers screamed and spasmed. Then their hairy carcasses bobbed on the surface of the bubbling water. The redheads looked at the corpses, then at each other. The spa attendant ran over, grabbed the closest woman, convulsed and tumbled dead into the drink.

Butterflye watched steam rise from the victims' hair. "Wow. French fries."

"Oh, dear," Marley said. "I didn't realize the drug lords had followed me on the cruise. If those people hadn't been so been so rude, we'd be dead too."

"Woo-hoo," Butterflye said. "This is our lucky day. We should go to the casino."

"Oh, yeah. It's a good time to buy a lottery ticket."

As the girls headed for the spa entrance, the spa's bartender approached them. "Hello, ladies. I am Jackson the bartender, and *Squalor of the Sea's* chief crime investigator. Did you ladies witness the accident?"

"No." "Yes," the girls said simultaneously.

"Yes." "No."

"Can you tell me what you witnessed?" He pulled out his order book and prepared to take notes. "I believe it was an accidental electrocution."

"I don't think this was an accident," Butterflye said. "Who did the shaver belong to? It certainly didn't belong to that bunch. Look at those pits. You couldn't cut that thicket with a weed whacker. Ugh. I just threw up a little in my mouth."

"Besides," MJ added, "It's connected to three extension

cords."

"Hey, I think we're close to the studio responsible for Bunny's movie." Zoe let the wind whip through her hair as she took a turn driving through California in perfect convertible weather.

"Do you want to stop?" Jake asked.

"How often do we have the opportunity to see a movie studio?" She glanced over in time to see Jake control some kind of ... face. "Really?"

"If you paid more attention to *where* we were sent instead of just the body counts, maybe you'd get out of the office more."

Zoe watched her knuckles go white as she tightened her grip on the steering wheel. "We're not having this discussion. I've ruined enough shoes in blood and guts to keep doing the pickups."

"Not even for your favorite actor's stunt double? The stunt guys are actually kind of him. Not as weird as rodeo clowns, but the car carnage can't be beat."

Zoe had no idea how to respond. She grabbed her phone from the console and tossed it to Jake. "I think there are some messages from Bunny on there. Remind me to *thank* Wreak and Havoc for introducing her to texting ... or attempting to teach her. In my own *special* way."

She heard Jake gulp, and a quick glance saw him pale. "Yeah, okay, or ... how come her texts are *pink*? Did you do that?"

"No," Zoe said through clenched teeth. "They come through that way. No matter how you change the setting."

"This just keeps going. What did they do? Default to voice recognition and activation? Oh, here it is. She's on the studio lot today. We can meet her at the commissary for lunch. That'll be new. I've never actually *eaten* there." Jake punched some buttons on the phone. "I'm attempting to confirm so the gate guard will have us on the list."

"Oh, please, who's going to keep us out?"

"Famous last words," Jake muttered about forty-five minutes later, as they held up traffic at the studio gate while Zoe argued with the guard.

"Get Bunny on the phone." She gestured toward the device.

Before the call completed, the car lurched out of Zoe's control. The rental crashed through the wooden gate arm with a crunching snap across the grill and rolled onto the lot with a squeal of rubber.

"Are you okay?" Zoe and Jake asked in unison.

Zoe's hands shook as she peeled them off the steering wheel, but a quick mental inventory revealed nothing broken or bleeding. "I'm okay. What about you?"

"Soft tissue, if anything. What do we do now?"

They turned in their supple leather bucket seats to witness the chaos surrounding the guard house. A once-expensive sports car had crumpled into a compact pile of wrinkled metal and glass bits, with a giant SUV on its back bumper like a weird metal dog in heat. People in designer clothes ran screaming and pointing. The guard yelled into his radio, as other uniformed men ran toward the scene.

"I say we find the Commissary. We're in and nobody's going to care about us now." Zoe knew she sounded callous, but there was nothing they could do.

"Oh, calvary's here anyway." Jake nodded toward the guard shack.

Zoe recognized the two as part of her minion staff, but couldn't place their names. "Must not be a celebrity pick up if Reaper sent those two."

"Perks of the job, choosing our pickups. Even though every soul is important."

She tried to hold back the snort as she put the Mustang in gear and pulled away from the accident, following the signs for the Commissary.

"Wow, there's a lot going on here," Jake said, helping Zoe navigate the busy café with crew members and actors hunched over plates and devices. They threaded through the tables to a fern-bedecked corner with a pink wrought iron ice cream table and woven cane chairs. Bunny perched on a wide-backed rattan chair in the corner with a view of the whole room.

"Zoe! Jake! You came!" Bunny stood and blew air kisses toward them, light sparking off her pink bedazzled outfit.

"Wow, that's ... shocking." Jake kept his voice low.

"Actually, it's *ultra*-pink," Bunny said, "a color created in 1972 by Crayola, but it's close to shocking pink, so I understand your confusion."

Zoe fought to keep a straight face. "Bunny knows her pink, Jake. You walked into that one."

Jake blushed a lovely cerise. "I did."

She turned back to Bunny. "So, how's it going?"

Bunny gestured broadly. "It's all about *me*, the star. It's great."

"Miss Baker! Let's go! We only have the recording studio until the end of the day. We have to do your looping now." A harassed functionary with a radio and a tablet computer hurried up to the table with barely a look at Zoe.

"What's looping?" Zoe asked more toward the studio minion rather than Bunny.

"Oh, nothing special." Bunny waved a perfectly pink manicured hand. "It can wait until we've had a chance to catch up."

"No, it can't. If we don't get this done today, no one will understand a word of your dialog." The functionary seemed adamant. "We have to get you into the recording studio."

"Isn't that the place with the headphones? I don't care for those. They're hot, and they mess up my hair."

"We can work around that if we have to." The functionary turned and lowered his voice. "And here I thought she'd love hearing the sound of her own voice."

Jake snorted, turning it into a cough. Zoe shot them both a "Zip it! Now!" *Look.*

"We're sorry, Bunny," Zoe said. "We didn't know we were going to interrupt your work."

"Then come with me. See the magic." Bunny popped to her feet, teetering only slightly on her cotton candy, Swarovski crystal strappy sandals.

"Okay."

The functionary shrugged. "Anything to get her moving."

The foursome headed toward the door when Zoe caught a glimpse of movement out of the corner of her eye. She turned to catch a good view of the man in a Hollywood toga. "*Orcas?*"

"What?" Jake stopped and turned back to her.

"But ... there's got to be some mistake." Zoe's voice came out strangled.

"You okay, Zoe?"

"I just saw a ghost."

"Oh, that might be DB," Bunny said, coming to link arms with Zoe. "He's the butler at my house. I thought he was stuck there, but ghosts will be ghosts. Right?"

"No. Not that kind—" Zoe blinked. "No, I'm not getting sucked in. I thought I saw someone I ... knew."

"Ms. Baker, we really need you to move. That dialog won't

re-record itself." The minion shimmied Bunny away from Zoe and toward the door. Zoe and Jake followed.

Zoe turned back just as the toga-clad mirage bolted toward the kitchen, knocking into a server bearing a fully-ignited cherries jubilee, sending flaming fruit across the Commissary. Splattering dessert sparked on tablecloths, curtains and overly styled hair. Special effect latex prosthetic masks instantly flashed and melted. Screams in artistic arias filled the air.

As the door clunked closed behind them, Bunny said, "How sad. Those screams are weak. They need to come from the diaphragm."

"Maybe you could teach a class." The functionary pulled her along. "*After* we finish the looping."

The quartet marched across the uncontrolled chaos of the parking lot. As the ancient wooden building went up in a ball of fire propelled by the gas-fueled oven and chef's stove, flames roared. The guard gate scene had firefighters cutting apart the sports car while traffic backed up around the block.

"Oh, I didn't get to finish my salad!" Bunny turned back toward the Commissary.

The functionary grabbed her arm and turned her toward the door to another building. "Hopefully we can get you to finish *something*."

Zoe exchanged a quick glance with Jake. The studio functionary's sarcasm wasn't lost on them, as it apparently was on Bunny. "Um, we should let you work. We'll just take a quick look around and take off when the smoke clears a little."

"Well, if you're sure." Bunny bit her lip. "It's hard being the *star*, you know. I'll see you at the Halloween Party."

"If we all survive until Halloween," the functionary muttered, pushing Bunny inside.

"He kind of has a point," Jake said as they headed deeper into the studio lot. "These coincidences are starting to pile up, and we really haven't talked about it."

"Zoe? What are you doing here?"

"Reaper?" She turned to the new, familiar voice. "What are you doing here?"

"I asked first." Reaper pointed to the fire. "But it should be pretty obvious why *I'm* here."

"Oh, Bunny's movie is through this studio, so we came by to say hi."

"Well that explains the *magnitude* of this event. Two

Redheads were here."

"What's that supposed to mean?" Something in his tone made her bristle.

"Ever since you four went on vacation, we've been at full staff. You've been leaving havoc behind wherever you go."

"Havoc's here? I thought he and Wreak were banned from Earth after they 'appropriated' that electron microscope for Sara Lee."

"Okay, you've been around Bunny today, so I'll let that slide." Reaper shuddered. "I don't know what's going on with you four, but our intake is way up this month. It's almost as if someone's pretending to kill you and succeeding with bystanders."

"*Pretending?*" Jake didn't even bother hiding his snort. "Being inept is more like it."

"You mean someone's actually trying to kill the Redheads? Well, that would explain a whole lot." Reaper scanned the area to make sure no one else was around. "Listen up, because I'm only going to say this once, and I'll deny it if either of you mentions it again."

"Spit it out, Reaper." Zoe poked him in the chest.

"Be careful, will you? It's silk." Reaper smoothed his shirt front. "But you don't actually suck as Death, and I'm not all that excited to break in a new one."

"Aw, Reaper, I didn't know you cared."

"Yeah, well, you're family now, and Jake would be useless if anything happened to you, and *him* I need."

"And that's more like it." Zoe patted Reaper's cheek, which she knew annoyed him. "I have no intention of dying— oblivioning?—on this trip. I don't want to hurt Jake either."

"You know I'm standing right here, right?" Jake asked, sounding miffed. "I can hear everything and actually have an opinion."

"Of course you do, dear. Why don't we let Reaper get back to work, and let's get back to our honeymoon?"

Reaper put out an arm to block them. "Not before I ask Jake, *what are you wearing?*"

Jake checked his t-shirt and shorts, neither of which were smoke-stained or ripped. "What?"

"'Don't Fear the Reaper'? Really?"

Zoe tried not to laugh at Jake's innocent expression. "We saw Blue Oyster Cult the other night," she said. "Great concert."

"You two are hopeless." Reaper threw up his hands and went back to work.

Moments later, Jake and Zoe drove out of the now unmanned security gates. The fire spread rapidly to another building. An explosion shook the ground.

"What was that?" Zoe asked, looking over the back of the convertible.

"Special effects department. They have explosives." Jake kept his eyes on the rapidly decelerating traffic.

"I almost feel sorry for Reaper."

"Don't." Jake dodged emergency responders as they drove further away. "He's collecting starlets. It's as close to Heaven as he gets."

"Good to know. Now, what do you know about oblivion?"

The car swerved as Jake's head snapped in her direction. "*WHAT?*"

"Oblivion is permanent, right?" Zoe chewed her bottom lip.

"Very. Why?"

"I thought I saw Orcas back there. In the Commissary. He started the fire. And I've had this weird feeling someone ... familiar has been following us. Is it possible?"

"No."

She stared at him. "That was abrupt. No, there's not someone following us? No, it's not possible? No, what?"

"Oh, I'm sure someone's after us—you—but it's *not* Orcas. Not possible. Now to prove it."

Zoe wasn't sure what button she pushed, but she'd never seen Jake so adamant or determined. She rather liked it. "How much time do we have before the next reunion?"

"A few days. But the drive will take most of that time. Why?" His tone shifted to suspicion.

"It might be time to face up to this trying-to-kill-us thing. Get to the bottom of ... everything. Don't you agree?"

"I've been saying that all along."

"Wow, have you practicing elegant ways to say, 'I told you so' for a long time, or just since you met me?"

Jake wisely said nothing and kept his eyes on the road.

Chapter Seven

As Butterflye opened her suite door, she noticed an ivory envelope propped against a vase of fragrant scarlet and white roses. "Look at this." Butterflye showed Ralph the linen envelope, addressed to Mrs. Butterflye Plague-Pestilence in a swirling font intended to resemble calligraphy. Inside the envelope, she found a smaller blank envelope containing a wedding invitation, a hand-written note from, Dado, *Squalor of the Sea's* chaplain/ chief bartender and a photocopied page from the *Sailor's Book of Hymns*.

The note read, "Mrs. Plague-Pestilence, Passengers Edward Looney and Catherine Warde will be exchanging their vows this evening. After the tragic passing of the ship's captain, I'll be officiating. The couple just learned that you are sailing aboard this cruise. They'd be honored if you would pre-record their favorite hymn for the service. If you can bless their ecumenical nuptials with your music, please come to the DJ's booth at the disco and chapel on deck ten, one hour before the ceremony."

She glanced at the blinking 6:00 on her phone. "Oops. I wish I'd noticed this sooner. I need to head down there *right now*!" She shed her white capris and grabbed a dress. "You want to come, Ralph?"

He scrambled to the door and looked up expectantly.

She danced around while she zipped the back of her flirty sequined number. After slipping her crystal-studded lanyard over her head, she turned her attention to Ralph. She re-tied his bonnet and pulled down his "Nobody Cares About Your Blog" t-shirt. "This is a wedding. You have to look presentable." She spit on her thumb and dabbed at an invisible smudge on his face. "There, that's better."

After navigating the ship's narrow passageways, Butterflye and Ralph climbed the spiral steps to the disc jockey's elevated glass-enclosed studio. Inside the booth, the DJ swiveled away from the control console, selected a couple of CDs, then spun back to the player. When he pulled his headphones down, he also wore a set of earbuds. Under his breath, he rapped in limerick.

After recording the hymn over a pre-recorded ninety-piece orchestra, Butterflye strolled down to the Liquid Fire, *Squalor of the Sea's* open-air disco. Four-person round tables surrounded the famous lighted dance floor. The bar, which doubled as an altar, had been decked out with flower arrangements and a unity candle. At the back of the dance floor, an arch decorated with white silk flowers awaited the bride and groom's appearance.

Dressed in a mini-dress for the first time in decades, Butterflye strutted her stuff. With her entourage of six-legged groupies safely back home in the Nether Region, she was free to bare her shapely legs. Overcome by the beat of the music, Butterflye did a few sexy dance steps and spun about, letting her straight, light copper hair fly. In the light of the strobe, the strands appeared bluish, almost starved for oxygen.

Couples in cocktail attire trickled onto the dance floor. Some sidled next to the altar/bar to order drinks. Others formed a human ring around the disco floor awaiting the arrival of the wedding party. On the blinking LED dance floor, a twenty-something woman writhed and wiggled her body in ways that Butterflye didn't know were physically possible. When the woman's dance partner picked her up, flipped her around and set her back down, her freakishly high heel missed Butterflye's eyes by mere inches.

Butterflye backed away and found a vacant table located safely on the opposite side of the room. She couldn't take any unnecessary chances; she was mortal. Butterflye picked up the drink menu, scanning until she found her favorite.

The server approached her. "Can I help you?"

She checked his name tag. Handsome young Vladimir sounded so exotic with his Romanian accent.

"I'd like scotch on the rocks." *Wait, I've got the premium liquor package.* She reconsidered her order. "Macallan's, thirty year."

"Verrry good, madam." He took her Have-A-Blast card. A few minutes, later he returned with a glass of amber joy.

She signed the ticket.

"Would you be the same Butterflye Plague-Pestilence from the Bunny and Butterflye Tour several years ago?"

Butterfly blushed a bit. "That's Butterflye and Bunny. You've heard my music?"

"No," he confessed. "Your concert in Bulgaria was cancelled. So I didn't get to see you and Bunny. My girlfriend and I were really disappointed. Would you autograph a napkin for me?"

Butterflye took a slow sip of icy scotch, allowing the flavor to linger on her tongue. "I'd be happy to." She scribbled, "All my love, Butterflye Plague-Pestilence," then blotted her lipstick in the shape of a kiss.

Vlad pocketed the napkin. "Thank you so very much! I can't believe this. I'm so excited."

Two tables away, another waiter slammed a beer can in front of Donald Trump. He picked up the can, then showed it to the waiter. "What's this? I ordered a Dos Equis Free."

"Sorry, sir. This is all your Have-A-Blast card permits you to order. Uno Equi, for the most boring man in the world."

Trump growled, jumped to his feet and waved to the three men wearing earpieces and black suits, who stood nearby. "Let's get out of here. I have some people I need to yell at."

High above the center of the disco, a three-foot diameter disco ball hung by a metal clamp. As it spun, a hot pink spotlight sent brilliant magenta beams of light dancing across the floor and the passengers.

"Butterflye?" asked a man wearing a plaid tux and a Kermit the Frog tattoo down the left side of his neck. He held a piece of paper in his hands.

"Yes. Would you like an autograph, too?"

"That would be nice, but the waiter said you're the famous rock star who's singing at our wedding. We really appreciate your filling in for us. The vocalist we booked has her head in a toilet and can't attend."

"That's too bad. She had too much to drink?"

"No," the groom said. "She drowned. We'll start in about fifteen minutes. I hate to impose further, but would you mind singing 'our song' too?"

"I'd be honored."

He smiled broadly and handed her a sheet of music. "You're okay with this?"

Butterflye scanned the notes and lyrics. "No problem. I don't have to sight read. I know this one."

"Great. I'll see you later."

From behind her, Butterflye heard a deep smooth voice. "Madam?"

She turned around. "Yes?"

There stood Stanley, her Groucho fan, this time dressed in a white shirt and pants. He extended a tray with a champagne flute of green sizzling bubbly. "Would madam like some champagne on the house?"

She took the glass. "What a cheerful color. Thank you."

"Very good, madam." He nodded his head. "Do you have any plans in Cozumel?"

"I've got reservations on the submarine excursion."

Groucho nodded. "I think you'll find it exciting." He quickly walked away.

The music stopped. The dancers applauded and left the dance floor.

"Hi," another voice said, so familiar it could have been Butterflye's own. And indeed, there stood Butterflye's Other Self, MJ. She wore a tie-dyed t-shirt so tight Butterflye could see her heart beat.

"Have a seat." Butterflye held up the glass of green smoking champagne. "When I see the waiter, I'll order you one." She set it down. "When yours arrives, we'll drink a toast to reunited family." Butterflye scanned the disco, but Groucho was nowhere to be seen. "I'm sure he'll be back soon."

"How was your excursion in Belize?" MJ asked.

"I was supposed to go on the shark dive. I missed the dive boat because I was in the clinic getting a toe fungus checked out. I guess I got lucky. I heard somehow the wetsuits had meat sewn into them. Twenty divers were eaten by great white sharks. At our next port, I think I'll take Ralph on a submarine ride. You want to come?"

"That sounds like fun. I haven't decided what I'm going to do."

Feedback squealed through the speakers. "Good afternoon everyone," the disco DJ said in a South African accent from his booth on the second floor. "Welcome everyone to one of Helvetica Cruise Line's oldest and most decrepit ships, *Squalor of the Sea*. I'm your host, Wushe. Tonight I'll be taking you to a place where the waves are small, the sailing is smooth and your troubles don't exist. The drinks still cost more than the national debt of Kyrgyzstan. But you'll always have a blast."

Everyone clapped.

"But first we have some business to attend to. Dado, *Squalor's* bartender and matrimonial guide, would you do the honors?"

Dado moved to the standing mic near the bar. "Meet Edward and Catherine. Tonight they will exchange vows."

Nearby, an interpreter for the hearing impaired signed Dado's speech.

The groom waited next to Dado at the bar. Beside him stood the groomsman and a little ring bearer. A few feet away, the maid of honor wove back and forth, wearing what looked like a chartreuse shade of makeup.

An electric guitar interpretation of the Mendelssohn's bridal procession blasted through the speakers, and the bride, dressed in a white miniskirt and missing one shoe, waddled next to the top of the disco's spiral staircase.

"We are honored to have a celebrity with us," Dado said. "Butterflye Plague-Pestilence, the renowned alto voice of Bunny and Butterflye, will sing our couple's special song. And later, we'll hear their favorite hymn. *Squalor's* audio/visual team will be recording this service, so anyone who wants a copy can get one from our photography kiosk for twenty dollars later on today." Dado reached out toward Butterflye. "Ms. Pestilence, the deck is yours."

Dado handed her a microphone. Butterflye stood and gave the Queen's wave to the crowd. "Thanks, Dado. And for the record, that's 'Butterflye and Bunny.'" Butterflye motioned to MJ with her hand. "Stand up. We can do this together. We have the same voice. Live, in stereo."

Butterflye nodded to the DJ up in the booth. The record jock punched the button that launched Queen's bassist John Deacon. Three quarter notes rang out the vibrations of the Fender Precision bass guitar, "Dun, dun, dun."

MJ took the music in her left hand and joined her cell donor singing, "Another one bites the dust."

"Dun, dun, dun."

"Another one bites the dust," the Deadly Duo belted out, both girls on the same notes.

All movement and conversation in the disco stopped. All eyes and ears focused on Butterflye and MJ. One man stood, snapped to attention and put his hand over his heart, then fell over, his pupils fixed and dilated.

At the altar, the groom reached behind the bar, grabbed a bottle of Everclear, doused himself with the entire fifth, then set himself ablaze with the unity candle. The deaf interpreter repeatedly ran her flat hand across her throat in a slicing motion before running to the guardrail and flinging herself into the sea.

MJ's eyes grew wide as the bar ignited. "Another one bites the dust." They belted out in brilliant unison. "And another one bites the dust."

The crowd went crazy, literally. Within the first few measures, the man next to Butterflye grabbed a plastic knife and plunged it into the heart of his lady companion before using on himself. The DJ fumbled with the control slides, but raised the microphone to full volume.

The girls paused allowing the lead guitar to play some fanfare.

"What's happening?" MJ asked.

Butterflye counted notes. "Obviously the groom got cold feet. Apparently everyone's upset. What a shame. Let's try harder to cheer them up."

MJ nodded and took a deep breath.

"Another one bites the dust..."

The bride, who had been awaiting the signal to descend the spiral staircase, tied her veil into a hangman's noose, attached it to the landing newel, then flung herself over the banister.

When Butterflye and MJ hit the chorus, Vlad the waiter grabbed Butterflye's champagne glass, broke off the base against a table and sliced his throat with the jagged edge. On the deck, Vlad's blood mingled with green smoking champagne.

"Wow, we've got them in a frenzy—just like the Beatles used to," Butterflye said.

The rotating disco ball wobbled, then plunged to the floor, squashing three ladies wearing "We're from North Texas" t-shirts and breaking into thousands of shiny pieces.

The clear enclosure surrounding the music booth cracked, then shattered, spraying glass all over the room. Guests scrambled for the jagged shards and used them in surprisingly creative ways to sever vital blood flow pathways.

As MJ watched the chaos, she fell into silent shock. But being the consummate professional, Butterflye continued to sing. By the end of the song, every member of the wedding party lay motionless. The recorded instrumental finally stopped only seconds before Butterflye's last notes.

As Butterflye's remaining notes throbbed to an end, the few guests who clung stubbornly to life moaned and convulsed on the floor. Within a few minutes, the seizures ceased. The only sound that Butterflye heard was the ocean spray splashing against the bow of the ship.

A familiar face appeared from the ocean off the ship's starboard side of the ship, then floated toward the disco. Reaper began to count bodies with a stylus. He looked at the assortment of self-inflicted wounds, then at MJ. "Really, Plague? You had to start singing? We're already slammed. Couldn't you let other vocalists torture them? Like Barry Manilow?"

MJ gazed blankly through him.

"Really, Reaper?" Butterflye mimicked him and tapped her coworker on the back. "Everyone's a critic."

Reaper spun around to face the real Butterflye. "Are you telling me there's two of you?"

She glanced at MJ and whispered. "Yep. She's my clone."

As Reaper went about collecting souls, Butterflye set the sheet music on the table. She turned to MJ. "Come on, girl. Let's find something else to do."

"Yeah," MJ agreed. "This place is dead."

"Cut, cut, CUT!" the director yelled.

Bunny didn't have a clue what had set him off this time. After all, the actual lines weren't important. Only the gist counted. As if *anybody actually memorized* a script.

"Can't you get *one word* right?" The director flapped the script under her nose. "After Space Thingy reaches for you, you scream 'Help!' Not 'Where did he come from?' Let's take it from the top, people, and try to reach the end of the scene!"

The new clapboard man slipped into the camera's view. On cue, he slapped the wooden slats, shouting, "Scene 4, Take 39!"

Bunny and Wil, already on their marks, started walking hand in hand uphill. "You'll love this spot," Wil said. "It's the perfect place for a picnic." To emphasize the dialogue, he raised the picnic basket he held in his other hand.

Bunny pulled him to a stop, pointing at the hilltop. From above rose a spotlight on a crane—which the director claimed would be replaced with ultra-cool special effects and appropriately scary music. For now, eerie blue and green lights with some red smoke snaking across the hilltop set the scene.

"Whatever could that strange alien light be?" Bunny asked.

Wil gasped. "It can't be possible. We reconfigured his rocket to crash into the sun. Surely that monster was destroyed. Unless it's another Space Thingy."

A booming voice echoed from behind the hill. "It is not another. It is I—the original Space Thingy. I survived your insidious plot to destroy me." He let out a maniacal laugh, then a man's head appeared on the starkly bowed horizon. Slowly all of him rose, hauled by ropes. His skintight, green suit covered everything but his face. Over that, he wore a rubber mask.

According to the director, that, too, would be replaced by special effects, creating, in the director's own words, "the most awesome, fantastical, scariest monster the world has ever seen." Right now, it was a bit underwhelming.

Nevertheless, Bunny, a trained actress who almost finished acting school, shrieked. "It *is* the monster. I would know that hideous face anywhere!"

Wil took a wide step in front of Bunny, spreading his arms. "Stay behind me, Amy. I, Dr. Wentwood Brown, will protect you."

"Oh, Dr. Wentwood Brown, you are my hero!" Bunny clutched his shirt and peered over his shoulder, making sure she stayed in the shot. She flashed the camera a big smile.

"Amy," the man in the green suit wailed-out. "Amy! I've come back for you, my love. All the while my ship melted in the sun, I thought of you."

"If your ship melted," Wil said, "how did you get away? Why didn't you die in the sun's fiery furnace?"

"That doesn't matter. What's important is that I'm here now and I've come to take Amy away, to the stars and beyond."

"I won't go," Bunny said. "My life is here, Space Thingy. Can't you see—we're from two different worlds. I can no more live your life than you can mine. Now leave us and leave Earth alone. Do this, if you love me."

"The other reason you can't have her," Wil said, "is because she is my fiancée. We are going to be married."

"No, no, no," Space Thingy wailed. Bunny noted the actor wailed a lot—so it must be in the script. He shambled toward them, swinging his arms like a gorilla.

Space Thingy grabbed Wil's arm and, stage-style, tossed Wil aside. Actually, Wil poised, jumped, then rolled aside as if thrown. Bunny thought it looked pretty good, but Wil grimaced like he wasn't satisfied.

The Space Thingy stuntman reached for Bunny.

Bunny froze. She widened her eyes. She raised her hands to the side of her face. Then she forgot the line … again. Turning aside, she shouted, "Line?"

The director threw the script in the air. "Cut!"

From the side, Mimi said, "Ooh la la!"

"That can't be the line," Bunny said. "This isn't a foreign film. There won't be subtitles."

"C'est ooh la la. Ooh la la!"

"The line is, 'Help!'" Will translated. "Just a simple cry for help. But given the direction we've had so far, I'd say the director wants something over-the-top. Try a little shriek and a lot of arm waving. Wait—make that a big shriek."

Bunny perched her hands on her hips. "Maybe it's the line that's the problem. *Who's* going to help me? Space Thingy just threw you aside, and there's no one else here!" She snapped her fingers. "Suppose I beat up Space Thingy!" After all, Semyaza, Michael and Adam all trained her to fight. Surely, she'd learned something. Screen-fighting was all fake anyway.

The director fumed, not quite as vividly as Satan, but a good runner-up. "If you beat up Space Thingy in the first half-hour of the film, what will we do with the rest of the time?"

"Oh." He made a valid point. It wouldn't make sense in the plot if she beat him up now. "That is a puzzler, but there's got to be a solution."

"There is," the director said, his voice rising. "You yell for help!" He ran his hand through his thinning hair—no doubt the reason he was going bald. "Now people, let's try to get this scene sometime this decade!"

"I don't have a decade," Bunny said. "I'm only on vacation for the month." The world becoming a blur before her eyes, Bunny stared off into space, trying to remember something. Anything would do.

"Miss Baker!" the director shouted. "You're daydreaming again. Focus on the here and now! You have one simple line, and you're blowing it all out of proportion. Just call for help!" The director stormed back to his canvas-backed chair. "From here on out, *nothing* had better go wrong! Pick it up from Space Thingy's arrival."

By now, the effects crew had reset the scene. The lights created an eerie glow while the smoke machine belched out clouds. As soon as the director yelled, "Action," the clapboard man smacked the slats together.

"Whatever could that strange, alien light be?" Bunny asked.

"Oh, no," Wil said, repeating his line. "It can't be possible."

A loud rumble interrupted as the ground trembled with a growing intensity.

"Oh, no," Wil said. "Not again. It can't be possible." He grabbed Bunny's hand and gazed into her green eyes. Surprise shone in his dark eyes and echoed in his voice. "Hey—the dialogue isn't as unnatural as I thought." Then he added, "We better get out of here fast."

As they raced downhill, Bunny caught another glimpse of Mars watching from afar. Her poor brother-in-law just couldn't catch a break. Every time he tried to watch the filming, some disaster ensued. How unlucky could a guy be?

While they ran, she thought how much the quake reminded her of her Warstomp—at least the light tap version. Yet this was California, the land of earthquakes and mudslides—not necessarily the good kind, with Vodka and chocolate sauce. Which reminded Bunny, she could do with a drink.

The ground rumbled louder. It split down the middle, cleaving the hilltop in two. Great chunks of earth and rock fell into the ever-widening maw. Cameras, lights on poles, cameramen and a bunch of people who didn't matter—just extras—fell into the chasm, their cries barely audible over the cacophony. Though people ran from the event, they weren't all fast enough.

Bunny and Wil, however, ran fast enough. Wil possessed a sleek, athletic build—so he was probably a jogger, like Adam. And thanks to Candace, Bunny's legs were both fast and shapely.

Together, they dodged collapsing building fronts. They ran past a Jeep as the ground swallowed it, chewed it into a metal spitball, then ejected it. The twisted lump of metal, tires and cheap cloth seats hurtled through the air and crash landed in front of Wil and Bunny.

Wil, his brow sweating, exhaled sharply. "That was close. If I didn't know any better, I'd say someone was out to kill this movie." His eyes widened, "Or kill *us*! I do have a couple of crazed fans—or un-fans, you might call them. Man, some people love Wesley Crusher and some really hate him." Then he stared hard at Bunny. "Is there anyone who'd want to kill you?"

Bunny shrugged. "Why bother? I'm already dead. Or I will be again at the end of the month."

By the time the quake ended, more than a dozen extras and crewmen lay in a mass grave of the Earth's own creation. Another dozen people were missing, among them, Mimi. Poor girl. If she cried for help, no one would understand her.

Suddenly, Bunny knew her motivation—or at least her character's mindset. The sheer horror of the scene revolved around Bunny's unrequited cry for help when no one was there to answer. She looked for the director to tell him the good news.

Instead, she ran into Reaper.

"Hi, Reaper. Why are you back?" she asked.

He blinked at her then shook his head. "You have to ask? There've been over twenty deaths here. I'm *working*—which I realize is a concept you haven't grasped."

"I do too grasp it. What do you think I'm doing? Just standing around in front of a bunch of cameras?"

"No offense," Wil said softly, "but that is what you do a lot of the time." He struck out his hand in Reaper's direction. "Wil Wheaton. I take it you know Bunny from"—he raised his eyebrows—"the Underworld?"

"I don't work for War, if that's what you mean," Reaper said. "Heaven and Hell know I have plenty of challenges with the Redhead I've got—and she's the best of the bunch. But nothing short of a mandate from Heaven and Hell would make me work for War. While I shouldn't say anything, I'll introduce myself. I'm Reaper. I collect souls for Death."

"Cool job … I suppose." Wil withdrew his hand. "I trust you aren't here for me? I think I would remember dying."

Bunny said, "Oh no. You'd be surprised. Death happens when you aren't even paying attention."

Reaper scoffed. "I'll let that comment slide. It's much too easy. But no, I'm not here for you, Wil Wheaton." As he said the name, it echoed ominously. "Not yet." He let slip a wicked grin.

Wil arched an eyebrow. "Can you tell me *when* I'm likely to see you again?"

"No can-do. Against the rules." Another wicked grin spread across his chiseled features. "Besides, I hate spoiling the surprise."

"I wouldn't mind," Wil said.

"Then *I* wouldn't enjoy the surprise," Reaper added.

"Boys, boys, boys," Bunny said, stepping between them. "There are much more important things going on."

Reaper's jaw dropped. "*You* realize there's important work to do?"

"Of course. I'm the female lead. We can't film until we clear the set so the crew can fix it."

Wil rolled his eyes and so did Reaper. They looked at each other and said together, "I should've known better."

Reaper shook it off. "*I* have important work to do, and I'm already *way* behind schedule. Ever since you four went on vacation, the work load has doubled. If I don't get caught up before Zoe comes back, I'll be toast." At Wil's quizzical expression, Reaper added, "Yes, I mean literally. Or rather, I'll be toasted. Satan doesn't accept anything less than perfection. Why the Redheads aren't held to her standards, I can only guess."

Bunny folded her arms in a huff. "Satan holds us to high standards. Just last month, she reminded me it was past Labor Day and time to quit wearing white shoes."

Reaper sputtered. "She told you *what*?"

"Let me remember her words exactly." Bunny tapped her lips. She dropped her voice to a timber closer to Satan's deep-throated growl. "Labor Day has come and gone, and you've done nothing to push through the latest war technology. All you've done is putter around Hell in those stupid, sparkly white shoes."

A wave of understanding washed across Reaper's pasty face. "That makes more sense. Anyway, I *really* need to get on the job. As it is, Zoe will hang me out to dry." Again, he looked at Wil. "*Yes*, in Hell, a lot of punishments are literal."

"Maybe I could help," Bunny said.

"You want to collect souls?" Reaper shook his head.

Bunny laughed. "Heavens no. I meant I could help you look good in front of Zoe. On one condition: You can't collect his soul until our vacation is over. He's too much help to lose right now."

"What are you talking about?" Reaper asked.

"Ooh," Wil said, "you might regret that question."

"Too late," Reaper said.

"I'm saying, I know where you can find a lost soul."

Reaper gaped at Bunny. "A *real* lost soul—as in one who's managed to slip the system?"

"I don't know what system you're talking about," Bunny said, "but he's dead and stuck on Earth as a ghost."

Reaper's eyes lit up. He grabbed Bunny's shoulders, then released her like dropping a hot potato. "Don't kid me, Bunny. Lost souls are like gold. Where is he?"

"First, promise to *wait* until after Halloween to collect him."

Reaper chewed his lip and shifted from foot to foot. Finally, he raised his hand and swore, "I promise."

Bunny checked to make sure his fingers weren't crossed. "His name is D.B. Cooper, and he's been staying with me. He's the best butler I've ever had. So"—Bunny wagged her finger—"you better not break your promise!"

"D.B. Cooper?" Reaper trembled all over. "*The* D.B. Cooper! This is great! Even Satan will be impressed!" Reaper grabbed Bunny and gave her a quick hug. "Thank you so much."

"You can thank me by keeping your promise."

Reaper nodded. "One minute after Halloween, he's mine!" He snapped his head around, almost exorcist-like. "What's Mars doing here?"

"I think he's watching me make a movie like Ares used to do. It's kinda sweet, really, but I hope it doesn't mean he has a crush on me. I have my hands full seeing Adam and Michael. Thankfully, I'm not Semyaza's type."

"Semyaza has a type?" Reaper raised both hands, palms out. "No, I don't want to know."

"What's to know? He is a fallen angel. He likes *living* women. Once they've died, he loses all interest. Frankly, I think he has commitment issues."

"I have to get back to work," Reaper said, walking away.

A man in a cheap suit approached, carrying a notepad and pen. "Who was that?" he asked.

"Nobody you need to know," Wil answered quickly.

"I'll decide who I do and don't need to know," he said.

"Who are you?" Bunny asked.

"I'm Detective Darrows, and I'll be asking the questions."

"I know my rights," Bunny said. "If I raise my hand, I can ask all the questions I want." She raised her hand and waited. "Well? Aren't you going to call on me?"

"What is it?" he asked, exasperation tinging his voice.

"Why are you asking questions?"

He glowered. "There've been a lot of accidents here, and I'm a police detective. And that's suspicious."

Bunny blinked. "Don't you know how you became a detective?"

"What?" Now he blinked.

"You said you were a detective and it was suspicious. That doesn't happen by accident. I understand how you might become all sorts of things by accident—for instance, I didn't set out to be an actress, but I was discovered at a soda shop. A big spider was crawling on the floor and I screamed, and a man said I would be perfect for his film. The rest is history."

"That's irrelevant."

"Not to me! Surely you must have some similar story as to how you *accidently* became a detective."

Detective Darrows squeezed his pen so tight, his fingers turned white while he muttered something about dumb actresses. With a look of calm restored to his forty-something face, he asked, "Have you seen anyone suspicious on the set?"

Mars had been hanging around, but Bunny knew him, so he couldn't be suspicious. There were always numerous faces on a movie set that she didn't know, so how could she be suspicious of them? Then she thought of someone.

"The producer," Bunny said. "He's been hanging around, and he doesn't have anything to do but dole out money."

The detective blinked in surprise. "That's not a bad direction. It isn't unheard of for a producer to wreck a show that's guaranteed to lose money. Unfortunately, he's already been vetted."

"He got a car!" Bunny exclaimed. "I want to be Vetted! No, wait … I want to be Porsched!"

Darrows shook his head and muttered, "Like that, she's back to dumb actress." Plainer, he said, "He didn't get a car. I should've said, I've already investigated and cleared him. We're looking for someone else." He jerked a thumb in Reaper's direction. "Who's that guy? Something's not right about him."

"Zoe says that all the time, but she has high standards. His name is Wilhelm Grimm and he's a reaper."

"What's a reaper do?" Darrows set his pen to paper.

Bunny wrinkled her nose. "And you think I'm dumb. Reapers collect the dead."

"Cleans up on the set," Darrows muttered. "Still, I'd better talk to him."

As he stalked off, Bunny called out, "I wouldn't. The last guy who interrupted him while he was working had a heart attack before his time."

Sara Lee, Duncan and JD laughed and stumbled away from the Mission Space ride at EPCOT.

"Maybe we should have taken the version of the ride without

the spinning," Duncan said, wavering.

JD snorted in a most unaristocratic manner. He'd even lost the tie a few days ago, though he still wore a sport coat. "Or maybe we should have ridden *before* we did the 'drink your way around the world' challenge."

The latter involved getting a drink at all thirty food and drink stations set up for the International Food and Wine Festival.

"I think it was that dragonberry colada that got me," Sara Lee said. "Or the Tzatziki Martini in Greece. Yogurt and vodka do *not* mix."

"Man, you're making me thirsty," Duncan said. "Still, I feel kind of bad about the way we left the simulator car."

"They're supposed to have barf bags," Sara Lee said. "Besides, the way that ride simulates G-forces, I'm sure they're used to cleaning up a little vomit."

JD chuckled. "A *little*? There was more puke in there than in a Roman vomitorium."

They all laughed again. The days had become a blur of rides, fun, alcohol and great food. JD and Duncan had hit it off like old fraternity brothers.

"Sooo, what now?" Sara Lee asked.

"I'm hungry," Duncan said.

"I'm sure you are, since your stomach is empty," JD said.

They staggered across a series of bridges to the World Showcase side of EPCOT.

"Let's go to China," JD suggested. "I could go for some potstickers."

"Okay, we just need to make sure there's no peanuts in the sauce," Sara Lee said. "I'm deathly allergic." If Satan ever found out, peanuts would be the only food that wouldn't turn to dust in Sara Lee's hands.

"I'll check with the booth," JD promised.

They wove through the light weekday crowd past the Aztec pyramid that served as the Mexico pavilion and the weathered "dark ages" Norwegian church, then arrived in the China area, patterned after the Temple of Heaven in Beijing.

They looked over the menu at the food booth.

"Ooh, Kung Fu Punch," Sara Lee said. "How'd I miss that on the last go-round?"

"You had the Happy Lychee martini," Duncan reminded her.

"My turn to buy," JD said. "Why don't you two find a place

in the shade while I get our order?"

"Thanks," Sara Lee said. "It's really hot today—though not hot as Hell."

Duncan cocked his head. "Is anyplace as 'hot as Hell'?"

"Just Texas in August," Sara Lee said.

She and Duncan claimed a shaded bench and sank down gratefully.

"I thought I was in good shape," Duncan said, "but I'm not used to this much walking."

"I'm *really* not used to it," Sara Lee said. Especially not with so much extra weight. Though apparently Satan's weight curse only applied when Sara Lee was in Hell, because she *had* lost a few pounds, despite their bacchanalian behavior. Still, she weighed quite a bit more than the last time she and Oscar had come to Disney World.

"You being out of shape is kind of pathetic, considering your body is still in its thirties," Duncan teased.

"Yeah, one of the really short list of perks of being dead is you don't age," Sara Lee said.

Duncan gave her a rueful look. "Oh, sure. Rub it in. I'm staring at fifty. It's all downhill after that."

It was like he *wanted* her to ask him. "What if you could..."

"A little help?" JD called from the food window, where he struggled to balance three plates and three plastic cups of Kung Fu Punch.

Sara Lee was quite certain *he* had never waited tables. Leaving Duncan to hold their seats, she hurried to help JD.

"Quick, grab that plate," he said, nodding toward the one teetering on his arm.

Sara Lee took the plate and two of the cups. JD led the way to the bench. He handed a plate to Duncan, then sat so he would be in the middle. Sara Lee fought a smile. JD did seem to be making an effort to be near her. She could get used to having him around. He was handsome and fun to be with, once you got past his stuffiness, which he apparently abandoned after a few drinks. And he looked different enough from Oscar that dating him wouldn't be too creepy. Maybe she should wait a little longer before having "the talk" with Duncan. Maybe it wouldn't be necessary. After all, if JD was interested, and God and Satan approved...

Sara Lee sipped her Kung Fu Punch. Vodka burned down her throat. "Wow, I see how it got its name. I'm pretty sure this is going to kick my ass."

"Lightweight," JD said with a twinkle in his eye.

Sara Lee laughed. "No one's called me *that* in a long time."

She set the cup on the bench, then took a bite of the chicken potsticker. Almost immediately after she swallowed the spicy sauce and chewy dumpling, her throat swelled, trapping the food and blocking her airway. The plate tumbled from her fingers, and she clutched at her throat.

"Sara Lee!" Duncan dropped his plate and cup and rushed to kneel before her. "Oh, God, I think she's having an allergic reaction."

Struggling to scrape even the smallest breath around the wedged food, Sara Lee gave her brother a "no shit" look.

"They said it was okay," JD said in bewilderment.

"There must be peanuts in the sauce," Duncan said, grabbing Sara Lee's purse. "Do you have Benadryl in this bag of yours?"

She nodded, feeling pressure swelling in her brain.

"Do you have food stuck in your throat?" JD asked.

Sara Lee nodded. JD pulled her up, got behind her and placed his interlocked fists at her stomach and jammed them into her abdomen.

Nothing happened. *Too low.* Sara Lee flailed to move his hands upward, but oxygen starved her muscles of strength. Panic choked her even worse than the food and swelling.

Someone broke JD's hold and pushed him aside. Two furry paws wrapped around Sara Lee's waist. After three expert pops, the food ejected from her throat like a fighter pilot from a damaged jet.

JD stared at the ground, while Duncan kept asking if she was okay. Her throat was still swelling—

Then suddenly it shrank back to normal. She turned to find Duffy the Disney Bear standing behind her in his little sailor suit and hat. Sara Lee had always felt scorn for the Duffy character, originally created solely to be sold in theme parks (ka-ching!). But right now, she felt a bit more charitable toward him.

"Thanks," Sara Lee said, still breathing hard to restore a normal level of oxygen to her cells.

"I'll get you some water," JD said, hurrying toward the food booth. Duncan still scrabbled like a hamster through the stuff in Sara Lee's purse.

Duffy handed her a pin that read "I've been saved."

"Jesus?" Sara Lee whispered.

Duffy nodded.

"Thanks!" She gave him a teasing look. "Does this mean I'm *really* saved?"

Duffy gave a noncommittal shrug, then rested his paw on her cheek. "Be careful. Something's not right here."

"I'll say," Sara Lee said. "Satan's trying to send me to oblivion. I should have known she'd be aware of my peanut allergy. Bitch. Thanks for the Heimlich."

"JD was doing it all wrong," Duffy said. "I had to step in."

"Why bother?" Sara Lee asked, a sudden wave of depression washing over her. "I mean, really, what does it matter if I go to oblivion?"

"God knows the fall of every sparrow, remember?" Duffy said. "How much more do you all matter to Him?"

"Once we're in Hell?" Sara Lee shrugged. "I have no idea."

"Found it!" Duncan triumphantly waved a plastic bottle labeled "Benadryl." Sara Lee didn't have the heart to tell him that it contained diet pills.

When she turned back to Duffy, he was gone. Sara Lee took a deep slug of Kung Fu Punch. As the vodka burned down her throat, she tried to shrug off the mood swing.

JD pressed a cup of water into Sara Lee's other hand. She opened the bottle and swallowed a diet pill, so Duncan wouldn't feel bad.

"You're sure you're all right?" JD asked, concern in his blue eyes.

Sara Lee nodded.

Duncan blew out a relieved breath and threw an arm around Sara Lee's shoulder. "Thank God."

"Pretty close," she muttered. The brotherly hug, the first real affection Duncan had shown since Sara Lee's return, chased away her blues. "Who's up for the Grey Goose Cherry Slush in France?"

Butterflye and Ralph stood in line, waiting to go into Cozumel's Sea Life Submarine Adventure. She wore her blue dolphin-design shorts and a white sequined tank top, while Ralph, standing upright on his back legs, wore a kid's *Squalor of the Sea* t-shirt and a chartreuse baby bonnet.

The man in line behind Butterflye winked at her. "What's the little feller's name?"

She smiled. "Ralph."

"I bet he looks just like you."

"He's my late husband's. We don't share any DNA."

"Really? I bet he's still a handsome young'un. I'd sure like to buy his little mama a drink."

Ralph turned, leaned forward and hissed at the stranger.

The man backed away. "That's the ugliest baby I've ever seen."

Down a gangplank, at the entrance to the submarine, stood a teenager wearing a nineteenth-century British naval uniform with broad horizontal stripes and a hat similar to Donald Duck's. In a thick Latino accent he said, "Be patient. We'll be boarding the *Nautilus* in five minutes."

"Butterflye!"

Butterflye turned to see MJ waving from the pier. "Hey, why don't you come with me?" MJ asked. "We can have a drink. You can bring your little boy too."

What luck! The perfect chance to pitch the job to her. She waved back. "That's a great idea. My treat. Come on, Ralph."

They grabbed an outside table at the Juan-in-a-Million Mexican Cantina across the street from the submarine adventure. Even in October, the Mexican sun beat down on them. At least the banana leaf umbrella offered a little relief from the heat. Butterflye sipped a McJose Scottish-style Whiskey, Mexico's premiere scotch, on the rocks. MJ drank an icy Cerveza Lite beer. Ralph pressed his mouth over a Senorita Temple, only with vodka, garnished with a cherry and a plastic palm tree swizzle stick.

They sat in silence and watched the line monitor close the door behind the last submariner.

Butterflye's stomach knotted. *How can I approach the topic of afterlife occupations?*

As the metal cylinder slowly lowered, air bubbles raced out of the sub's underwater jets and rose to the surface. Within thirty seconds, water completely concealed the vessel's presence, except for the fake periscope that scanned the crowd like a perv looking up a lady's skirt. Slowly the periscope slid away from the dock and disappeared into the lagoon.

"I have a confession..." Butterflye tested the waters of truth. They were bitter waters. "We're not actually sisters."

MJ stared at their almost identical reflections in the polished glass table. As the story progressed, MJ slammed down the remaining contents of her Cerveza and polished off a second before the bottle's sweat even reached the table.

"You're telling me we're not twins separated at birth? I'm your clone?"

"Yeah, that's pretty much what I said ... verbatim." Butterflye spilled it all: the rich stalker Jonathan Harrington Latimer, Jr., his hi-tech medical research firm, Butterflye's fatal flight across the English Channel, Jonathan's well-funded geneticist grandson and a hippie baby momma that produced a perfect reproduction of one of Satan's favorite underlings.

MJ folded her arms across her chest and leaned back. "You're saying you're dead and I was made from DNA from your hair brush?"

"Technically I'm on vacation. But, yes, you're made from my DNA."

"Lady, you are *crazy*! ... Hey, Pedro," MJ yelled at the waiter. "I need more." She held up four fingers.

"You said your company is failing and the drug dealers are coming after you. How would you like job security someplace where no one can threaten your life again?"

"You want me to make a deal with the devil?"

"That's the spirit!" Butterflye showed her an old photo of a tall muscular man wearing a tight-fitting white breastplate sitting atop a rearing horse the color of snow. "That was my husband Ossie. He was one of the biblical Horsemen of the Apocalypse. The job is mine, and now I'm offering it to you."

"Which Horseman?"

"Plague or Pestilence, or both. Your choice. I go by Plague-Pestilence."

"Bummer. I was kinda hoping for Death or War."

"Sorry, MJ. They're already taken."

"What's the catch?"

Butterflye pointed at the roach wearing the bonnet. "Ralph. He was Ossie's pet. He comes with the job."

Ralph turned his head toward MJ and tightened his mandibles into an arthropod smirk.

"And," Butterflye mumbled, "a few hundred thousand of his friends. Oh, yeah. You'd sort of have to die, but only for a moment."

MJ shrank back in her wrought iron chair. "What's in it for me?"

"The usual. Job security, eternal damnation, a health plan.

Oh, and minions. That's the best part. Everyone's too afraid of you to complain if you're hormonal—" Ralph tugged at Butterflye's shorts with his spiky foot. She looked down. "What?"

He hissed.

"Here." She handed him a twenty dollar bill. "Yes, you can get a souvenir. Hurry." She turned back to MJ.

"You're telling me you're immortal?"

Butterflye nodded. "I like to call it sempiternal."

"But you said your husband died. How can that be if he was immortal?"

"Well, the Four Horsemen drowned in a nasty ice fishing accident while they were on holiday topside. There's no protection on vacation. If someone blew me up right now, I would die for good. But when I come to Earth for work, I'm untouchable. It's the same way your health insurance works. It doesn't cover you for illness or injuries that happen in another country. Check your PPO. It's in the fine print."

MJ's eyes scanned the horizon. With a new epiphany, she cringed. "But that means I'd go to Hell."

"MJ, you sell drugs embedded in clothing to teenagers. Where do you think you're going when you die? You don't get the Up elevator for starting kids on pathway drugs. Did you see the movie, *The Mummy*?"

"Which one? Boris Karloff or Brendan Fraser?"

"Fraser. Remember that sleazy little guy, Beni? He told O'Connell, 'It's better to be the right hand of the devil than in his path.' Trust me, you'd rather be spreading diseases than getting them." Butterflye stirred her drink. "Besides, I've seen what those Mexican drug lords do to competitors. Those are not pleasant exits. If you go to your great reward naturally, you'll just be one of the faceless damned. But once you're Plague, you can strike those scumlords with whatever lingering disease you want, or kill them super-fast. Your choice."

"What happens if I refuse?"

"Not a thing." Butterflye sipped her scotch. "The Big Guy is into that free will thing. But to answer your question, the same thing that happens to every human being. You'll grow old, ugly and die, if those drug lords don't get to you first. As Plague ... or Pestilence, you'll never look older than you do now. And, bonus, you don't get sick."

"Wow. I'd be my own boss. I wouldn't have to answer to stockholders."

"Yeah, sure," Butterflye said dubiously. She pictured Satan chewing out her future replacement. "If you say so."

"It's tempting. What's not to love? Hellfire, eternal damnation, perpetual torment."

"You've been reading too much of the Big Guy's propaganda. You never get sick, no gray hairs, no wrinkles." Butterflye gazed at her own eyes in the table top. Even being on vacation this short time, the faint crow's feet had become slightly more pronounced. "Except when you go on vacation."

Ralph scurried back to Butterflye. He wore an official MJ t-shirt with Cozumel embroidered over the pocket, and an infant-sized sombrero. He waved a cockroach-shaped key chain at Butterflye and pressed the souvenir's head. He danced around on his back two sets of legs to a digital rendition of "La Cucaracha."

Butterflye laughed. She turned her attention back to the dock, catching the glint of the submarine periscope gliding just above the water's surface. "Hey look, there's the sub. Time has really flown."

"I bet they had a better time than we did," MJ said.

"I doubt it." Butterflye stood up. "We're going back to the ship." She paused. "What do you say? You interested?"

The sub slowed its approach thirty feet short of the slip, turned a hundred and twenty degrees, then stopped for a moment. Butterflye spied something streamline, gray and shiny skimming across the water's surface near the lagoon's entrance. "Is that a shark?"

"Can't tell," MJ said, squinting at the water.

The maybe-shark smacked nose first into the submarine. A huge fireball emerged from beneath the water, billowing forty feet into the air.

"Look, fireworks," Butterflye exclaimed. She loved fireworks.

The sub's diesel tank shot straight up, spinning end over end, and at its apogee exploded into a million tiny glowing pieces.

"Oooh. Awwww."

On a bright, clear Cozumel afternoon, touristas found shrapnel from the sub and assorted body part raining down on them. The banana leaf umbrella didn't protect the girls from bulkheads and control panels, but it certainly slowed down entrails and the occasional severed hand.

MJ pursed her lips as she watched the diesel-fed flames dance across the surface of the water. "Can I give those drug lords leprosy?"

"Yup. Leprosy, scabies, erections that last shorter than four seconds. Anything you want."

The head and torso of a female submarine passenger splatted beside MJ, covering her in bloody goo.

"You won't have to worry about the drug lords anymore. All you have to do is sign on the scarlet line."

MJ stared down at Ralph, who rubbed his head against her shoe. "It's tempting. I'll have to give this some serious thought."

Chapter Eight

Bunny hung up the mansion's corded princess phone. She
sank into the plush comfort of the chair beside the phone table,
her heart sinking even farther. Feeling numb, she stared through
D.B. Cooper's diaphanous form, saying, "The film's finished—
and not in the good way."

"I'm sorry to hear that." D.B. scooted his newspaper away.
"Boy, you lose a few extras and the producer calls it quits.
Back in my day, extras were a dime a dozen. Why didn't the
studio just hire stuntmen? They would've known how to fall in
a chasm without breaking their necks."

D.B. raised his ghostly eyebrows. "I hope this doesn't mean
you'll be leaving. I've really enjoyed getting the paper again.
I've fallen out of touch with the world—no pun intended."

"There was a pun?" Shaking her head, because she didn't
care and because her attention had snapped onto the
newspaper's headline, Bunny said, "What's that about Congress
giving the defense department a two billion dollar bailout?"

"What? No, that's not what it says. You're reading straight
across and putting two article titles together. Congress isn't
bailing out the defense department; they're bailing out the
President's favorite band. I suppose, though, it's not too far off
to call a government contract a bailout."

"Then I want a bailout," Bunny said, "or a government
contract. They seem to pay better than Hollywood contracts."

"I wouldn't expect either," D.B. said, "unless you're going to
buy weapons for the military."

Bunny pushed to her high-heeled feet. "That's it! First, I
lose my expense account. Secondly, Kitty won't take over my
job. C, my movie gets canceled. Now, fifthish, the Pentagon is
spending more money that I no longer have!"

Bunny dug her cell phone from her Gucci purse. She scrolled
through her directory for P, finding Paramount Studios, Paris,
Pentagon. With her finger poised over Pentagon, her thoughts
oscillated between Paramount and Paris—two places she would
rather call.

Her call rang straight through to the highest-ranking general. He answered with a dull, "Oh, dear, what do you want?"

"Quit wasting *my* money!" Bunny thought it best to be direct when talking to anyone involved with the government. Those sorts of people talked in circles so much they were as dizzy as their rhetoric.

"*Your money*?" the Pentagon general uttered. "I'm not sure I follow your meaning … as usual."

Bunny let out an exasperated sigh for his benefit. "I'm War. Therefore, the war budget belongs to me." She grabbed the newspaper and waved it at her phone. "I hear you're about to spend billions on dromedary technology—as if camels need to be upgraded."

"You mean drone technology, and it has nothing to do with camels."

"That's even worse," Bunny said. "Who uses bees in battle?"

The other end of the line fell silent. Then the general said, "Not that kind of drone. Listen, War, I can't talk now."

"Make time, Alfred!"

"My name isn't Alfred," he said.

"What is it?"

After a prolonged silence with a distinctly uncomfortable vibe, the general said, "Frankly, I'd rather not have War know my name. Alfred is fine. General is fine. I don't care."

Bunny scowled, hating when she didn't get what she wanted. Yet she had to admit his name wasn't important. In life, he had a cameo role. Not everyone could be stars. "Fine, I'll call you Albert."

"It was Alfred a minute ago."

Bunny waved her hand in dismissal. "Listen, buddy, you'd better make time for what I have to say, because I've recently fallen on money troubles and I'm going to need that budget back."

"We need the money for weapons. What's more important in a weapon budget than weapons?"

"Don't give me any doubletalk or try to confuse me with logic. I know that *anything* can be a weapon. So, from now on, tell your soldiers to bring stuff from home for weapons. Think of the savings."

The general sputtered.

"Just do it. You aren't the only one with better things to do than argue. I'm expecting a magazine photographer and writer at any moment." Bunny hung up.

She reclined on the couch and tried to relax. Worry led to wrinkles that never photographed well—unless you were a Shar-Pei. She tried reclining on the divan, imagining herself the great Theda Bara. Instead of resting, all Bunny felt was stretched out, like on a mental torture rack. How, when and where had her afterlife gone so wrong?

Her phone claimed it was 2:00. The magazine people weren't due until 5. Even Bunny couldn't lounge and do nothing for four hours. Or was it two? Digital readouts made it so hard to tell time. What was she supposed to count?

Beyond the French doors draped in lace, a beautiful garden beckoned. When she wasn't shopping on Earth, Bunny appreciated nature's beauty—especially in the form of planned gardens and manicured lawns with neatly trimmed trees and shaped bushes—the way God intended.

Bunny reclined on a lawn chair with striped cushions. The California sun shone gently on her skin, which had become much too pale after death. If nothing else, she'd return home with a nice tan. In Hell, lying out for a tan only resulted in blisters and scorched skin.

As Bunny half-dozed, a large potted bush burst into flames with a near-sonic boom that sounded like "Bunny."

She leaped to her feet. Her stilettos clicked against the stone pavement surrounding the kidney-shaped pool. She grabbed a child's pail, scooped water from the pool and doused the fire.

She'd never thought the California sun could be so hot. Maybe the Texas sun. Relieved and proud that she'd stopped a wildfire, she tossed the pail and stretched back out.

Before she could close her eyes, a pine tree erupted with dozens of tiny flames, resembling Christmas lights. Again, "Buuuunnnnnyyyy" shook the air, this time accompanied by a faint jingling sound.

Bunny raced to the coiled watering hose. She twisted the spigot then ran with water gushing out. She sprayed the tree, putting out every tiny flame. Standing with the water running over her expensive, open-toed shoes, she frowned.

"I'd better phone the fire department and have them send someone to man the garden." Looking at her wet feet, she amended, "After I change my shoes."

With the spigot turned off, but the hose left straggled across the yard, Bunny headed inside, her shoes dangling from her fingertips.

A loud boom whooshed down the chimney. Crusted old logs erupted into flames, dispersing accumulated dust motes. A cloud of dust seemed to form a face. From it came a distinct, booming, "Ho ho ho, Bunny!" The tune "Jingle Bells" followed.

Bunny dropped her shoes, and up arose such a clatter. She ran towards the fireplace, causing a mouse to stir. "God? Is that You?"

"It's been Me all along. Didn't you hear Me calling your name?"

"I thought it sounded familiar—but then, no plant has ever talked to me before. I figured it was a case of mistaken identity. Smokey the Bear always says 'Only you can prevent forest fires.' I never realized he meant it so literally."

"I suppose Smokey does give out a good message."

"Why didn't You knock?" Bunny asked. "Or ring the bell? Even if I didn't hear it, D.B. would've answered the door."

"Oh, yes," God murmured, "I'd forgotten about D.B. Meant to send Reaper after him years ago." The still-hovering, cloudy, bearded face smiled and winked. "I'm sure I'll get around to it. For now, there's a more important matter at hand, and it involves you."

"Oh, dear Lord—and I mean that in the nicest way—I can't take on more duties right now."

The cloudy Santa-face, continually reshaped by the rising smoke and dust from the fire, raised an eyebrow. "Are you *actually* busy with war plans?"

Bunny laughed. "Oh, heavens no. Why would You ask? I'm worried about my lack of funds. Satan closed my expense account."

"Don't worry, Bunny. Haven't I always taken care of you?"

"You did let a cam light fall on me and kill me," she said.

"That was a matter of murder, which unfortunately falls into the category of Free Will."

Murder? Bunny furrowed her brow. Remembering that caused wrinkles, she opened her eyes wide. "It was an accident."

The Santa-face shook His head sadly. "Bunny, that happened years ago. Focus on what's happening now. You're in danger."

"Not anymore. The movie's been shut down due to so many accidents." Bunny sat on the couch, drew up her knees and wrapped her arms around them. "There goes my income." Then she brightened. "Are You here to tell me about another movie deal?"

"Even if I were, your vacation isn't long enough. So just listen to Me. *You are in danger.* Beware of Mars."

"Is it in retrograde? Because that would explain the accidents."

"Oh, oh, oh," the cloudy Santa-God lamented. "Bunny, I'm talking about Mars, your brother-in-law. He intends to kill you while you are mortal and assume your job as War."

"That's not very nice. We're like family," Bunny said.

"Just heed My warning."

"I'll bet the other Redheads are having a better vacation. This kind of stuff never happens to them."

"I never bet. I always know the outcome. But you're wrong; stuff *exactly* like this is happening to them."

"Have You warned them too?" Bunny asked.

God hummed, making the smoke seem to thunder. "No. Jesus is watching over Sara Lee, and Zoe wouldn't listen anyway. Besides, she's got Jake. Unfortunately, Butterflye is in international waters and outside My jurisdiction."

"There's someplace *You* can't go?"

Another rumble. "In a moment of weakness, when negotiating for Earth, I gave the Bermuda Triangle to Satan and allowed a neutral zone around it." The billowing shoulders around the floating head shrugged. "It's allowed for a little mystery on Earth, and that's a good thing. Yeah."

"Say, God, why are You talking through a fire anyway? How come You don't sit on the couch with me?"

"My presence is too awesome for mortals to withstand on Earth. This is the safest means—that or sending an angel with a message. And I wasn't sure I had any angels capable of getting through to—I mean, getting the message right."

"It was a complicated message. There are two Marses. Whoever named the planets should have thought it through." She cocked her head thoughtfully. "Were the planets named first? After all, they were here first ... right?"

"As always, you cut right to the problem," God said. "Promise Me you'll be careful."

"Oh, sure." Bunny waved a hand. Piece of cake. It wasn't like she wouldn't recognize Mars. He had the same sweet face as Ares. *Sweet.* "Hey," Bunny said, "there are three Marses.

There's also the candy bar. Was the candy named after him or the planet?" Either choice seemed a weird one.

"It's too difficult to explain in the short time I have left. I really need to be going. There are literally millions of things I have to do—all before nightfall."

"Before You go," Bunny said, "could I make s'mores over the fire? Talking about candy bars has made me hungry."

The fire crackled and let out a resigned hiss. "Sure. Just toss in a roasted marshmallow for Me."

Zoe and Jake had made no headway in their attempt to find out who was trying to kill her, partially because there had been no new attempts during their trip to the next reunion. While she was glad not to have another attempt on her life, she felt frustrated that she had to keep looking over her shoulder.

"Well, this reunion is already better." Zoe studied the art deco building as Jake handed off the car keys to the valet.

"You're just saying that because we're standing in front of a four-star hotel." Jake reached for his bag, only to have it snatched away by a uniformed bell hop.

"Welcome to the Ritz. I'll take your bags." The bell hop whisked into the building with their bags before either one could respond. They had no choice but to follow or lose their belongings.

"Checking in?" A perky, perfectly coiffed young woman in a suit asked from behind a massive marble counter.

"Yes, thank you." Zoe handed over her credit card and an ID built specifically for their vacation.

"Welcome to the Ritz, Mrs. Grimm. You're part of the Skinner party. You'll be on the fourth floor. All ... festivities will be on the second floor conference level. Here's your welcome packet."

"Packet?" Zoe looked up from the receipt she signed.

"Yes, ma'am. Everyone in the Skinner party gets a packet. The itinerary and instructions were very ... detailed."

Zoe wasn't sure she liked the slightly frightened look on the desk clerk, Jenny from Aspen's, face. Zoe took the packet and nearly dropped it, not expecting the heft.

"This is going to be an experience, isn't it?" she asked.

Jenny from Aspen didn't meet her eyes as she coded the key cards. "I really can't comment, ma'am. But they're very ... organized."

"Well, thank you, anyway."

Jenny's smile erupted once more as she handed over the keys. "The elevators are behind you and to the left. If you'll follow Roger, he'll take your bags to your room."

"That's okay. We can manage," Jake said.

"Oh, no, sir. It's hotel policy. We can't let you do that. Roger?" The bell hop, who suddenly seemed much larger and more intimidating, gestured toward Jake.

"Make sure we get his full name before we leave," Zoe said. "He'll be good on the Squad when his time comes."

Jake nodded. "Especially with the stubborn souls."

They rode the elevator to the fourth floor in uncomfortable silence. Roger waited while they swiped the door open, then set out the bags. He hovered a moment until Jake pressed a tip into his palm. Roger nodded in thanks and closed the door behind him.

"Glad that's over," Zoe said, unzipping her bag. "I was starting to think Roger was permanently attached to us."

"That would've been awkward, especially on our honeymoon." Jake hefted the packet. "Speaking of which, should we see what we're in for?"

"Not on an empty stomach. Let's look at it over dinner."

"You sure you don't want to find out if the Skinners have some mandatory mixer or dinner or something?" Jake sounded uncertain.

"Come on. We work for some of the most demanding souls ... anywhere. What can a few relatives do to us?"

No sooner did the words leave her mouth when a staccato knocking on the door answered her question. Zoe shrugged to Jake and opened the door. A hotel staffer scurried in.

"Sorry for the interruption, ma'am. This is your welcome basket. I was instructed to tell you there's a Welcome Reception tomorrow at 10:20 a.m. in the second floor Ballroom C." The hotel staffer fled before either Jake or Zoe could say a word or offer a tip.

"I guess that answers the question about tonight, and looky, a welcome basket." Zoe ripped off the cellophane and rummaged through the goodies. "Wine, cheese, cookies ... and a spa gift card with an appointment already set for 9 a.m. tomorrow morning."

"Is that weird? It seems weird." Jake hesitated over a recyclable-paper-wrapped cookie the size of a saucer.

"Yeah, this isn't ... normal. But given our experiences so

far, did you expect it to be? We have to check them out. Who knows, the next Death might just love"—Zoe read the cookie label—"Gluten Free, Dairy Free, Vegan Carob Chip Cookies."

Jake shuddered. "Suddenly I really, really want a hamburger or a steak."

Zoe yanked him toward the door. "Let's go."

Zoe arrived for her pre-arranged spa appointment at precisely 9 a.m., before any other customers registered. She was whisked into shampoo and facial. She let the salon's quiet sink in and ease tensions she didn't even know she had. The manicure and pedicure would've impressed Bunny with the vibrant shade of pink they applied before Zoe could object. The hair style and makeup were more "Sorority Chic" than she would've liked, but Zoe didn't want to offend whoever picked up the tab.

When Zoe was alive, cosmetics had been limited in scope. Though thicker in composition, she'd never felt foundation as caked on as the troweling she received in the spa. She didn't love the color palette either. The blue eye shadow did nothing for her eyes. When she dared look in the mirror, she felt like a live-action Barbie doll.

A man in a white, flowing spa uniform slipped through the salon, keeping to the walls. For a second, Zoe frowned. All the employees she'd seen so far were female. She was struck by his familiarity. She felt she should know him, but never got a clear enough look at his face to place him. Maybe he just reminded her of Orcas, simply the doppelganger effect?

Zoe was about to ask about the man when the stylist enveloped her in a cloud of hairspray, sending her into spasms of coughing. When she could finally breathe, she said, "Can I ask—" Before she could finish, the stylist whipped off the cape.

"You're done. Have a nice day."

The chair spun around so fast Zoe felt like she'd been launched toward the door. Since she was propelled in that direction, she didn't stop to offer a tip—not that the woman acted like she even wanted one.

A wisp of white movement caught Zoe's eye. The man skirted the outer wall heading toward the lobby. She moved along the opposite wall, trying to get a clear look at his face. He managed to stay out of range except for one brief flash when he glanced behind him.

"Wait? Wait. That's *not* Orcas, it's—"

Before she could complete the thought, a series of pops and a bright flash of light and heat erupted from the salon on a toxic wave of hairspray and nail polish remover. The shockwave drove her to the floor. Shrieks rose and fell from inside the salon followed by the unmistakable sound of sprinklers wetting down the room. She was tempted for a split second to find a sprinkler and let it ruin the stylist's hard work. As the smoke and chemical fumes burned her eyes and lungs, a pang of fear propelled her out the door.

Zoe caught another glimpse of the man in white. Through watering eyes, she could tell he had dark hair and vaguely familiar features, but like a recurring dream, just out of reach.

"Okay, Jake's right. Something hinky's going on." Her phone pinged an alarm. "Oh, crap. Brunch. Can't be late for that."

Zoe scurried toward the elevator, putting the man in white and the salon fire out of her mind as she fought against the current of concerned onlookers streaming toward the salon.

As she and Jake approached the ballroom less than an hour later, Zoe finally had enough of the weird looks he shot her. "What?"

"It's ... you're ... that's a very different look." Jake blushed, as if afraid of saying the wrong thing.

"It's only for a day. It'll all wash out when I shower." Zoe's teeth clenched. She didn't care for the Sorority-Barbie look either and really started to hate it as they approached the ballroom.

Every woman sported the same Beauty Queen Big Hair and wore similar outfits. They all turned to stare at Zoe and Jake with wide, impossibly white smiles and shiny eyes. She dug her nails into his arm.

"Let's go, Jake. Right now. Turn around and walk away." The nervous churn in her stomach bled into her voice.

"Don't you ... why?"

"We need to go. Right now. But no sudden moves."

"But your family?"

"That's not family, Jake. That's a Multi-Level-Marketing *cult*. Maybe even Amway. If we go in there, we're never coming out."

Jake jerked her back toward the elevator, the warning for no sudden moves disregarded. As Zoe fumbled with the TV remote for express checkout, he threw their belongings back in their bags. They crept out of the room, checking to make sure the hallway was clear, before sneaking down the stairs.

"Let's hope the last reunion works," Jake said as he sped away from the hotel. "We're running out of relatives."

Butterflye swiped her card and opened her stateroom door. "Mine, all mine," she said, surveying her earthly domain, temporary though it was.

Ralph sat on the couch, a brandy snifter in his claw. He glanced up from his book, *Insect Adventure*, to wave his antenna at Butterflye.

"Wow. That wine tasting in the chef's lounge was amazing. Sorry I had to leave you here. It was for adults only. I hope you don't mind."

He shrugged and scratched his neck with his back leg, then returned to his novel. On a nearby coffee table, the remains of a rolled up t-shirt smoldered in an ashtray.

"It's just that—"

A pounding at the door broke off her sentence.

"Open up, Mrs. Plague. Open up this minute!"

Butterfly cracked the door and peered out. She was greeted by the new head of security/bartender, along with her steward Fred and Donald Trump.

Fred forced the door open. He pointed his finger at Butterflye and said, "Adkjfsk eljtp dlaptj sd."

Butterflye planted her fists on her hips. "What's going on here?"

Trump pointed at her. "This is *my* suite."

He speed-dialed a number on his phone and set it to speaker. "Nice try, Satan. We had a deal. I don't have to your pay your bill until I die. I had to buy the cruise line to get out of that coffin of a cabin. I'm billing you for the time your Redhead had possession of my suite."

Satan's voice came over the phone. "No problem, Don. It's worth it."

"That's so sweet," Butterflye called out. "You think I'm worth it."

"That's right," Satan said. "I totally didn't mean it was worth the cost of the Presidential Suite to get rid of you, Plague."

The billionaire set his Trump Smartyphone 2100 down on the coffee table and fixed himself a club soda, while Fred wadded up Butterflye's clothes and souvenirs and threw them in the blue leopard-spotted trunk. Ralph, sporting a Turtle Farm t-shirt, ambled past Fred, who also stuffed him into the trunk.

Panicked, Ralph jumped out, skittering from place to place and toppling the lamp on the end table. He scampered through the broken ceramic fragments on the floor and tried to make a break for it. He wasn't fast enough. Fred grabbed him and the "Better not open before Halloween" gift from Satan, then slammed the trunk shut. The steward pushed the trunk end-over-end into the corridor, to an awaiting forklift.

The bartender handed Butterflye the remaining carry-ons and pointed to the hall. As she closed the door, Trump said, "What did I do with my phone?"

Butterflye followed the forklift out of the elevator on Deck Zero, down the corridor five hundred feet to the far aft of the ship. The forklift operator, whose name tag read "Carlos from Uruguay," set down his load. He put his hand out waiting for a tip.

"You've got to be kidding," Butterflye said, not reaching for her purse.

Seeing there was no gratuity in his future, Carlos raised and lowered the lift arms rapidly, violently slamming the trunk against the deck five or six times. He kicked the trunk off the platform and raced away at full speed with the flag of Uruguay fluttering behind him.

Butterflye turned the doorknob and pushed the door open as far as it would go. The door slammed against a twin bed, the only one the shoe box room could hold.

Butterflye lay on the bed. It was hard to believe that this cabin was designed to house two adults—maybe Munchkins. Ralph sat at the foot of the bed, playing Cockroach Crush on his misappropriated Trump Smartyphone. By the look on his face and the hum coming from his wings, he had just taken out an entire swarm of praying mantes.

The room was almost perfectly quiet, except for Ralph's game sound effects and the constant hum and vibration of the ship's engines located a deck or two directly below.

The ship pitched back and forth, and with each movement of the vessel, Butterflye's stomach flipped 180 degrees, like a bronco ride that extended long past its obligatory eight seconds. The aft of the ship raised up, then smashed down into the sea. As Butterflye slammed into her cabin's ceiling, bright lights burst inside her head. Dropping to the bed, she squeezed her eyes shut and rubbed the back of her neck. "I think that last one gave me whiplash." She moaned and grabbed a barf bag. It was going to be a long last day.

Once the sea finally calmed to a slow rock and roll, Butterflye grabbed the phone from Ralph and searched through the photos and videos, hoping to find something she could use to blackmail Trump into returning the Presidential Suite. As one video started playing, an evil laugh bubbled up from Butterflye's throat. This was even better. She forwarded the video to her work email, attached it to a text to Satan, then handed the phone back to Ralph.

She looked around her room. Two paintings faced each other on opposite walls. The one on the port wall was a bright orange bird-of-paradise bloom surrounded by a splotchy green background. "Is it me, or are these the exact same artwork?"

Ralph looked up from his game and nodded.

He was right. The framed print on the starboard wall was pixel-for-pixel the same painting on the port side.

Butterflye dozed off, but woke a few minutes later when her cell phone rang. It was Wreak, red-faced and breathless. "Butterflye, I just wanted to warn you Trump found out about the stateroom hack."

"I know." Butterflye turned her phone around and displayed all one-hundred square feet of her cabin with the camera. "How do you like my new digs?"

"Oh, wow. Bummer. It's worse than I thought."

"Is Angelica there?" she asked.

"I'm here." The nun's nostril monopolized the screen.

"Sister, I think I've got an idea about getting your ciggies back. I've uncovered information that Satan plays with the ponies." Butterflye motioned to Ralph to hand her Trump's phone. He smashed a couple more praying mantes with a virtual hammer before surrendering it to Butterflye.

"Gambling's a sin, and this is Hell. What's the problem?" Angelica asked.

Butterflye held up the Trump Smartyphone displaying a video of Satan prancing a rainbow-colored, plastic horse around her desk. Behind her, in her private bunker, was a carefully displayed collection of inanimate equines. "I didn't say she was playing the ponies, I said she was playing *with* ponies. I just texted this photo to her, along with the tracking number for a cigarette dispensing machine for our break room and one for your private quarters. After all, tobacco was one of Ossie's best inventions. I can't let it disappear because of political correctness. ... Oh, and Sister, make sure you send in those scotch requisitions. We don't want any disruption in supply."

The nostril expanded as an off-camera smile crossed the nun's face. "Will do, Boss. Good work. How'd you find out about the ponies?"

"Donald Trump's phone. He's got dirt on everyone. By the way, what's this website I found on Facebook, 'The Truth about Hell'?"

"Sorry, Boss." Angelica simulated static noises. "I'm afraid we have a bad connection."

The Darth Vader Theme played on Bunny's laptop, which meant Wreak and Havoc were Skyping her. In no mood for more bad news, Bunny groaned and opened the computer. Once the magazine people heard about her film being canned, they called off the spread. No money. No fame. What a lousy vacation.

Forcing a little cheeriness for the benefit of others, she said, "Hello, boys. What's the catastrophe *soup du jour*?"

Greed shone in their eyes. "It's *not* a catastrophe!" they chimed—actually chimed in song.

"Let me tell her," Havoc said, his baritone blotting out Wreak's tenor notes. "You always ramble. By the time she gets the news, she'll be on a second vacation."

"Like Satan would give the Redheads another vacation," Wreak said. "But go ahead. You're better at speaking Bunny-ese."

Havoc's face puckered. "Bunny, we finally found where you stashed—"

"Dumped," Wreak corrected.

"*Stashed* Ares's book collection. Along with his smut, you tossed out his accounting books—both sets."

"Who needs two sets of the same books?" Bunny asked.

"Focus, Bunny," Havoc said while Wreak smirked. "I'm talking about ledgers." At Bunny's blank stare, he added, "Books used to manage a budget."

"Who needs books for that? You charge something and a bill comes. Someone else comes along to pay that bill with another charge card." Bunny sighed. "Things used to be so simple when I could use my *carte blanche* and Satan got the bills. Why did things have to change?" She stomped her foot, but nothing happened. "I hate change! Change is bad. Anybody who says change is good is a liar."

"Bunny!" Havoc snapped his fingers rapidly. "Ares kept track of money coming in and going out ... but a lot more came in than went out."

"That's called profit," Bunny explained.

"It can be ... when it's done legally," Havoc said. "However, Ares siphoned funds from every defense department around the world. He took bribes—"

"—from both sides," Wreak interrupted.

"—and charged fees for everything from consultations to inspections. He had an A to Z list of money-generating schemes."

"More like an Alpha to Omega list," Wreak said.

"You're both crazy," Bunny said. "'Consultations to Inspections' only runs from C to I."

Wreak rolled his eyes, while Havoc drew a long breath and let it out, counting to ten.

"Bunny," Havoc said, "the point is, you are *rich*. Forget the loot in your 'junk room.' You have more hidden accounts with loads of money than a Democrat."

"We're talking 'ten Bill Gates' rich and 'one hundred oil sheiks' rich," Wreak said.

Bunny cocked her head. "So? I know all sorts of guys working in gas and oil, and they earn minimum wage."

The boys exchanged confused stares, then Havoc nodded knowingly. "We aren't talking about gas station attendants."

"I'll put it in terms Bunny understands. Just let me Google blockbusters." Wreak's fingers flew over the keyboard, typing like a madman at a pipe organ. "You're easily a thousand *Avatars* rich with a couple thousand *Titanics* to spare."

Bunny squinted at their gibberish. Clearly they had been in Hell too long. Maybe Satan should institute a regular vacation plan for everyone in Hell.

"Boys, I know a lot of avatars from hanging around with angels, and they aren't rich. Ares used to have the titanics over for cards, and believe me, they're just huge and mostly broke."

"Okay," Havoc said, "I'll grant there's plausible confusion with the word avatar, but I think you're confusing an enormous cruise ship with the Greek Titans."

"Let me help." Wreak typed some more. "Adjusting for inflation, and the fact you think the world is stuck in 1972, you're as rich as a thousand times the total ticket sales from *Gone with the Wind*."

Bunny cooed. "*I have money.*" Suddenly, she didn't mind so much that the Pentagon wasted money on weapons. Let those monkeys in Washington (as Michael called them) spend billions. After staring dreamily, Bunny snapped back reality. She gripped both sides of the laptop. "As soon as I get back, you two need to clear up the misuse of *my* funds on Earth. Since I've been in charge, the Pentagon has taken advantage of me, because I don't recall receiving any payments—which is wrong."

"No, Bunny," Havoc said gently, "it was *wrong* of Ares to *take* payments."

"But War is a job, and people get paid for doing jobs."

"Okay, Bunny, *that* brings up a whole other issue. But hold that thought—if you can." Wreak's face turned profile as he spoke to Havoc. "You're confusing her." Then he was back. "Bunny, it's perfectly all right to take bribes and kickbacks. That's how the world works."

Havoc smacked Wreak upside the head. "You *earned* your place Down Below. Quit lying to her. She's only here because of the job."

"Boys! Fix the problem—if there is one. You two aren't making any sense."

Havoc gave a neat, bobbing nod, similar to the bobble headed dachshunds popular in cars. "All you need to know, Mistress of Devastation, is that you have plenty of money and all is right with the world again."

Wreak scoffed with a loud, sneering cough—a difficult sound and expression to manage simultaneously. "Since when has *all been right* with the world?"

"All I meant was *Bunny's War* is right with the world."

"You bet I'm right," Bunny said. "It's like I told General Alvin at the Pentagon ... they're wasting money on more weapons when *anything* can be a weapon."

"Uh, Bunny, the chairmen of the joint chiefs of staff is Martin Dempsey," Havoc said.

"Then who's Alvin?" Bunny asked.

Wreak smirked. "One of the Chipmunks."

"Never mind," Bunny said. "But you might help him out when you have some spare time and look at his books."

"We'd love to go through the government's books." A greedy gleam lit Wreak's baby blue eyes. He rubbed his palms together and let out an evil "hee hee hee."

Havoc gave him a second wallop. "Do you like being reminded

of the many steps that led you here? Or doesn't the word 'atonement' mean anything?"

"Like *that* ship hasn't already sailed," Wreak said.

"Is that one of my battleships? Don't they have names like 'Atonement' and the 'Starship Enterprise'?"

While Wreak chortled, Havoc smiled and said, "I'll give you points for being close, Mistress."

"It's not like she's lobbing hand grenades or horseshoes," Wreak muttered.

The doorbell chimed, its music echoing in the expansive mansion.

Bunny perked up. Maybe the magazine people had changed their minds. She closed the computer and said, "Gotta go." Then she added, "Drat. Did that in the wrong order." She raced to answer the door, but D.B. arrived first.

"Who's calling?" the ghost-butler asked, sticking his head through the wood and glass door.

Seeing her handsome suitor in his signature black through the glass pane, Bunny yanked open the door. "Adam! What are you doing here? Are you on vacation too?"

Adam rushed inside. He swept her into his arms and kissed her. "No, I'm not on vacation. Michael sent me to look after you."

"Why didn't he come himself?" Bunny asked.

"He can't. After your TV show, he used up all his trips to Earth for a millennium. So he pulled some strings with Gabriel and sent me on one of Gabriel's allowed visits."

"Pulled what strings? Gabriel's pretty tight with his privileges. He wouldn't likely give up a 'trip to the zoo,' as he calls it."

"It was literal strings. Michael has to sit in on ten jam sessions, playing the harp, with Gabriel and his horn."

That impressed Bunny. "Wow. He must really think this is important. Michael hates the harp. But all angels are required to play it—except Gabriel, who's lorded that over Michael for as long as they've known each other, which I gather is a long time."

"Bunny, it's *very* important because *you* are important."

Bunny stroked his cheek. "So you came down to protect me."

Adam grinned back. "Michael wasn't too happy about the notion, but even that mule-headed angel concluded I would work harder to protect you than anyone else.”

“I can't believe Michael thinks I'm important. He's always telling me I'm a terrible War and I need to 'get into the game.'”

Adam winked. “I'll tell you a secret—there's a debate in Heaven as to whether you're the best or worst War. Some think you're the worst because the Earth was predicted to have a lot more wars going on by now and that you're falling behind.”

Bunny shrugged. “Michael would agree.”

“Others, myself included, think you're the best War, for precisely the same reason. Some of us think your job is to *end* all wars.”

Bunny laughed. “That would be tough. People will fight over anything.” She gave his arm a playful push. “Just the other day, I told General Alister at the Pentagon ... no wait, his name was Marvin ... no, that's a Martian ... it was Marlin ... no, that's Nemo's father ... oh, well, whoever he is, I told him what you said—that *anything* can be a weapon.”

“It sounds like you were trying to do your job,” Adam said, encouragement in his tone.

“Not really. I wanted him to quit spending money, because I thought I was funding him and that I didn't have any money because Satan is broke. It turns out the Pentagon is supposed to pay me—or they were paying Ares—but Havoc says it's wrong to pay me, because I'm a terrible War—but Wreak says it's fine; it goes with the job. It sounded like money laundering, because every government on Earth paid Ares, so the currency wouldn't match. Laundering is about matching things like socks, right? Right now, no one knows where the money belongs. Although the Pentagon wants it for goats ... no, it's to weaponize camels— the kind with one hump. Don't ask me why. I guess that's the only mounting that would fit.” Bunny shrugged. “Anyway, money matters are confusing with all the demonstrations.”

“Denominations,” Adam said softly.

“It's really better to use charge cards and take money out of the picture. Not that it matters anymore. The boys told me that Ares wrote a couple of books that were making me a fortune. Probably from reprints. Who knew Ares wrote a bestseller?”

Adam gripped Bunny's shoulders. “Sweetheart, it's probably better if you don't handle financial issues.”

“You're right, Adam. You're so smart. Maybe you could look into whatever the boys were talking about.”

“I'll be happy to, but you really need a qualified accountant.”

He bit his lip. "Bunny, you've called me Adam twice now. Didn't you promise me something?"

Bunny stared upwards—as if answers might magically appear on the ceiling. "I'm not good with trick questions."

"Didn't you promise to call me by another name?"

"You'll have to be more specific." Wow. Some people expected a person to remember every detail of a conversation.

Adam let out a calming exhale. "Didn't you promise to call me *Pernell*?"

"Oh yes, that Indian name for 'cowboy in black.'" Bunny wiggled his black sleeve. "Are you sure you want me to call you that? It sounds like a girl's name."

"I'm sure."

"Okay, but you cowboys are sure funny." Cheyenne and Sioux were girls' names too. "I guess that's how you manly types stay in touch with your feminine side."

"Yeah. That's it." Adam wrapped an arm around Bunny's waist. "If you're not doing anything, how about we go out for a nice dinner, then a stroll on the beach in the moonlight?"

"It's a date," Bunny said, suddenly very glad Adam had come to protect her instead of Michael. Michael would've probably spent the evening turning the mansion into a fortress.

That was when Bunny noticed the pistol at Adam's hip.

"I've never seen you armed," Bunny said, adding a hesitant, "Pernell."

Adam smiled upon hearing his nickname. He patted the revolver. "Mars is also on vacation. It's the only way he could stay on Earth this long. And this will stop him permanently."

"You'd think he'd have better things to do on vacation than try to kill me," Bunny said.

Chapter Nine

"You okay?" **Jake asked as** they cruised through the mountains.

"Just thinking, and loving the scenery. The cliffs are a little disconcerting."

They whizzed past a yellow sign warning of falling rocks. Almost on cue, a loud rumbling led to tumbling pebbles followed by larger rocks and boulders. Jake hit the gas and zoomed around a bend and out of danger.

Zoe twisted to scan the top of the mountain from the back of the convertible's open top. A figure backlit by the sun stood on the shoulder. The shadow's line reminded her of Orcas, but it wasn't him. Then it hit her—Dolph, Orcas' brother. She hadn't had any contact with him since the memorial for the Horsemen. Zoe and Dolph had only Orcas in common, and he was gone forever. But why would Dolph be trying to kill her? She blinked and the shadow was gone.

"So, what's next?" She settled back in her seat. A shadow of fear nagged at her like an itch she couldn't scratch, but she didn't want to worry Jake.

"Our last stop," Jake said. "The last family with potential replacements."

"Then let's hope this is better than the last two." Zoe shivered. "Is it wrong that I'm actually looking forward to getting home? Don't get me wrong, this has been great, but..."

"You miss your home and bed. I get it. I do too."

"Homebodies R Us, I guess. Now that that's out in the open, let's do silly stuff between now and the last stop."

Jake pointed at a sign. "You mean like the Santa Cruz Mystery Spot?"

"Exactly like that."

An hour later, as they wound through twisted and tilted "gravity-defying" walkways in bright, colorful gardens, Zoe asked, "How long can we stay?"

"At least as long as the guided tour. Maybe longer. Enough to have a good break. Enjoy the mystery."

She took advantage of the Mystery Cabin, which made her seem taller and Jake shorter, and put them on an even height, to easily kiss him without stretching.

"What's that for?" he asked.

"For not debunking all this with science and logic."

"I could." Jake stood on a ledge that put him on a steep angle to the apparent floor. "But why? Mystery can be fun. Besides, *aliens!*"

A ball, seemingly rolling uphill, suddenly shot off the track and narrowly missed Zoe's head. "And there it is again. Can't we have one stop without an 'accident'?" She made full use of air quotes and sarcasm. "Come on. Let's go before we run into Reaper."

The seaside park a couple of hours farther up the coast exploded with color and scents from dozens of flower varieties in full bloom around a stone and wood pavilion resembling a castle. Birds chirped in the trees and bushes. Children chased each other while adults watched in groups on benches and blankets.

"Looks relatively normal," Zoe said, climbing out of the car.

"Experience so far suggests those two words don't go together." Jake joined her in surveying the scene.

"What words?"

"'Relative' and 'normal.'"

"Ha, ha."

Zoe's family tree did seem to have more than its fair share of cuckoo bird nests. Burned by the past two encounters, they approached cautiously, but were greeted warmly.

"We're so glad you could make it. Our family's so spread out, we've lost track of all the tendrils," a genuinely nice woman about thirty said while keeping one eye on the active game of tag. "I'm Suzie. The internet has been an amazing resource for bringing us all together."

"Bang!" A carrot-topped boy about six pointed a finger at another child. "You're dead! Now your soul is *mine!*"

"Damion!" The woman's shout was a scold. "It's not nice to kill your cousins."

Zoe started. Her eyes went wide. Jake wore a similar, stunned expression. "You don't think?"

"Let's just watch for a bit."

Suzie introduced Zoe and Jake to various relatives. Zoe tried to concentrate on all the kindness showered on them, but her attention kept returning to Damion.

The boy—if he'd been born sixty years earlier—could've given Ron Howard a run at being Opie Taylor, with his innocent face, red hair and freckles. He now had a toy space gun to replace his imaginary finger gun.

"It's my Death Ray!" he said proudly.

"Forgive him," Suzie said, flopping down on a bench beside them. "We introduced him to *Dr. Horrible's Sing Along Blog* and now he's into being an Evil Villain."

Zoe smiled, genuinely amused. "There are worse things. Evil scientists are very smart."

"So is Damion. When we watch *Phineas and Ferb*, he takes notes on the boys' inventions and criticizes all the Inators."

"That's my kind of kid."

They stayed in the park until sunset, when bit by bit, relatives headed back to homes or hotels. Zoe and Jake were among the last to leave. Before they packed it in, Damion bounded up and plopped in Zoe's lap—much to Suzie's chagrin.

"I like you. You don't die today," he said seriously.

"Why, thank you, Damion, I appreciate that."

Zoe met the little boy's eyes and felt ... something she never expected. A connection. A jolt. And ... *aw, crap.*

Suzie plucked the little boy off Zoe's lap. "Come on, Damion, I'm sure we'll see Miss Zoe again."

"You can count on that," Zoe said as Damion scampered off. She fought the lump in her throat as she gripped Jake's hand. "We need to go."

"What's wrong?"

"I found him. The next Horseman." She sighed. "Last place you look."

"Which one?" Jake scanned the remaining relatives.

"Damion."

"The kid?"

"The kid."

"Oh, man, Zoe."

"Not here, Jake. We'll talk about it someplace ... else."

"You know it would drive *Her* completely crazy to work with a six-year-old for the rest of eternity. That could be fun to watch." Jake was apparently determined to find some kind of positive spin when they were in the car.

"But think of what it would do you and Reaper and the rest of the minions." Zoe chewed her lip. "It was hard enough to learn to work with me."

"And what does a six-year-old know about Death anyway?" Jake asked.

"Probably as much I did." Zoe crossed through the list of Pros and Cons before it really got started. "I can't do it, Jake. I can't. He needs a chance to grow up. He needs to be able to live before he can be Death. I can wait."

"That's very … astute and reasonable."

Zoe's half-smile held a bit of sadness. "You say that like it's unusual. I do try."

"You know what this means?"

"It's time to go home," Zoe said.

"Not this very moment." Jake wrapped her in his arms. "We still have a little time left."

"And no other place I'd rather be than right here."

Sara Lee half-dragged her brother down the hall of the Animal Kingdom Lodge. Duncan looked thin, but was six feet tall to Sara Lee's five-foot-four, and weighed 180 pounds to her … whatever. Her weight was one subject on which she preferred to stay blissfully ignorant.

"The world is spinning," Duncan slurred. His legs gave out and Sara Lee stumbled, slamming him into the wall.

"And the walls are moving," she said, hoping that in his drunken state, Duncan would buy it.

When they'd left EPCOT, Sara Lee hadn't realized how bad off her brother was, or she'd have asked for JD's help. They were supposed to change and meet him for dinner at Victoria and Albert's, Disney World's finest restaurant. Sara Lee suspected Duncan wouldn't make it.

Not that she minded the idea of spending time alone with JD. She just pitied Duncan for the hangover he'd have tomorrow.

Finally, they reached his room. Huffing and sweat-soaked, Sara Lee wrangled her brother through the door, dumped him on the bed, then pulled off his shoes.

Duncan gave a relieved sigh. "Thanks. I haven't had anyone to take care of me since Pam left."

"Who's Pam?" Sara Lee asked.

"My ex-wife."

"You were *married*?"

"For about five years," he said, still slurring his words. "Didn't take. She claimed … I never let anyone in."

"I guess not." Sara Lee suddenly realized how little they'd talked about Duncan's past. He always turned the conversation to her, and Sara Lee, being a lawyer and therefore, by definition, self-centered and self-important, never noticed.

"I'm glad I came on this trip," Duncan said, squeezing her hand painfully hard.

Sara Lee just smiled and smoothed his hair with her free hand. Living in Hell, she was used to pain.

"I didn't realize how much I missed having family," he said, his words slowing and his eyelids drooping. Within thirty seconds, he started snoring faintly.

"Me either, Brownie Baby." Sara Lee sighed. She couldn't do it. She couldn't even bring herself to ask Duncan. This was all Jesus's fault.

She fetched a glass of water and set it on the bedside table, then headed to her room to shower and change.

A few hours later, Sara Lee and JD walked down a softly lit path on the Animal Kingdom Lodge property. Moonlight bathed the world in silver.

The path forked. A sign stating "Pool" pointed to the left. JD went right. Towering hedges formed a natural, curving wall that kept her from guessing what lay ahead.

"Duncan missed a terrific dinner," Sara Lee said, gripping the chiffon skirt of her black evening gown and swinging it as she walked.

JD chuckled. "I think he got a little too much sun."

"And a lot too much alcohol. I swear that boy didn't get any of our family's Irish blood. So where does this path lead?"

He adjusted the bow tie on his tuxedo. "You'll see."

"Ooh, a surprise. I love surprises."

He cast her a sidelong look. "Do you?"

"Well, good surprises," Sara Lee amended. "After ten years of practicing law and over twenty years in Hell, I should remember to qualify things."

"I find it hard to imagine you as an attorney," JD said.

"Just get into an argument with me, and you'll see. My mom always said I'd argue over the color of the sky. Law seemed a natural fit. What did you do before Hell?"

"I oversaw one of my family's vineyards in what is now Tuscany," JD said.

"That's why you know so much about wine."

JD looked a little sad. "Oscar never talked about me?"

"Not about any of his family," Sara Lee admitted. "I only met you those few times while Oscar and I were dating, and I never met your parents. I kept asking him to invite you all over, to see if he could mend fences, but he said—" She resisted the urge to smack her own forehead.

"What? Truly, I want to know."

"That he didn't want to inflict all of you on me," she rushed out.

"I suppose my family can be a bit elitist."

A snort escaped Sara Lee before she could stop it. JD tried a glare, but his quirking lips ruined his effort.

They emerged through an archway into a small, cobblestone courtyard. The tall shrubs enclosed three sides and a Plexiglas wall on the fourth provided a view of the Animal Kingdom savanna. On a café table flanked by two folding chairs rested a plate of chocolate-covered strawberries, two glittering flute glasses and a bottle of champagne chilling in an ice bucket.

"Ooh, definitely a good surprise," Sara Lee said.

JD popped the cork and slowly poured champagne, tilting the glasses to minimize foam.

"Perrier-Jouet Flower Bottle," Sara Lee said in approval. She'd bought that a few times for clients in New York. She felt a little surprised he JD hadn't gone for Cristal, not that she minded.

He handed her a glass, then lifted his own. "To an exciting finish to our vacation."

Sara Lee lifted her glass in salute, pleased she'd remembered not to clink it against his, and even more pleased that he'd set up this tête-à-tête. Oscar had been fond of grand gestures too. Once, he'd starved out an entire village to get land to surprise Sara Lee with a mountain vacation home. He always liked mixing business with pleasure.

From beyond the hedge, a string quartet struck up Mozart's "Waltz of the Flowers."

"That song was in *Fantasia*," Sara Lee said, visualizing animated blooms twirling in midair.

"It seemed appropriate," JD said.

Sara Lee gave him an incredulous look. "You've seen *Fantasia*?"

JD shrugged, his cheeks reddening. "I've had an ill-spent last twenty-odd years."

He and Jesus might have a lot in common after all, what with Jesus's mid-afterlife crisis—

"Wait," she said. "That time frame corresponds roughly to the time Oscar and I were married."

"So it does." JD set down his glass and held out his hand. "Would you do me the honor of a dance?"

Sara Lee placed her glass beside his. Feeling awkward, yet a bit breathless, she slipped into his arms. He executed the waltz with flawless, smooth steps and turns, his lead easy to follow.

"Oscar was a terrible dancer," she said with a fond smile.

JD laughed. "He had to keep count."

"I loved that about him."

"You loved his flaws?" he asked in puzzlement.

"I loved that he danced with me, even though he sucked at it, because he knew I enjoyed dancing. Though I'd have enjoyed it more if he hadn't stepped on my toes so often." Sara Lee followed JD's lead into a spin, then came back to the basic waltz position. "Besides, you can't enter marriage expecting your partner to be perfect. You'll definitely be disappointed."

His warm hand stroked her bare back, scattering her thoughts.

"You've got some muscle on you," he said.

"Um ... I work out with the Master Trainer From Hell."

"Candace? Me too." JD shuddered. "Though mostly she's trained me to beg for mercy."

He moved into a more complicated series of turns, which Sara Lee easily followed, thanks to the guiding pressure of his hand. There was something incredibly intimate about a waltz— the closeness, the secret communication by touch, the dizzying turns. Or maybe her dizziness was due to the high volume of alcohol she'd consumed.

"Sara Lee?" JD said, his voice suddenly soft.

She looked up at his blue eyes and found them staring back with open desire. His rare show of unguarded emotion both touched and scared her. She wasn't sure if she was ready for another relationship, especially one this complicated. Dating her dead husband's brother sounded like a soap opera—or an episode of Jerry Springer.

The song ended, but JD kept his hand on her back. His other moved to stroke her cheek. "I need to tell you something..."

Light burst above them and a boom shook Sara Lee almost

off her feet. Red and gold sparks rained down, setting fire to the tablecloth and some of the shrubs. From behind them, musicians shrieked and instrument strings twanged as they snapped.

"What is it?" JD shouted.

"Fireworks!" She grabbed his wrist and pulled him toward the deathtrap's exit. Another rocket exploded ten feet above them, forming a Mickey Mouse head and ears. High-pitched, demonic Mickey laughter rolled through the air. Smoke burned Sara Lee's throat as sparks drifted toward them. Searing pain shot up her arm and she cried out. JD brushed an ember from her forearm with his jacket sleeve and they started running.

"Pool!" Sara Lee said.

"Right!"

When they reached the fork, the Iron Underwear cut off Sara Lee's breath. She slowed, huffing.

"What's wrong?" JD asked as she released his hand.

She waved him toward the pool. "Go!"

Another rocket exploded, then another, creating a pink cube within a cube. It would have been cool if it weren't right overhead.

JD pulled her arm around his shoulder and half-dragged her toward the water. Echoes of demon-Mickey's evil laughter followed them. Fiery pink death rained from the sky—almost like a collaboration between Bunny and Zoe. The hem of Sara Lee's dress burst into flames. JD made a mighty lunge, and they tumbled into the pool.

"Hey, you're not allowed in the pool except in a bathing suit," a cast member said from where he stood skimming leaves from the water. "It's against—aaakkkk!"

A shower of sparks set the man ablaze. He staggered into the pool. JD dove and dragged Sara Lee under the surface—before she got a breath. Sparks sizzled on the water above. Choking on over-chlorinated water, Sara Lee fought toward the surface.

JD shook his head violently and held on, evidently unaware she had no air. Sara Lee's lungs burned. She twisted her wrist and yanked upward against his thumb, breaking his hold. You didn't survive long in New York—or Hell—if you didn't learn basic self-defense maneuvers. Her head broke the surface, fortunately just as the sparks died. Treading water while her sodden dress tried to pull her back down, she coughed and tried to drag air in at the same time. Finally, she wheezed in a breath, then another.

JD surfaced beside her. "Are you okay?"

"What ... were you trying ... to do—drown me?" she asked between gasps.

"I was trying to keep you from burning," he said.

"Well, next time give me some warning." She softened her words with a weak smile. "I didn't get a breath."

Around the pool deck lay the charred remains of a towel girl amidst smoldering cotton towels and a watchman in a scorched blue uniform. The pool man floated like debris on the water's surface.

Sara Lee looked skyward and saw only stars. "Do you think it's safe?"

JD stared off into the darkness. "Not at all."

Another watchman entered the pool area and shone a flashlight's beam on the mayhem. He sucked in a sharp breath, then his light stopped on Sara Lee and JD. "Are you folks okay?"

JD half-shrugged and shook his head. Sara Lee dog-paddled to the ladder and the guard helped her out. Seeing Jesus in the watchman's uniform didn't surprise her.

He touched the weeping burn on her arm. The throbbing pain faded, then the wound healed over.

"Thanks," she said as JD hauled himself out of the pool. Water sluiced off his ruined tuxedo.

"Jumping in the pool in formalwear looked a lot more fun in *It's a Wonderful Life*," Jesus said softly.

Sara Lee glanced at her gown and sighed. Between the burned patch and the bleach stains, her dress was toast.

Bunny poured Adam a glass of homemade lemonade. Lemonade was trickier than orange juice. She'd had to add sugar and cut slices for the pitcher, although D.B. never gave her a precise answer as to the exact count of slices in a lemon.

Adam's lips drew up in a teensy bit of a forced smile. "It's really ... sweet."

"I thought it came out good too," she admitted. It tasted like pure sugar with a hint of lemon zest.

Adam took another small sip, then set his glass on a coaster. He leaned back against the striped couch. "I'm surprised Mars hasn't tried anything more by now."

"I still say everyone is worried over nothing. Mars was watching us film. He's just too shy to come up and talk to me."

"Don't make the mistake of thinking he's not out to kill you," Adam said.

"Oh, Ada—Pernell," Bunny said, quickly correcting herself, "it's sweet of you, Michael and God to worry, but I'm sure it's nothing."

"Are you saying God is wrong?"

Bunny took a long sip of lemonade. "Satan would never let Mars go on vacation if she knew he'd try to kill me. So either God or Satan made a mistake—and both possibilities seem unlikely." Bunny hummed thoughtfully. "There's a first time for everything, I suppose. God does stay really, really busy. Say—maybe it's a clerical error. Maybe God's secretary goofed. She always seems flustered when I check in with Him."

The doorbell chimed.

Hope sprang eternal in Bunny's heart that the magazine people had returned. As she leaped to her feet, Adam jumped up even quicker.

"Let me answer," he said.

"Good luck. No one can get to a door faster than D.B."

Sure enough, the ghost hovered before the opening door. While the resident spook could open things—doors, cabinets and drawers—he lacked the spectral manipulations to pick up and carry objects. All he could manage was to shove things around.

"Who is calling?" D.B. asked.

"Tell her it's Mars. Wait, you'd better tell her it's her brother-in-law. No, make it the brother of her deceased husband, Ares. Be as specific as possible."

During the deeply growled spiel, Adam rushed to the door. He rested his hand on his revolver. "Don't make me use this," he said, his own melodious, baritone voice menacing.

Bunny stepped up behind Adam. Mars filled the doorway, holding a box of Russell Stover chocolates with a drawn-on bow and a bouquet of calla lilies. Bunny gently nudged Adam aside.

Sweeping a hand toward Mars, she asked, "Does that look like he wants to kill me?"

"The candy could be poisoned," Adam said.

"What self-respecting *man* would kill someone with poisoned candy?" Mars asked.

Bunny cocked her head. "Russell Stover isn't *great* candy,

but still, you'd buy cheaper if you were going to poison it."

Adam knocked the box from Mars's hands, hurtling it toward the rose bushes. He drew his revolver from its holster. "It's oblivion for you."

"You won't shoot an unarmed man, *cowboy*." Mars waved the flowers in Adam's face and pushed inside. "Nothing is poisoned or poisonous." He raised his arms. "Look at me. Completely unarmed. Not even a butter knife."

Bunny accepted the flowers, saying, "Maybe he's here to apologize."

Adam squeezed between them. "Bunny, love, stay out of his reach." His voice dropped. "No man is ever unarmed. Remember, there are many ways to kill using only your hands."

Holding out her manicured hand, Bunny said, "Not with mine."

"Hear me out, Bunny." Mars bumped his shoulder into Adam's. For a moment, the two jostled back and forth, neither gaining any ground. Then, Mars blurted, "Bunny, how about marrying me?"

"But that's illegal. You're my brother."

"Brother-in-law," Mars corrected. "In many cultures, it's traditional for a man to marry his brother's widow to take care of her. Don't you see? This would solve both our problems."

Bunny felt confused as to how marrying Mars would get her movie back into production ... unless that was why he'd been watching them film. "Are you a producer?"

"No. What?" The question whipped Mars's head around.

"She thinks your proposal comes with a promise to fund her movie," Adam said.

"You got that from what she said?"

"*I* understand her. *I* actually care about *her*."

Mars shrugged. "It's not like I dislike her. She's family ... in-law. Bunny, answer me. Will you marry me?"

"Wait—the candy and flowers were for a proposal?"

Mars nodded to Bunny's question.

Slowly, Bunny said, "You brought Russell Stover chocolates? Not Godiva?" As she worked through the logic, Adam smirked at Mars. "And you brought calla lilies? Not roses? Aren't calla lilies for funerals?"

Mars muttered, "I figured they would work either way." Louder he said, "Bunny, let me have the burden of being War. It'll make Satan happy. God would be hap—well, God's already given His approval for whomever you marry, and whatever He says is written in stone. You'd be rid of the job and I wouldn't have to kill you. It's a win-win situation." Mars's lip curled. "Not something War usually deals with."

Adam growled. "Yeah. You're more the winner-take-all kind of guy. So there's something more here."

"He makes sense, Pernell," Bunny mused, hoping it was okay to use his pet name in front of Mars. "Once I'm rid of the job, I'll have more free time to spend with you."

"You'd also be a married woman—to another man," Adam said. "Tell him no."

"Come on, babe," Mars pleaded. "You know I'm your type."

He *did* look exactly like Ares.

"Bunny," Adam said, his voice even, with a hint of sternness, "Ares *murdered* you, then dragged you to Hell."

"When you say it like that," Bunny said, "it loses all the romance."

"Don't you see, Bunny? Mars has been trying to kill you. He's just like Ares."

Mars glared at Adam. "Doesn't that make me *exactly* her type? Besides, I should've been War all along. Instead I got a planet named after me while my brother got to be War."

"A planet *and* a candy bar," Bunny said. "Besides, one out of five planets is pretty good."

"There are nine planets," Mars said, "or there used to be until a bunch of astronomers pulled Pluto's status."

"You're wrong. My sister's an astronomer, and she loves dogs."

Mars stifled a grunt. "Bunny, sweetheart, your answer?"

"I'd say keep Pluto. He's Mickey's best friend."

"No," Mars growled. "Are you going to marry me or not?"

All the while, D.B. hovered to the side, his finger to his ghostly lips. Finally, he let out a mournful moan.

"What's wrong?" Bunny asked.

"I just wanted to get your attention," D.B. said. "Bunny, I'm probably not the best person to give advice on how to live one's life, but consider what would make you the happiest."

"Well, not being killed would be good."

"Bunny," Adam said, "you hated your life with Ares. Think hard about all the things you've told me. How he left you alone. How you were practically a prisoner."

"A prisoner of love," Mars argued. "My brother took good

care of her. He bought her anything she wanted. He looted more than half the world for her."

"That's true," Bunny admitted. "He brought home junk from everywhere. I used to think he went to garage sales, because everything was so old. A lot of stuff was even broken or faded."

"Bunny," D.B. said, his voice a whisper on the wind, "you should focus on the matter at hand. Do you *want* to marry this man?"

"Which one?" After all, they had both proposed to her— Mars just now and Adam after her game/reality show.

"I'm referring to the scary one with the hard eyes," D.B. said. "The one who showed up waving candy and flowers."

"You mean Mars." Bunny glanced at Adam and sighed wistfully. "Pernell has very nice eyes."

"What's your answer?" Mars glared at Adam, then the ghost. "I can't wait all of eternity. I am working on a deadline, and Halloween is almost here."

"Why can't I give you my answer when I get back to Hell from vacation?" Bunny asked.

A hurt expression flitted across Adam's face, then he looked thoughtful and aimed a comprehending grin at Mars. "Nice tactic, Bunny."

She blinked, unsure what Adam meant. Putting off things— especially unpleasant things—was what everyone did. She knew she would turn Mars down. Marrying her brother-in-law sounded just plain creepy. But why ruin his vacation too?

Throughout the exchange and pause, Mars's face grew steadily more red. Finally, he exploded with, "NO! I can't wait until your vacation is over. That defeats my purpose! Sure—if you planned to say 'yes,' it'd be fine. But I'm not as dumb as Ares was. I have the distinct impression you're going to say 'no!' So, *no* deal. Just remember, I *tried* to be nice!"

Adam, whose gun hand had never wavered, gave it a quick flick to draw attention. "Take one step toward her and I shoot. Don't think because I was an actor I won't kill you. Before that I was a Marine and a butcher."

"Couldn't hold down a job, eh?" Mars asked. "Dishonorable discharge?"

"My enlistment was up," Adam said, grinding out the words.

"Besides," Bunny added, "his father needed him to help run the Ponderosa Ranch."

Adam briefly furrowed his brow at her, then returned his

attention to Mars. "Just leave. No one has to die forever. Satan can live with the disappointment."

"But can I?" Mars asked.

Bunny shook her head sadly. "Satan's not so bad. You just have to understand her and overlook her social awkwardness. You know she doesn't mean half of what she says."

Adam and Mars both stared at her.

D.B. cleared his throat with another ghostly moan. "Bunny, I don't think Satan making false promises falls into quite the same category."

"It's all right. Every year she 'promises'"—Bunny used air-quotes—"to come to my parties, but she never does. It's her loss. Poor thing. Large groups of people make her nervous."

"I don't think that's it," Mars said.

"It's time you left," Adam said.

Mars shrugged one shoulder and turned halfway around. Then he lunged into Adam, one hand grabbing the wrist of Adam's gun hand. Bunny squealed in fright. D.B. sailed before her like a gust of wind, driving her backward to safety.

What should she do? It wasn't as though she knew anything about fighting! Michael and Adam should've prepared her for something like this! Bunny covered her mouth—not because she felt like screaming, but because it seemed the right gesture.

Mars and Adam wrestled over the gun. Their arms flailed back and forth, overhead, down by their sides, out in front, everywhere. Then Mars's hand slid over Adam's and he squeezed the trigger.

The wild shot shattered a vase. Long stemmed roses—from Adam—scattered on the table and plummeted to the floor like a red and green waterfall. Actual water flowed and pooled on the tiled floor too.

D.B. Cooper whirled around Bunny so fast, he looked like a white tornado. "Hide!"

Bunny whipped her head around, seeking a good spot—safe, but with a view. Men were fighting over her, just like they had during her show, "For the Love of War," and like they had when she'd been alive. She hadn't lost it.

Bunny scurried behind the fainting couch. The boys had better not damage it. She planned to take the couch to Hell. Re-upholstered in pink, it would be perfect in her office—just the place for a nap or to stretch out dramatically.

Forgetting about redecorating, Bunny, her stomach in knots,

watched her boyfriend fight the man who looked identical to her late husband.

Mars looked exactly like Ares. He sounded like Ares. He swaggered like Ares. And he was trying to kill her, just as Ares had done. *Ares murdered me. Right at the height of my career! And I'd just renewed my studio contract!* The words people had told her so many times finally sank in. Ares wasn't as nice as she'd thought. *He ruined my chance for real fame!* How could he have done that, if he truly loved her? She perched her hands on her hips in indignation. How rude! How very selfish!

Bunny clutched the arm of the fainting couch and called over the side, "You can win, Adam—I mean Pernell!"

Adam's gaze flicked in her direction.

Mars snatched the gun, twisted it toward Adam and fired.

Bunny jumped up. "Nooooo!"

Adam's body wavered, turning more and more diaphanous by the moment. "Remember what I taught you! You can do it, Bunny!"

"You won't forget my party, will you?" Bunny called after his fading body.

"I won't forget. I'm supposed to bring—" Adam poofed.

Holding the revolver, Mars faced Bunny. As Adam completely vanished, so did the gun, because all property returned with the owner. So, in some instances, you did take it with you.

Bunny glared at Mars. "Just because you won doesn't mean I'll marry you! I've decided you *aren't* my type. Adam is my type." *The Cowboy and the Actress* ran through Bunny's mind as the perfect title for their love story.

"It's your loss, honey. And for the record, the reason Ares brought you so many gifts after every battle was because he felt guilty for all the women he'd ravaged."

Anger well up inside Bunny. She stomped her foot with all her strength.

Mars's head should've exploded. The ground should've opened up and swallowed him whole. But nothing. No Warstomp.

Mars laughed, sounding eerily like Ares recounting a victory. "You don't have War's abilities when you're mortal. Right now, you're nothing but a silly, helpless girl."

Something snapped—and it wasn't Bunny's garter belt holding up expensive silk stockings. Her anger flowed from the roots of her dyed strawberry blonde hair down to her open-toed, diamond-studded, six-inch stilettos, size 7½. Nobody called her silly and got away with it. Sure, she'd admit to being helpless now and then, but never silly. Arguing the fact she was a girl seemed pointless, with her curves, kept toned by Candace and kept soft by Haagen Dazs and Godiva chocolates—the appropriate choice for wooing a lady. No wonder Mars was still single.

Her thoughts seeping back to the present, Bunny clenched her fists and shook one menacingly. "Take that back, you ... you ... mean old man. It's like we're not even family!"

"We *aren't* family! You're the stupid bimbo my brother married. I knew you'd be trouble. I just didn't know you'd be *my* trouble."

"In-laws *are* too family. So who's stupid now?"

"I only count *blood* relatives. An in-law can't give you a kidney." Mars squinted and gazed far away, the same look of concentration Ares used. "Most murders are of family members. So"—he grinned viciously—"I suppose we are family."

Mars took a menacing step toward Bunny.

"Watch out," D.B. called. "Mars attacks!"

Backing away, Bunny threw up her hands. "Think about what you're doing. Murder will condemn you to Hell for eternity."

"Where do you think I came from? How do you think I got there? Ares was only chosen for War because he killed two more people than I did. If I'd slaughtered one more family, I'd be War."

"Then you'd be dead—really dead—in oblivion."

Mars snarled. "If *I'd* been War, none of the horsemen would've gone to oblivion. *I* wouldn't have started a fire in an ice-fishing shack. They'd all be alive—whatever—*and,* since my brother wouldn't have had vacations on Earth, Ares would still be in Hell. So everything is really *your* fault."

"I admit I make a few hard-to-follow logic leaps, but you're crazy. There's no way any of this was *my* fault. I didn't even know Ares before he became War."

"But you and the other damned Redheads drove your husbands nuts. Why do you think they needed a guys' getaway? If they hadn't married you four, they'd have been happy with all work and no play."

Bunny straightened a little bit. "I concede your point, but they didn't have to go ice-fishing. They could've done something safer, like surfing or snow skiing."

Mars worked his jaw like it was stuck together with taffy.

"Okay, I concede *your* point. But I'm still going to kill you."

He lurched for her, reaching for her neck.

Bunny hopped backward. "D.B., help!"

The ghost shoved long shards from the shattered Waterford vase toward her. As the crystal pieces scraped across the table, Bunny stared at him. "Really? You want me to glue the vase together *now*?"

D.B. sighed.

"I need a weapon," Bunny said, backing away from Mars.

D.B. sighed harder. He knocked over the fireplace poker set with a metallic clang.

Bunny stepped over it. "Are you trying to trip me?"

D.B. set a pair of scissors lying next to the newspaper to spinning where Bunny had intended to cut out articles about her film. For a minute, the scissors wobbled around.

"Quit playing and help me!" Frantically, Bunny scanned the room. Had there been any wooden chairs, like in a saloon, she could hit Mars with one. But she couldn't lift any of the over-stuffed pieces of furniture. A saloon would also have booze bottles. Clearly, a saloon was a better place for a fight than a living room. All she had was a broken vase, fireplace pokers, a metal doorstop shaped like an iron, a heavy table lamp, some modern art figurines with lots of sharp angles, scissors and a newspaper. Absolutely nothing.

"D.B., *help me!*" Bunny shouted.

"I can't do everything for you, woman! Think on your feet!"

Bunny's gaze dropped to her retreating feet. Mars's shadow loomed closer, overshadowing her toes that peeked through her open-toed stilettos. *My shoes.* Once, when she'd stepped on Wreak's foot, driving her heel onto his big toe, he'd sworn her shoes were lethal. Bunny was pretty sure lethal meant something like a weapon.

She took a big hop backward, kicked up one heel and removed her shoe. Holding it with the six-inch stiletto pointing outward, she shook it at Mars. "I warn you—I'm armed."

Mars laughed. "With a shoe?" He spread his arms and wiggled his fingers. "Come on. I dare you."

Bunny made a running lunge at Mars. Wearing only one shoe, she stumbled. As she fell forward, her arms flailed. Mars laughed harder.

Her flailing shoe struck Mars in the neck, and Bunny's 120 pounds drove the heel deep. Blood gushed out like a chocolate fountain—except it was red, and it was blood, not chocolate.

Mars collapsed to the floor. An unbalanced Bunny followed, landing on top of him.

Blood splattered her pale yellow gown, adding crimson blobs and speckles. "Now see what you've done," Bunny lamented. "It's ruined."

Mars gurgled and choked, a weak hand clawing at the shoe stuck in his throat.

"You'd better not have ruined my shoe too," Bunny said, plucking the heel from the wound.

A lot more blood gushed out.

Bunny wiped her diamond-studded heel on Mars's shirt and inspected it for lost stones. "You're lucky; none are missing."

Mars pressed a hand to his neck. "I can't believe you've killed me," he rasped. "At least, I won't be in Hell anymore. It's 'Hello, oblivion.'"

He closed his eyes. His hand fell from his neck. Then he rapidly decayed into dust and blew away, like a really good special effect.

Bunny looked at the blood covering her gown. "Am I unlucky or what?"

D.B. hovered over her. "Frankly, my dear, I'd say you were insanely lucky."

Chapter Ten

"You killed him with your shoe?" Wreak said incredulously.

Bunny nodded, nestling the bloody shoe in a tissue-lined box to go out for cleaning. "It's like Adam said, anything can be a weapon. Although, I think *everything* is a bit of an overstatement. It was dumb luck I figured out my shoes were dangerous."

"I've told you that a million times," Wreak said.

Havoc patted Bunny's hand. "It's like I've always said, Bunny may not be conventionally smart, or smart in any measurable way, but she has street smarts—sort of."

"Yeah," Wreak retorted, "if that street is Rodeo Drive."

"You have to be sharp to catch a good sale there," Bunny said.

"What I don't understand, Mistress of War, is why you're back in Hell. You still have two days of vacation."

Bunny looked at Havoc with all seriousness. "Exactly. I'm running out of time before my annual Halloween party. Besides, it's safer down here. I learned from a nice fellow, who goes by Teepee Copper—no, it's Debbie Topper, no, it's a funny name." She hummed then snapped her fingers. "D.B. Cooper. Anyway, he taught me that even the most carefully laid out plans can end in death. By the way, he'll be hanging around once Reaper collects him. I told him he could work with you."

"D.B. Cooper?" the boys echoed. "*The* D.B. Cooper?"

"You're sure you don't actually mean Debbie who lives in a teepee and drives a Coup, riiiiight?" Wreak added.

"I mean the man who jumped from an airliner into a rainstorm." Bunny shook her head. "Must've been a really bad movie to leave a plane early, and in a storm no less."

Wreak's blue eyes lit. "I'll bet he comes up with some really good schemes." He rubbed his palms.

"Schemes that could end in death," Havoc said.

"So we recoporealize," Wreak drawled. "It's not like that hasn't happened a few hundred times."

"Anyway," Bunny continued, "I thought since he was good

with money, he could keep those accounting books y'all told me about."

"Uh, Mistress," Havoc said, "he might not be the best choice for an accountant."

"Yeah," Wreak added, "if you want him to *clean up*, you'll be better off making him a housekeeper."

The doorbell rang.

"I wonder who knows I'm back?" As Bunny rose to answer the door, Wreak and Havoc blocked her path.

"It's probably nobody," Havoc said hastily.

"Probably a wrong door," Wreak added. "Let us answer it."

"If it means that much to you, go ahead." Bunny waved them away.

A few moments later, the boys returned with Adam.

"It *was* for you," Wreak said in loud relief.

"Of course, it was. It's my house." Bunny opened her arms wide. "Pernell! My hero!"

Adam embraced Bunny and gazed into her eyes. "How am I the hero? *You* killed Mars."

"By accident. But you risked your life for me."

Adam smiled, with a touch of embarrassment. "I *would've* risked my life for you, but I wasn't in any real danger. I wasn't on vacation, remember?"

"Still, recorporealizing is pretty painful—or so I've heard." Though Satan had promised to wring Bunny's neck or break every bone in her body, she'd never actually done anything to her. Satan was all talk. Underneath her gruff exterior, there beat a heart of gold ... or maybe coal.

"Recorporealizing isn't a big deal—when it happens in Heaven. Accidents still happen, even Up There. It's actually kind of funny then. The Three Stooges—although there are more than three of them—are always clowning around and being recorporealized." Adam kissed Bunny's nose. "You saved yourself, and I'm very proud of you."

"I couldn't have done it without my training. But it's what you taught me that saved me." She glanced at her shoes. "Wherever I go, I'm never without a weapon." Then she snuggled closer. "I'm glad you weren't mortal or I would've lost my soulmate."

Adam's hold tightened. He drew in a breath. In a whisper, he asked, "Does this mean you love me more than Michael?"

"More than Michael ... and more than Ares." Bunny met

Adam's hazel-brown eyes. Physically, he was much like Ares—tall, swarthy, black hair, brownish eyes and broad shouldered—but they were completely different in all other aspects. It finally dawned on her that Ares had murdered her, ruined her career and kept her a prisoner, because he wanted to possess her, like all the "treasures" he collected. But Adam loved her.

"Sweetheart," he said, his tone far more gentle than when Mars had used the term, "then why aren't you wearing the engagement ring I gave you?"

"Because you haven't asked me to marry you—*again*." Sometimes the simplest things had to be explained to men. Bunny found most people needed her to explain things. Sometimes it felt like she spoke a foreign language, though her words were so obviously straightforward.

Adam dropped to one knee and took Bunny's hand. "Bunny, will you marry me?"

Bunny eyed him askance. "While I don't mean this as a criticism, because I'm not a reviewer, your first performance was better."

"Let me try again," he said.

Just then, Satan stormed into the living room. Wreak and Havoc disappeared down the hall, which ultimately led to Ares's junk room. Adam curled his fingers tighter around Bunny's hand and stood between her and Satan.

"You!" Satan pointed accusingly at Adam.

"The one and only," Adam said.

"Oh, Satan," Bunny chirped, "once he does the proposal right, I'm going to marry him! Aren't you happy for me?"

"I'm never *happy* for anyone!" Satan snapped. "Wait ... marry?" Satan's red face turned a deeper shade of purple. "I disapprove of him! I know I approved of him in the past, but that was before all the damned trouble he's caused. In your absence, he's started several petitions and pickets for better housing and fairer treatment in Hell! In Hell!!! I will not, I repeat, I will *not* have him for War."

"You'll be going back on your word," Bunny said.

"So what else is new?" Satan asked.

"Is that why you're here? Because Ad—Pernell—and I are busy."

Satan snorted. "Amazing. You finally got his name right." She growled and balled her hands into fists so tight her fingernails bit into her palms, drawing drops of blood which splattered and hissed on the pink carpet. "I'm here to give you back your unlimited expense account," she said in a rush, like taking medicine fast.

Bunny blinked in surprise. "Why?"

Satan fumed and grumbled. "It came directly down from Him." She pointed upward and winced. "Whenever He sends a directive, it always starts with: 'You know how I hate to interfere.' Right."

Bunny almost told Satan she didn't need an expense account because the boys had told her she had tons of money. But who turned down more money? Besides, it might hurt Satan's feelings. "Okay, that's great. You can go now." Bunny swished her hands toward the door.

"You're *dismissing* me? Nobody *dismisses* Satan!"

"Then what's another word for saying you can leave now?" Bunny asked. "Because we're busy."

"Oh, right, it's true love." Satan sneered. "As if that's a real thing."

Suddenly, from behind Satan came a strong harrumph and a tapping foot. Lynn looked just like Rodan's statue of *The Motivator*. "What's that, *honey*?"

Satan turned slowly, but not before Bunny saw the red creeping into her cheeks. "I didn't realize you were there, dear."

"What's this about true love?" Lynn asked not-so-sweetly.

"I was talking figuratively," Satan said. "Of course, *we* have true love. *We're* special."

Lynn pointed at the door. "I believe we're intruding. We should go."

Satan heaved a sigh. "Yes, dear." She slunk from the room with her forked tail between her legs.

Alone at last with Adam, Bunny said, "Where were we?"

Adam gave her a wicked grin and winked. "I was proposing, *dear*." He said that last word just like Satan.

Bunny laughed. "Yes, I believe you were." She clapped her hands together like a clapboard, saying, "Proposal scene; take three."

"You're in luck," the impossibly beautiful desk clerk said when Zoe and Jake arrived at the resort. "We're usually booked a year in advance, but we've had a last-minute cancellation. Is the Honeymoon Suite all right?"

The suite, unlike the one at Niagara Falls, was elegant and

luxurious in soft earth-tone brocades and silk. Fresh-cut flowers added a light fragrance to the sea breeze wafting through fluttering sheer curtains stretched across open French doors. A bottle of champagne chilled in a silver ice bucket by the bed.

"Now *this* is a honeymoon suite." Zoe gave in to the urge to run across the room and throw herself on the giant, pillow-piled bed.

"What? You didn't like the one in Niagara?"

At the hurt tone in Jake's voice, she rose out of the fluffy heaven she landed in. "Oh, honey, of course I did. I loved it ... just in a different way."

"So you just want to be friends with that other suite?"

Zoe blinked at Jake, trying to wrap her head around him making a relationship joke of any kind, then let forth a peal of laughter. "There's room in my heart for all kinds of honeymoon suites. Especially if you're there to enjoy them with me."

"Wait, we're still talking about the *room*, right?" Jake's expression clouded.

She shot a decorative throw at his head. He managed to get his hands up in time to deflect it. "Of course I'm talking about the room. I'm just as old fashioned in my relationships as you are. You're all I can handle."

Jake seemed mollified, then abruptly changed the subject. "Now, about these attempts on your life."

Zoe buried her head in Egyptian cotton clad pillows. "Do we have to? Can't we just, you know, pretend there's nothing wrong and wish it way?"

"We could, but the damage has been getting bigger. The next attempt might take out a town."

"Then no one would give me grief over numbers." She knew she sounded petulant and didn't care.

"Okay, what's going on with you? This isn't right. You're ... more ... *more*." He flopped down on the end of the bed.

"Don't wanna." She felt him get off the bed, and in her mind it was in a huff.

"Here, have a chocolate-covered strawberry," he said.

"What? Why?"

"Because you get childish and whiny when you're hungry."

Zoe popped up from her pillow haven. "I am not a Snickers® commercial. Aw, the little tuxedo kind. I love those."

Jake handed over the plate of six huge, succulent strawberries artistically decorated in at least three kinds of chocolate. As she bit into one, she moved quickly to catch pieces of shattered candy-coating and strawberry juice.

"Better?" he asked when she'd finished all six.

"Better."

"Now, are we ready to get to the bottom of this?"

Zoe sat up. "You're not going to let it go until I say yes, are you?"

"Germans can be just as stubborn as Redheads when we want to be."

Zoe blew out a breath. "I know I've been very ... oblivious. Is it wrong to want one little honeymoon trip without worrying about plots or body counts or Satanic fits? Sometimes I miss being ... ordinary."

"I doubt seriously you were ever *ordinary*. Don't forget, I worked for Orcas before you were a sparkle in the Universe. He didn't do ordinary. Neither do I."

Zoe managed a weak smile. "Mortal then. It's been nice being human again for a while. So facing some Hell-spawned conspiracy wasn't on my 'to-do' list."

"Oh? What was on your 'to-do' list?"

"It's a honeymoon, obviously, my husband."

Jake blushed. "I get a feeling there's a 'but now.'"

Zoe pushed off the comforter and paced the room. "I can't let people die because they're nearby, no matter how much it would benefit me when we go back. We need to find this joker. I assume you've done some research."

"I have a theory." Jake dug the tablet out of a duffle bag. "You said you saw Orcas?"

"That had to be a mistake."

Jake tapped the screen. "Maybe not. I did some digging the other night while you were sleeping. I have to give Wreak and Havoc some props for the souped-up network connection to the Underworld."

"Jake..."

"You knew Orcas had a brother?"

"Dolph. They had a ... complicated relationship, I guess."

"So do I with my brother."

"You guys look like the Brady Bunch compared with them."

Jake handed over the tablet. "You don't need the files cross-referenced with myths and legends, then."

Zoe scrolled through the file, feeling a little guilty about not telling Jake about Dolph when she'd recognized him. "You went to a lot of work. Yeah, the classic Greek tragedy. Dolph got caught with one of Poseidon's daughters and was banished to rule fish or something. Epic jealousy that Orcas became Death while Dolph was stuck with seaweed. But why me? Why now?" Zoe's eyes went big. "You don't think?"

Jake nodded. "Succession Clause. If the Horsemen have no wives, the jobs go to their brothers."

Zoe tossed the tablet on the bed. "Okay, now I'm pissed. Dolph could've had the decency to come to me about this. This sneaking around stuff is ... wrong."

"As opposed to—"

She stopped him with a forefinger under the nose. "I didn't try to kill anyone. I scouted. If there had been a good candidate, we would've sold whoever it was on the job *then* killed them. This ... this was rude and messy."

"So, what should we do?"

"Find me the most dangerous-looking place around here. We'll draw him out and put an end to this."

Jake swallowed hard, but didn't argue. "Can we at least have dinner first? The restaurant here is Zagat-rated."

Deep in the night, after a four-course gourmet meal, Zoe slipped out of bed. Jake never moved. She ran a hand down the side of his face before dressing quickly and heading out. The resort boasted not only the four-star restaurant but also mountain trails with majestic views. She picked her way to the top of a trail. Loose rocks, steep drops and dim light made the trek attractively dangerous.

"It's about time you showed your face, Dolph."

A shadow stepped out from the trees. When moonlight illuminated his familiar features, her breath caught. In the dim light, she could almost believe it was Orcas ... but the hard lines and harsh features shattered the illusion. How could she have mistaken him for Orcas at the movie studio?

"I should have inherited his job. Not you." His high-pitched, Michael Jackson-like tenor shocked Zoe out of her reverie.

"You dropped off the face of the ... whatever. You disappeared right after the memorial. You could've made a case back then. It's way too late now."

"Why?" Dolph's squeaky voice grated on her nerves.

"Well, one, I don't like the way you work. This job requires some standards. Two, I don't intend to fall into oblivion for you. And three, there's no way I'm leaving my staff to someone who sounds like the love child of Alvin the chipmunk and Donald Duck."

Dolph squealed in a piggish way and threw himself at Zoe. She sidestepped him with a speed only hours of Candace-demanded cardio could explain. He lunged again. Zoe scrambled for higher ground while groping for anything to use as a weapon. Her hand landed on a thick stick, and she started swinging with all the heart of a minor-league baseball player hoping for a shot at the majors. Several blows connected with Dolph's head and shoulders. His attack turned to defense. She beat him back down the trail.

"Listen, Dolph. I didn't ask for this job. I never wanted it, but it's mine now. *Mine.* I"—she punctuated her speech with blows from the stick—"I protect what's mine. Orcas's memory. Jake. Death. I will not. *Will not.* Let you take it from me. I might not be the best at it, but it's mine."

Dolph's child-like sobs grated on her ears, but she didn't let up. When he deflected the stick back on her, he got in a few blows of his own. Her foot caught on a rock. Her ankle turned. She went down on her rump. Dolph lunged. She got her feet up to catch him in the gut. He grabbed for the stick. She pushed with her feet while aiming the stick and propelled him over her head and off the cliff.

She struggled to her feet as he screamed all the way down into the canyon. "Now, *that* came from the diaphragm. Bunny would approve."

Exhausted and sore, Zoe hobbled back into the resort. She didn't see Jake until he yanked her off her feet in a huge bear hug. "Ow ... ow ... ow."

"What happened? You're hurt!" He guided her to a chair and started to check out her ankle.

"Now it's over. Really over. Dolph won't be haunting us any longer."

A thin, high-pitched laugh and a phantasmal chill filled the lobby nook. "That's what you think."

"Can that happen?" Zoe asked. "You said someone who's already sent to oblivion can't be a ghost."

Jake shrugged. "Anything's possible on Halloween."

Chapter Eleven

Since it was the last day of vacation, JD and Duncan decided they should spend the evening at Universal Studios Halloween Horror Nights. They ignored Sara Lee's objection that it reminded her too much of "home." In addition to the usual rides, the park had set up several haunted houses and "scare zones"—foggy areas with employees dressed as zombies, axe-murderers and chainsaw killers jumping out at guests. So, a typical walk down Hell's darker alleys. Creepy music and sound effects—creaking doors, rattling chains and distant screams—reminded Sara Lee of the nicer parts of Hell.

She determinedly pushed away thoughts of eternal damnation. She still had a few more hours of food, drink—and food.

"We should do a haunted house before the lines get ridiculous," JD said.

"As if standing in line to be scared isn't already ridiculous," Sara Lee teased.

"What about the insane asylum?" Duncan suggested, looking at the board listing the various haunted houses and their wait times.

"Ugh, no," Sara Lee said. "Oscar and I did that one once. They had feces smeared all over the wall and the whole haunted house reeked of shit. It made me even sicker than when we rode Mission Space."

After JD bought three super-sized margaritas, they headed to the "Fun House." On seeing the entrance, a giant clown head, with an open, leering mouth as the door, Sara Lee regretted their choice.

Duncan suddenly clutched his stomach. "Oh, man. I really don't have the stamina that you two do for all this eating and drinking."

"That's what you get for eating sensibly and drinking in moderation all those years," Sara Lee said.

He grinned weakly. "Yeah, well, I think I'd better sit this one out. You two go ahead."

"You sure you're okay?" Sara Lee asked, touching his arm.

Duncan patted her hand. "I'll be fine. I just need water and some quality time on a bench." He clutched his stomach again. "Or maybe a bathroom."

"Text me if you need anything," Sara Lee said.

He waved her off and ran toward the bathroom line.

Sara Lee stood in indecision.

"He'll let you know if he needs you. It's not like you can go into the men's room with him," JD said, gripping her wrist. "Come on. It's our last night of vacation. We may never get to do this again."

Already, JD seemed more closed off, as though back in Hell with his snooty family. He again wore a tailored suit and a bland expression as they walked through the clown's mouth.

Inside, a green strobe light flashing on fog created a stop-motion effect on everything that moved. A pounding bass note set Sara Lee's heart to thudding. Chains swinging from the ceiling drew her gaze as she waited for the inevitable costumed scarers to jump out.

She rounded a corner, then found another hallway filled with pulsing, hazy green light. It offered two directions—probably bad and worse.

"Oh, great, a maze," she shouted over the thumping beat.

JD pointed left and they headed down the hall. A body dropped almost on top of them—a grotesquely realistic dummy hanging from a noose. A clown with a deranged leer painted on his face staggered into Sara Lee. A fake dagger stuck from his throat and fake blood sprayed over her arm.

"Yuck! They're not supposed to get stuff on you," she said.

Amid terrified screams echoing through the halls, Reaper appeared in the fog. Dark circles ringed his eyes.

"What are you doing here?" Sara Lee shouted over the bass and shrieks.

He pointed at the hanging body, then the clown. "Collecting."

"These are real? Damn Satan all over again." She cocked her head. "You look like shit."

"Bodies are dropping like flies around you girls," Reaper said.

Sara Lee huffed. "Satan's trying to kill the other Redheads too? Why am I not surprised?"

Reaper looked puzzled. "Satan isn't after the other Redheads. It's—"

A spear tip punched through Reaper's midsection. He faded, then disappeared in a pop of smoke.

"Come on, Satan! Decorporializing Reaper is just mean!" She turned to JD, but he no longer stood beside her. She whipped her head around, but the stop-motion strobing—and the margaritas—made her dizzy. She closed her eyes until the world stopped spinning, then continued down the hall, growing more and more panicked. Reaper would recorporialize, no doubt in a worse mood than usual. But if Satan's random killing spree struck down JD, he'd fall into oblivion.

She took another turn and left the green fog and throbbing bass behind. "JD!" she called as she entered a room.

Dozens of her own reflection surrounded her. It reminded her of Bunny's dressing room.

"Hall of mirrors. Just great. Like I want to see this much of myself."

Suddenly, dozens of JDs stood just behind the dozens of Sara Lees. Metal glinted in his hand as he whipped it upward. The sting of a dagger touched her throat.

"What the hell are you doing?" Sara Lee demanded, grabbing his wrist and tugging. It didn't budge.

JD drew a determined breath. "What I should have done all along."

"I don't understand."

"Satan found a loophole of her own," JD said, his face an expressionless mask. "If you fall into oblivion, Oscar's job is mine."

Tears stung her eyes. How could she have been so wrong about him? If JD had cared about her at all, he could have married her to get the job. That was a loophole too. Everything had just been an act.

Her vision blurred, Sara Lee groped for her purse and popped the magnetic catch. "Why didn't you just kill me from the start?"

"I'd hoped to learn what Oscar saw in you," JD said, his lip curled. "But all *I've* seen is a graceless, gauche and frivolous creature who infected my brother with her crass ways."

Sara Lee pushed aside the paperback at the top of her purse. Maybe she should consider ebooks. "I taught Oscar to have fun without that stick up his butt—" The dagger bit her skin.

"Is that all you think of social graces?"

Sara Lee's hand closed around the blackjack's handle. "Oscar loved that I didn't hide behind stuffy manners. He loved that I showed my feelings."

JD sneered. "Oh, yes, he did love that. Oscar often went slumming with low women, but never for more than a decade or two. I expect you were nearing your expiration date—"

Heaving a guttural scream, Sara Lee slammed the blackjack against JD's knees. As the dagger clattered to the floor, he roared in pain and dropped to all fours. She kicked him in the groin, changing his roar into a squeak, then grabbed the dagger.

Sara Lee jerked his head back by the hair and put the blade to his throat. "Oscar loved me!"

"He loved them all," JD gasped. "But he always tired of slumming after a time."

Her chest heaved. "You … *liar!*"

He chuckled weakly. "You know I'm right."

Sara Lee's hand shook. She should just slit JD's throat, send him to oblivion. He deserved it.

You're better than this," Jesus's voice said in her head.

The hell I am. And get out of my head!

Yet she couldn't make the cut, not until JD admitted he lied, not until she understood *why* he lied. "Why are you saying this? Why are you *doing* this?"

"Because my mother and Satan reminded me of my duty to my family—and to Oscar's memory. You're not worthy of the mantle of Famine. You've disrespected everything my brother stood for, with your disregard for his legacy."

The words hit like a slap. Sara Lee's arm dropped of its own accord. She bit her lip. "You're right."

"What?" he snapped, still on hands and knees.

"You're right. I've done nothing to carry on Oscar's work, not really. He always treated the office of Famine as important, even though your mother essentially sold Oscar into the job in exchange for your family's status in hell. Oscar trusted that, as long as he worked for God as well as Satan, being Famine had value. He didn't have to understand the Greater Plan to know he was part of it. I've just treated this job like an unwanted burden."

"Why?" JD asked, his anger the first genuine emotion she'd seen all night.

"Because I *didn't* want it." Sara Lee choked on a sob and turned to hide the tears spilling down her cheeks. "I only wanted to be with Oscar!" And maybe he hadn't wanted her much longer.

"I did too," JD said bitterly. "I've spent the last twenty-five years hoping to find common ground by trying to understand what he saw in you and in living like a commoner. I read popular literature, watched blockbuster movies and television. I even"— he made a disgusted noise—"ate a Whopper ... with cheese."

"The horror," Sara Lee said, wiping tears off her face.

"But I never understood, not until you ... until you infected *me*."

Sara Lee whirled on him. "What the hell does that mean?"

"I've never let my guard down like this," JD said. "At first, I was just playing along while I decided whether or not to accept Satan's 'task' of sending you to oblivion and becoming Famine. But suddenly, I wasn't pretending anymore. To my family's shame—to *my* shame—I *enjoyed* our time together. I enjoyed debauching in public like peasants, and laughing out loud, and not being too sophisticated to take pleasure in simple amusements. I even started to root for you and your brother to make a true reconciliation, as I'd always hoped Oscar and I would—until I remembered that you only contacted Duncan in hopes he would take this horrible unwanted burden from you— the very job to which your husband dedicated his eternity—"

"I should have known."

Dozens of Duncans appeared behind Sara Lee. She kicked JD in the ribs, then turned to face her brother. The tears blurring Duncan's eyes stabbed her to the core.

"I *was* feeling better," he said with a bitter smile. "So the only reason you wanted to see me was to convince me to take your job."

"At first," Sara Lee said, forcing herself to meet his gaze. "But I couldn't do it."

"Oh, sure," Duncan said, folding his arms.

Sara Lee gripped his shoulders. "Did I ask?"

He shrugged off her hold.

"Well, did I?" She stepped back and massaged a throbbing spot on her forehead. What a mess. "These past few weeks have shown me what a stupid mistake I made by cutting you out of my afterlife. I'd forgotten how much it meant to have my little brother around, to be with family."

She grabbed Duncan in a hug. At first, he stood rigid, but after a few moments, his arms closed around her, weakly at first, then with fierce emotion.

"I'm sorry about how this started," Sara Lee said as they

released each other. "But I'm glad I got to see you again."

Duncan swallowed hard. "Me too—"

JD groaned and pushed to all fours. Sara Lee kicked him in the ribs again, then stomped on his back, knocking him flat.

"Um, why are you kicking JD?" Duncan asked.

"He's the one who's been trying to send me to oblivion, not Satan," Sara Lee said, adding another kick for emphasis. "All this time, he's just been pretending to be our friend."

Duncan's gaze narrowed and he kicked JD in the ribs. "Come on, sis. We still have a few hours left."

They finished the haunted house, then rode the Mummy roller coaster three times, because it was Duncan's favorite. At five before midnight, they exited the Men in Black ride.

Duncan put an arm around Sara Lee's shoulders. "It's been ... weird."

"I get a little comp time on Earth every month," Sara Lee said. "Can I visit you?"

He grinned. "Won't that cut into your shopping time?"

"Acceptable loss," Sara Lee said, grabbing him into a tight hug. He kissed the top of her head.

The alarm on her phone beeped, indicating midnight. But she didn't need the notification. The returning power of Famine knocked the breath from her lungs and made her body shudder under the tangible weight.

"Be good, Squirt," she said, then let Duncan go. She walked toward a foggy scare zone so her departure wouldn't draw attention. Before she could reach it, a zombie in ragged orange prison coveralls jumped from the bushes. Sara Lee screamed.

"Surprise!" the zombie shouted.

"Jesus?" She clutched her chest. "You scared the crap out of me."

"Yeah. I love Halloween—though technically, now it's All Saints Day."

"Time to go back to Hell." Sara Lee sighed. She hadn't realized how much she'd hoped she and JD could have a relationship, how much that hope had made the thought of returning to Hell a positive thing. Now her future in Hell just seemed ... empty.

"Don't hold a grudge against JD," Jesus said, squeezing Sara Lee's shoulder.

"Why not?" she demanded, rage pounding through her anew. "He took my memories of Oscar and what we had and made me question whether they're even real."

Jesus cocked his head. "What does your heart tell you?"

"I don't know anymore." Sara Lee's head throbbed harder. "A few months before Oscar went to oblivion, he hired an assistant, Gigi. She was elegant, well-mannered, cultured, a blue-blood—everything I'm not. How can I be sure JD isn't right? How can I know whether or not Oscar was planning to replace me with her?" A faint smile played across Sara Lee's lips. "Of course, after I decorporialized Gigi for the third time, she finally got a clue and quit."

"Grudges harm the bearer most," Jesus said, mussing Sara Lee's hair. "Besides, forgiveness often brings unexpected benefits."

"You sound like a fortune cookie," Sara Lee said, folding her arms.

"Wisdom is often found in unexpected places," Jesus said.

"How can you ask me to forgive him?" Sara Lee asked.

Jesus chuckled. "I'm all about forgiveness, remember?"

"Don't you know what JD's done?"

"Do you?" Jesus asked.

"Yeah, he tried to kill me a dozen times and ended up killing a bunch of other people instead." Yet that didn't make sense. During the fireworks attack, JD had been in as much danger as Sara Lee of falling into oblivion. But there was no doubting the dagger he'd put to her throat. His intentions in the Fun House were crystal clear. She wanted to kick him all over again.

"Sara Lee, Satan is behind the death attempts—except the last one," Jesus said. "If she killed you, JD would become Famine, whether he wanted to or not. No doubt Satan thinks he would be more bendable to her will."

Sara Lee shook her head. "So this is like the World Series—you've been helping me in order to balance Satan's interference?"

"Except that Dad approved this time," Jesus said. "Satan went too far."

"Thanks." Without thinking, Sara Lee reached to hug Jesus. At the last second, she pulled back. "Sorry."

Jesus drew her into a hug, sending a burst of happiness through her, like sunshine after a bleak winter. "I'm not giving up on you." He held out a pair of classic Mickey Mouse ears.

Feeling dizzy from the unexpected show of kindness, Sara Lee took the cap. Turning it, she saw her name embroidered on the back.

"A memento," Jesus said.

204   The Four Redheads: The Wrath of Satan

"Why are you so nice to me?" Sara Lee asked in mystification.

Jesus grinned. "Why? Because I like you."

She groaned at the Mouseketeer reference.

"You have potential," Jesus said. "And for all your negative claims, you haven't quit trying to improve."

Sara Lee scowled. "You see something that isn't there."

"Or you don't see something that *is* there."

The Gulf of Mexico still churned, but the swells had dropped to six feet rather than the fourteen-foot waves that rocked Butterflye's world earlier.

The last evening of the cruise was bittersweet. Butterflye rolled up her evening gown and laid it in the bottom of the portmanteau. Soon she'd be back in Hell, and life would go back to normal. She laid the dolphin-pattern hot pants on top of the gown. She gazed at them wistfully. Not the good kind of normal, but the "it sucks to be me" normal, where her work apparel touched the floor to hide the legion of cockroaches that followed her every step.

After Butterflye reapplied her makeup in the postage stamp bathroom mirror, she reached for Satan's present to be opened on Halloween. The box weighed almost nothing. And when she shook it, she heard only the slightest scraping sound. As threatened, Butterflye had left the gift unopened until the appointed day. She could only imagine the booby trap Satan had set for premature revelation.

"What do you think it is?" She weighed it in her hands. "I wonder if it's an Amy Winehouse costume. Maybe Janis Joplin? I'm going to look unforgettable tonight!" She ripped the blood-smeared wrapping paper off in one motion and gasped.

Rather than a tightly-fitted, shimmering mini dress, she found a pair of one-size-doesn't-really-fit-anyone camo pants, a shirt eight sizes too big, a camo baseball cap, a salt and pepper beard/ponytail combo and a pair of thick-framed polypropylene black eyeglasses. It looked like something out of Satan's closet.

"What the Hell? I'm going to be a hippie?" She looked at the label and realized it was even worse than she first thought. "Oh, no! It's Duck Dynasty!"

Butterflye and Ralph left their cabin and headed to the Liquid Fire open-air disco, where the Halloween festivities had already begun. The pair from Hell exited the elevator, Butterflye dressed in her Duck Dynasty duds and Ralph as Hello Kitty.

The flimsy polyester camo shirt and pants sagged on Butterflye's frame like oversized pajamas. She rolled up the-way-too-long pants legs and retied the drawstring waistband. She glanced in a mirror. Hopefully no one at the party would notice her attempt to make the shirt a little more form-fitting by using five two-inch safety pins. Instead of reclaiming an ounce of sexiness, it just created a huge ridge running up her backbone, making her a well-camouflaged, gray-headed Spinosaurus.

Pumpkins carved with the words, "Enter if you dare," greeted her at the entrance to Liquid Fire. Fake spider webs dripped so convincingly from the twenty-foot high awning, for a moment, Butterflye feared she had *already* teleported home.

The deck was elbow-to-gaping-ribcage with ghouls, vampires and walking dead. A passenger wearing a lifelike Mick Jagger mask looked remarkably like a zombie guitarist jamming with the band. Not surprising. Mick had looked undead when he was twenty.

"Look at that," Butterflye said to Ralph through her salt and pepper beard.

Beneath a twisted plastic tree, intricately carved jack-o-lanterns depicted the artist's interpretation of demons and ghouls. She pointed at a devil pumpkin with short pointy horns and a goatee. "That's not what Satan looks like."

Ralph shook his head.

Butterflye adjusted the bill of her ball cap and clawed at her itchy cheek under her ragged gray beard. "Act human," she reminded Ralph as she motioned him up. "Stand up straight."

He rose, teetering until he got his balance, then followed her into the dimly lit party. Flickering orange chandelier bulbs cast menacing shadowing on the walls, and plastic cauldrons fluttered with fabric flames.

Butterflye surfed through an ocean of Cowardly Lions, policemen, stormtroopers and Mr. Spocks.

Most of the blood from the wedding mishap had been cleaned up, but DNA stains of some kind still glowed bluish in the disco's black light. Upstairs, the DJ booth remained an open-air room with treacherous spears of glass jutting from the metal window frame.

Suspended above the dance floor where the disco ball once

resided, a pair of costumed skeletons, bound together with zip ties, danced a macabre samba in the sea breeze. Across the deck, giant latex octopus tentacles reached through the guardrails.

Butterflye sidled up to the bar. "Scotch on the rocks." She handed her Have-A-Blast key card to Radhatanaya, the bartender.

He returned in a few minutes and handed her the card and a glass. She couldn't escape the feeling of being watched until she looked closer at the garnish floating in the amber liquid, a hazel gummy eyeball. *That must be it.*

"Here's looking at you kid," she said to Ralph. She pulled down her beard and took a deep swallow. Its contents had the distinct flavor of battery acid with just a creamy hint of ethanol. She swallowed hard. "Rad," she said to the bartender, "this is horrible."

He shrugged. "Look, lady, you only have two dollars and eighteen cents left on your Have-A-Blast card. I did you a favor."

"I guess my boss had me on a pretty restricted budget after all. Thanks."

She left the bar and scanned the disco for a place to sit. Luckily, a party of four—a taco, the Little Mermaid with no cleavage, Marie Antoinette (post revolution) and a morbidly obese Wonder Woman—vacated a nearby table. Butterflye swooped on it like an eagle on a rat.

A few minutes later, a familiar face entered the disco, a face so familiar Butterflye saw it whenever she looked into the mirror. MJ wore a sexy devil costume, not unlike the image in the carved pumpkin, only prettier.

"Marley!" Butterflye waved and pointed to one of the vacant chairs. "Over here."

MJ followed the voice and smiled when she approached Butterflye and Ralph. She squinted at the bearded hunter. "Butterflye, is that you?"

"Uh-huh. Sit down."

As MJ sat, she said diplomatically, "Ah, Ralph, you're so cute as Hello Kitty. And Butterflye, I'd never have recognized you under that getup."

Like any disco, Liquid Fire played at a decibel level slightly below the Hiroshima nuclear blast. Between the band and the crowd yelling to be heard over the band, Butterflye could only catch the occasional word. She repeated back what she thought she'd heard. "What is smeared on the hall?"

MJ tried again during an acoustical lull. "Interesting costume."

"Thanks. It was a gift from my boss. She's not known for her fashion sense. You, on the other hand, certainly are dressed for your future role."

MJ's more robust figure accentuated her too-skimpy, too-short, too-tight red leotard. A pair of sequined devil horns crowned her flyaway red curls. "Did say you were hungry for a breakfast roll?" MJ asked.

"You'll be a beautiful Plague!" Butterflye yelled.

"We'll see. I still haven't decided yet—hey, we're sitting in the perfect spot. I understand they'll be shooting fireworks tonight."

Off the starboard side, the ship's official pyrotechnician shot a few bottle rockets over the water. They exploded into gold and blue spiders, then fizzled, leaving only smoke. A chorus of "ohhhs" and "awwws" arose from the crowd. Hello Kitty Ralph scampered on top of the table to get a better look. His screeches sounded more like "ehhh" and "uhhhh."

A fiery purple tail and white glitter shot from a Roman candle. Butterflye clapped her hands. Ralph jumped and fell forward.

An emerald air bomb shot above the water. The pyrotechnician sent up a couple of red and green fountains. "Oh, no. We're out of fireworks."

"Here." His assistant grabbed a handful of flairs. "Try these."

The tech lit the flair and a single white-hot flash soared above the ship, burning bright and hovering before fading away, replaced by the smell of gunpowder and smoke.

"It's the last night," Butterflye said, her mouth turned down. "I feel like Cinderella a few minutes before midnight."

In the aftermath of the disappointing fireworks display, the latest DJ set up a couple of poles and a crossbar. "Let's play Zombie Limbo!"

Ghouls and undead of all makes lined up and one by one danced under the bar to the beat of steel drums and bongos. MJ fell into line. She arched her back, took in a deep breath, let it out slowly, then moved forward, her crimson horns missing the bar by centimeters. Once MJ regained her balance, she motioned to Butterfly.

"Why not?" Butterflye shimmied, which in the camo dinosaur costume came off more like a seizure. But on her first pass a rough edge of the bamboo stick caught on her beard fibers, pulling the bar off its hooks. It tumbled to the deck. Disappointed, she circled around to watch those who hadn't been disqualified.

Twenty more people tried their luck and most made it through. MJ made another successful pass under the lowered bar. The third time around, her oversized boobs lifted the bar up and knocked it to the deck with a hollow rattle.

The music of the steel drum broke off, and the partiers' attention shifted to high above them. In the crow's nest, a brass bell rang. "Iceberg!"

MJ stared at Butterflye. "An iceberg? In the Gulf of Mexico?"

"Rogue iceberg!" The ringing continued to clang with urgency.

"Rogue iceberg," Butterflye repeated. "That explains it."

Squalor of the Sea shuddered violently, and a couple of Volkswagen-sized chunks of ice plunged down on the deck, flattening two passengers wearing a camel costume, a waiter with a tray of drinks, a lady wearing a Marge Simpson wig and a handful of people in unimpressive apparel.

It barely missed a guest dressed in a nun's white sari habit with the trademark blue stripes on the veil. A rather bulky Mother Teresa jumped out of the way and landed next to Butterflye's remaining free chair. Nearby, three ghouls wearing earpieces, shredded dark suits and sunglasses stood at attention.

"Mother, would you like to join us?" Butterflye offered. "My extremely efficient assistant is a nun. I couldn't do my job without her."

"Thank you," a male voice said. He sat down and faced Butterflye. "I don't mind if I do."

"Donald Trump!" Duck Dynasty Butterflye gasped.

"You." Trump pointed at MJ. "You're the one who stole my suite."

MJ shrugged. "Huh?"

"Yes, you. I saw you."

"Hey, dude. Not me. I bet you mean her." MJ pointed at her cell donor.

"No. She didn't have a beard. I know your face. ... Did you put on a little weight?" he asked.

Butterflye raised the bill of her cap. "It might have been me."

Trump looked at the horned woman. "You're not her?"

MJ shook her head. "Nope. I sell t-shirts, dude."

Butterflye smiled meekly. "*I* work for the Ruler of Demons. I'm afraid my minions were a bit overenthusiastic about my vacation plans."

Mother jutted his chin out and nodded approvingly. "Well done. I'd like to talk to them about a job. I could use some demonic hackers in my IT department."

"Transferring them out of Hell is above my pay grade. ... Oh, and there's another thing." Butterflye reached her hand across the table toward Ralph and wiggled her fingers. "Hand it over. You know it doesn't belong to you."

Ralph shook his head and hid his legs.

"Ralph, give Mr. Trump his phone back. If you're good, maybe he'll play Cockroach Crush with Friends with you after we get back home."

Ralph laid the phone on the table and sighed, his antennae drooping.

"Sorry," Butterflye said to Trump. "When Fred moved us out of your suite so quickly, he must have packed your phone with my stuff."

Trump picked up the phone and checked his messages. "There's an invoice for six-thousand dollars for an insect porn site."

Ducky Butterflye rested her hands on her hips. "Ralph, bad boy. You'll have to figure a way to pay Mr. Trump back. But for now, say you're sorry."

Ralph shrugged his wings and dropped his head. "Ehh."

Butterflye turned to Trump. "I'm afraid that's the best he can do. We're working on his enunciation."

Trumps eyes met Butterflye's. "I'll send *that* bill to Satan too."

"Ooo, Ralph," MJ said. "You're in trouble now. You're going to have Hell to pay."

The roach dropped his head. "Uh-oh."

"I'm sure Satan will be happy to make a deal with you. In the meantime"—Butterflye pulled her own phone out of her camo pants—"Mr. Trump, can I get a picture with you? My assistant Sister Angelica will be so excited."

"Why not?"

They all leaned in close. Butterflye raised her phone and targeted the group in the screen. "Smile," she prompted Trump.

Trump scowled. "I am smiling."

Butterflye texted Sister Angelica the photo. "Mother Teresa Trump."

Angelica texted back. "Damn, he looks good."

"No hard feelings," Mother Teresa said. "Let me buy you a drink." He waved Rad the bartender over to the table. "A bottle of Trump Vodka for the ladies."

Rad smiled at MJ, then turned to Butterflye. "Ladies? That nun needs a shave."

"I so wish I had my powers right now," Butterflye whispered to MJ.

"And while you're at it, bring me a Shirley Temple," Trump added.

"Do you mean the drink or an underage girl?" Rad asked.

"The drink."

"Your choice." Rad scribbled something on his pad, left, returned and set four glasses on the table.

Butterflye happily sipped her Trump Vodka, a huge improvement over the liquid battery acid she'd drunk a few minutes earlier. She placed the glass down and made imaginary circles on the Helvetica cocktail napkin. "That's odd." She eyed the lip of her vodka glass and cocked her head to the right. "Shouldn't the vodka be level?"

Instead of being moderately even, the liquid on the left side hugged rim of the small tumbler. On the right side, the vodka hovered around the middle of the glass. She opened her fingers and the glass slid off the table and shattered against the deck.

"We must be taking on water," Trump said.

Butterflye's fan Stanley, once again dressed as a waiter, walked by. "Yes, sir," he said to Trump. "There has been some damage." He handed Trump, Butterflye and Ralph life vests. "Here." He started to pass a life jacket embellished with polished scuba weights to MJ, but lost his grip on it and it plunged through the deck, leaving a gaping hole and a pile of splinters. "Hmm. Sorry, ma'am. That one must have been defective. I'll try to find a replacement."

Remembering all the airline safety briefings she'd watched, Butterflye put on her own life vest and then helped Ralph into his.

"You know," MJ said, "if Ralph goes into the water wearing that thing, he'll drown. Roaches breathe through their butts."

"How do you know that?"

She gave a lopsided grin. "Lady, I *know* my roaches."

Butterflye looked at the vest, then Ralph's butt, vest and butt, vest and butt. "They don't make vests for two foot long *Gromphadorhina portentosa* posteriors. That's specist." She took Ralph's vest off and turned it around, but it wouldn't stay on. "Hmmmm. Okay, Ralph, don't go in the water."

Mother Trump put on his gray pinstriped life vest with a silk peacock blue tie that set off his blue eyes, as well as the stripes in his Mother Teresa veil.

Suddenly "The Monster Mash" that had been booming from the disco speakers was replaced by the sounds of the general emergency alarm, sounding like a red alert from *Star Trek*. With each of seven klaxon blasts, the overhead lights dimmed.

"This is the purser in command. There is a minor emergency. Will all passengers please make your way to your muster stations? It's really nothing to worry about. Well, yes, you should worry, but don't dwell on it. That's not the word either. However, if you haven't written your will, this would be a good time to sit down with one of the fifty-three attorneys on board and fill one out. Oh, yes, and this is not a drill."

Minutes later, Butterflye, Ralph, MJ, The Donald, and a thousand other costumed passengers sat at the downstairs dining tables that doubled as muster station D-3. Trumps ghouls stood stiffly nearby. Few people seemed concerned as servers passed out life vests and took drink orders.

Unless people were paying attention, they might not have noticed the shivering deck below them, accompanied by the high-pitched wail of bending steel similar to the sonorous song of whales.

Trump stood up. "Come on, ladies. Let's go down to the lifeboats."

Butterflye scratched under her beard. "They told us to wait here."

Teresa Trump looked at his Rolex. "In the last few minutes, we haven't seen a single crew member. They're not coming back for us. Time and lifeboats wait for no man. Let's go."

A mature lady in a Lee Meriwether Catwoman costume, sitting next to Trump, asked, "Can I go with you?"

"Of course."

By the time they arrived on deck five, only one lifeboat remained moored in its davit; a small fleet of the orange boats peppered the water around the floundering *Squalor of the Sea*.

Trump unlocked the launch mechanism and brought the boat down to deck level.

"Get in," Trump ordered his small posse.

Butterflye, MJ, Catwoman, the ghouls and Ralph climbed aboard. At the last second Stanley, with the Groucho eyeglasses, jumped into the boat too.

Mother Trump swiveled the launch mechanism and lowered the boat into the water, thirty feet below into the choppy Gulf, then slid down the line and landed in the lifeboat himself.

Butterflye scanned her companions. Stanley eyed MJ, smiling and occasionally nodding. He pulled out his phone, punched in a long series of numbers and said, "Stanley here, ... Yeah. ... Almost. ... Yeah. ... Soon. ... Yeah. ... Release the kraken."

Across from him, Catwoman sat beside MJ. The pointed tip of her left kitty ear was missing.

"Aw, what a shame," Butterflye said. "Your ear broke off."

Catwoman ran her fingers along the edges of her cat ears. "It didn't break. I'm *feral* Catwoman."

"Of course." Butterflye exchanged eye rolls with MJ.

Back on the ship, the klaxon sounded again. Metal screamed as massive iron beams inside twisted unnaturally. Reeee ... eeee ... eeeee ... eeeeek.

"Good evening, *Squalor of the Sea* passengers," the purser said over the intercom. "Welcome to our annual Day of the Dead celebration. Tonight, as you can tell, we're taking our party theme to the extreme. I hope you've enjoyed our band, the Hellraisers. We just have one announcement. You may already be aware that we have made intimate contact with a rogue iceberg, and water is flooding our engine room as we speak.

"Stay calm," he urged the stampeding passengers. Then he yelled to someone in the disco, "Play some music. Something soothing."

As the bow of *Squalor of the Sea* slid below the waves, the public address speakers squealed, followed by the voice of a bewildered Albanian crewman. "This is Edi, the busboy. While we're waiting for the anticipated arrival of the rescue ship, I found some music recorded earlier by one of the many celebrities on this cruise."

After a few moments of dead air, four bars of introductory organ music rang across the sea.

Butterflye turned her head toward the ship. "Oh, boy! This is the hymn I recorded for the wedding. They never had a chance to play it."

The organ paused and the sound of Butterflye's voice filled the salty air surrounding the sinking vessel. "Nearer my God to thee..."

In a nearby inflatable lifeboat, a man clad in a thickly padded wrestler costume screamed, "Oh, God, make it stop!" and hurled himself into the Gulf. Hundreds of other survivors joined him. People clinging to floating wreckage let go, and those still clutching the floundering ship's guardrails threw themselves into the water.

Feral Catwoman winced, then plunged her fingers into her ears as far as the second knuckle before closing her eyes and smiling peacefully. "Ah, that's better."

A crew member assigned to an inflatable raft attempted to shield his ears as he threw a floatation ring to the wrestler.

Butterflye shook her head. *People really do stupid things when they panic.*

"Nearer, my God, to Thee, nearer to Thee!" screeched the speakers.

"No life preserver!" the man screamed, lobbing the ring back at the crewmen. "I want to die. Now." The man threw himself back into the sea. "Let me die. Let me die."

In Butterflye's lifeboat, MJ solemnly mouthed the words of the hymn, and Mother Teresa Trump appeared completely unaffected by both the chaos and the breath-stopping music filling the air. The three ghouls pulled out their revolvers, and in unison, inserted the barrels in their mouths and pulled the trigger.

Trump rolled his eyes. "Idiots."

The water roiled, and from the turbulent water arose a colossal squid head, the mantle alone measuring eight feet. The eyes bulged, and it appeared to throb in four/four time with Butterflye's hymn. The head disappeared beneath the Gulf, but within a few seconds, the creature's two feeding tentacles shot out of the water. One twenty-foot-long tentacle swung over the lifeboat. MJ dodged left and it missed her by inches, but it wrapped three loops about feral Catwoman. The other tentacle snatched the suicidal man floundering in the water.

"Still all my song shall be..." Butterflye's recording sang.

The creature's head reemerged, and the tentacles plunged its victims through the ashen skin into the squid's hearing organ near the base of the brain. The human earplugs kicked and squirmed.

"Catwoman, come back!" Butterflye stretched to grab Catwoman's foot, but before she could, the squid relaxed and eased back into the water. *Poor lady. What strange behavior from a squid! Why would it do that? Maybe the music volume was amplified underwater, and it hurt the squid's statocyst ear thingies.*

"Turn off the music," the deckhand ordered. "They're killing themselves. Stop the music!"

But the music continued.

A giant wave washed over the deck as water filled the last remaining compartments, sweeping many of the hangers-on overboard. Butterflye felt the shockwave of a muffled explosion from deep within the ship. When the stern rose into the air, the smoke stack creaked and collapsed under its own weight. As it slammed into the water, it crushed half the lifeboats. The funnel's force created a small tsunami that pushed Butterflye's lifeboat clear of the sinking ship.

The Helvetica cruise ship began her final dive almost perpendicular to the water. The ship's lights flickered a few times, then blinked out. The stern disappeared beneath the surface, and with it, Butterflye's inspiring recording. As *Squalor* sped toward its grave in the Gulf, the suction pulled all but Butterflye's lifeboat down with it. Suddenly, everything fell quiet, except for the soft splashes of waves, the gurgles of the drowning and the cries of people still begging to die.

Donald Trump pointed at the horizon. "Look, there's a ship. We're saved."

Off in the distance, a well-lit ship sailed toward them. Slowly the navigation lamps appeared larger and larger to the occupants of the lone surviving lifeboat oscillating in six-foot waves.

MJ stared at the hypnotically floating wreckage and the bodies bobbing up and down. She whispered to her Other Self, "You know, Butterflye, I've decided to take your offer. I think I'd make a good Plague."

"I think you would too," Butterflye agreed quietly.

"After all," MJ continued, "it's only a matter of time before those drug lords catch up with me."

Butterflye dug through her handbag and pulled out a rather

damp sheet of vellum, a blood-red pen and a pair of reading glasses. She handed the clone her specs. "You'll need these, MJ. The print is really, really small."

"Oh, what the hell," MJ handed the glasses back to Butterflye. "Why bother reading the fine print, if you're making a deal with the Devil?" She signed and dated the document and dotted the 'J'. "Done deal."

"Just one more little detail to complete," Butterflye said. *Time to die.*

MJ fell over and stopped breathing, but like a computer reboot, within a few seconds, life returned to her face and she sat up. "Well, that was different." She touched her face. "Hmm. I've been through worse."

"Woo-hoo," Butterflye shouted. "Congratulations Ms. Plague-Pestilence."

"I think I'm going to drop the hyphen and just go by Plague."

"Whatever you say, *Plague*," Butterflye said, saluting the new horsewoman. She sighed. "This is the end of our vacation. In a few minutes, it will be midnight, and you'll be transported to your new life, uh, afterlife."

Before long, the ship pulled alongside the lifeboat, exposing the cruise ship's name, *Carpathia II*.

A shot rang out from across the lifeboat. Marley Plague fell backward into the Gulf of Mexico. Her lifeless blue eyes stared into the Halloween night sky. The top of her head was gone, her brains floating in the water.

Butterflye scratched beneath her beard. *That could have been me.*

Stanley tossed his revolver overboard. He opened his flip phone, punched a couple of buttons, and said, "Mission accomplished. Plague is dead."

Stanley vanished.

Butterflye turned her eyes away from her Other Self floating alongside the life raft to Donald Trump, who was reaching for a rope that had been dropped from the massive ship.

"What time is it?" she asked him.

"Three seconds to midnight."

"Oh." Butterflye and Hello Kitty Ralph also vanished.

Sara Lee and her luggage—minus the obligatory one missing bag—materialized in her living room. She set her purse on the end table and looked around at the familiar sights—the broken recliner, the worn velvet couch, the photos of Oscar's triumphs. It felt … good to be home. How weird.

The photo of Oscar and JD brought a new wave of anger. Sara Lee yanked it off the wall and stuffed it in a drawer. After a few cleansing breaths, she grabbed a notepad and pen from Oscar's desk and wrote at the top, *Ways to Create Famine*. As she flopped onto the couch, a loose spring poked her butt. She moved to the one comfortable cushion and stared at the page. Nothing came to mind.

Five hours and a family-sized bag of stale Milky Way bars later, she'd still added nothing to the page. Her mind was stuck in a loop between JD's callous comments about Oscar and Sara Lee's last few months with her husband. There might have been signs that Oscar had tired of her. Had there been signs? Gigi's beautiful face and perfectly coifed hair flashed in Sara Lee's memory. Damn JD all over again!

A knock rattled her front door. Sara Lee sighed. She hoped it wasn't one of those damned door-to-door magazine salesmen. Hell was packed with them, and they were just so pathetic. In Hell, no one was gullible enough to fall for their scams.

Bracing herself, she unlocked and opened the door. JD leaned—no, lounged—against the door frame. He wore jeans, a Cubs World Series Champions t-shirt and a backwards baseball cap.

Sara Lee didn't know whether to kick him in the groin again or laugh.

Before she could decide, he said, "I've been a world-class jerk."

"I think trying to kill me goes beyond being a jerk," she said stiffly.

"My mother and Satan flogged me with guilt and duty. I panicked."

Her lip curled. "All those times."

"I only tried once—at Universal, after Satan attacked us with the fireworks as a final warning to me."

Though Sara Lee didn't doubt that Jesus had spoken the truth about Satan's murder attempts, she asked, "Why should I believe you?"

JD raised a hand and said solemnly, "I swear on my family's snobbery."

Good thing he hadn't said "honor," or Sara Lee would have landed on the side of kicking him in the groin. She still might.

It was early.

"Satan was pretty steamed that I couldn't bring myself to kill you. I have the burns to prove it." He showed her a hand-shaped blister on his forearm. Sara Lee could even make out the swirls of Satan's fingerprints. "Some are in places not so easy to show you."

"Why did you even resist?" Sara Lee asked, folding her arms. "You made it pretty clear what you think of me."

He looked at the cracked concrete stoop, then met her gaze. "At first, I delayed my decision out of respect for Oscar's memory. But I enjoyed our time together in Chicago and at Disney World—the crass laughter, the over-indulgences, the comradery."

"Really."

"It goes against everything I've been taught," JD said, anguish in his sapphire eyes. "But I realize now why Oscar stayed with you, why he married you even after I argued you weren't good enough for him—"

"What?"

"But now I understand. You, who were born without advantages and luxuries, overcame all that, made something of yourself, worked hard to expand your limited horizons. But most of all, you know how to have fun, how to feel, to live life."

Sara Lee blinked hard. "Dear God, is that your perverted way of saying you like me?"

JD hesitated, then nodded.

"That's more lame than a third-grader sending a 'check yes or no' note." She considered Jesus's request that she forgive JD, but shook her head. "I can't be around you—not after you made me question everything Oscar and I had."

JD bowed his head. "I shouldn't have done that. But in my family, we go straight for the jugular."

Oscar had been that way when Sara Lee first met him. And every once in a while, he backslid and hurt her deeply. No one can place a kill shot quite so well as someone who knows and loves you.

"After Oscar and I fought over him marrying you, he never confided in me again, what few times we saw each other," JD said. "So I have no idea whether or not he planned to leave you. But I do know that he never cut off his entire family for another woman. Only for you."

Sara Lee's throat swelled with emotion. She swallowed hard. She wanted to believe JD, but how could she?

Then she remembered something that happened a few weeks before Oscar died. She'd been feeling blue, something she'd struggled with her whole life and which followed her into the afterlife. Hoping to cheer her up, Oscar bought tickets to a Broadway musical, even though he detested them, considering them bastardizations of opera. He'd already planned vacation on Earth with the other Horsemen, so he couldn't eat, but he took Sara Lee to her favorite restaurant in Manhattan, *Le Grenouille*, for a pre-theater dinner. If he'd tired of her, he wouldn't have gone to all that trouble. The ache in her heart faded away.

"I wish I could unsay what I said. May we start over?" JD asked with his best hopeful puppy look.

"Sorry," she said hoarsely. "I'm not interested in being the 'low' woman you go slumming with when the mood strikes."

"Please," JD said. "Have you never said or done something horrible that you regretted?"

She snorted. "I'm a lawyer. Of course I have. But I never tried to send someone to oblivion."

She started to close the door.

He grabbed the doorknob, blocking her attempt. "Give me another chance? It'll take time and practice to change the habits of several lifetimes, but I really want this."

She huffed. "*What* do you want?"

"Friendship." He stroked the back of her hand, sending a traitorous tingle across her skin. "Maybe something more. I'm willing to move slowly, to prove that I mean what I say."

Sara Lee closed her eyes. Did she really want to go down a road paved with his good intentions? Everyone knew where that usually led.

But she was already in Hell and hadn't laughed so much since Oscar died. JD could be fun and interesting—when he wasn't being a total dick.

The odds of someone changing, though—not so good. Satan banked on that.

Yet Oscar had changed. And a person's desire to change improved their odds of success—

"You know, just because you can't see me doesn't mean I can't see you," JD said.

Sara Lee's eyelids snapped open. "You've read *Hitchhiker's Guide to the Galaxy*?

He grinned. "Under the covers with a flashlight—so my

mother wouldn't see."

"A grown man hiding non-pornographic reading from his mother?"

"You've never met my mother." JD shuddered. "She's practically a force of nature—the Category 5 meets F5 kind."

"What sort of books does she approve of?" Sara Lee asked.

"Non-fiction. Biographies. True Crime—especially if it's about her."

"I assume she vets your clothing choices too." Sara Lee swept a hand to indicate his outfit. "She let you leave the house looking like this?"

He lifted a shoulder. "She ordered me to go change. But I said no and left."

She pinned JD with a stare. "You said no and left. In that order?"

"No." He flushed and ducked his head. "Damn, you really are a lawyer."

"Well, congratulations on reaching the teenage rebellion stage of puberty," she said.

JD laughed. "Wait until I tell my family I'm moving out. That will rock them to their foundation."

The knot of anger inside Sara Lee loosened. Not hating JD felt good. Maybe Jesus was right. Maybe virtue really was its own reward—

Nah.

Beyond not hating JD, Sara Lee wasn't sure what she wanted from him. But she had as long as eternity to find out. "You want to come in for a while? Maybe you could help me with a project I'm starting."

JD blew out a relieved breath and followed her inside. "I hope you don't want me to paint your house, because I've grown fond of this outfit."

Sara Lee turned his ball cap so the bill was in front. "So have I."

He wiggled his eyebrows and turned the cap backward again.

"Good for you," Sara Lee said. "Bad fashion choice, but at least it's *your* choice."

Peering at the notepad on the scarred coffee table, JD blinked hard. "'Ways to Create Famine?'"

Sara Lee gave a self-conscious shrug. "I have to start somewhere. I didn't ask to be Famine, but that doesn't mean I can't try harder to be a good one, for however long I hold the job."

"Good for *you*." JD put a hand under her chin. His thumb traced her jaw line and he smiled. "Let's get to work."

Chapter Twelve

Bunny flashed her pink diamond engagement ring at her fellow Redheads. In the ghastly light of the Sulfur Well Bar, however, the glorious pink bore a sickly yellow-green cast.

Zoe eyed the stone. "Who are you marrying?"

Bunny furrowed her perfectly plucked eyebrows. She remembered his face perfectly, but was unsure which name to use. She didn't want to confuse her fellow Horsewomen. "Adam, of course."

"There's no 'of course' with you," Sara Lee said. "For all we knew, you hooked up with Michael."

"God said none of the angels could be a Horseman," Bunny said. "They all already have roles in the Apocalypse. Then again, Satan broke her promise to let Adam be War."

"So, you're finally going to marry that poor man," Butterflye said. "You've kept him on the hook long enough."

"When's the wedding?" Zoe asked.

As Bunny drew her arm aside, letting one of Butterflye's bugs scuttle past, it dislodged a crepe ruffle from her shoulder. "I believe in *long* engagements. We're not getting any older, *and* we have the rest of eternity. Besides, I need to let Michael down easy. Archangels can be so moody."

"So," Zoe said, drawling out the vowel, "how was everyone's vacation? Anything weird happen?"

"Nothing special," Sara Lee replied, though her hand tightened around the stem of her wine glass. "Except that Satan tried to kill me—several times. Oh, and she guilted Oscar's brother into trying to kill me too."

"Really?" Butterflye blinked in surprise. "My clone actually agreed to become Plague." She gave half a shrug and drained her scotch. "She signed the papers and everything, but a few seconds before Ralph and I returned to Hell, a drug lord killed her."

Zoe stared expectantly at Bunny. "What about you?"

Bunny nodded. "Mars tried to kill me—but I killed him instead—although that was hardly interesting. A producer had started on a sequel to my hit movie, *The Thing from Space*, but everything went wrong. You just think our lunch at the commissary was a disaster."

Satan and a man entered the Sulfur Well. They threaded between the crowded tables.

"Great job, Stanley," Satan was saying.

Stanley formed a pistol with his fingers. "You should have seen the look on her face. Blam!"

At that moment, Satan's and Stanley's gazes locked on Butterflye and her gaze on them. All three pointed at each other and shouted, "You!"

Stanley paled. "She *was* dead. Floating in the water with most of her brains missing."

"You idiot!" Satan smacked Stanley upside the head. "That wouldn't kill her. She never uses her brains!"

Stanley's body swelled. Recognizing the danger signs, the Redheads reached for umbrellas. Before they could open them, Stanley's body exploded. Bits of Stanley flew everywhere.

Butterflye dropped her umbrella and picked a chunk of entrails off the shoulder of her blue sequined gown. "Aw, I just had this cleaned."

The other Redheads picked pieces of flesh and bone from their clothes and drinks. Like everyone else in Hell, Stanley would eventually recorporialize, painfully but assuredly.

Satan charged toward the Redheads' table, knocking smaller tables aside and scattering the bar's regulars.

Nose-to-nose with Butterflye, she snapped, "You're supposed to be dead." Straightening, she added, "You were *all* supposed to be dead!" She turned her fiery glare on Sara Lee. "I should've known that mama's boy would wimp out of killing you. I should have taken you both out when I had the chance." Her fury turned on Bunny. "*You* killed my best candidate for War with a *shoe*? Wait. That actually makes sense." Satan sank into the only empty chair at the round table and grabbed her head with both hands, her horns peeking between fingers. "Why does all the crap happen to me?"

"You rip what you sew," Bunny said sagely. "At least, anything *I've* sewn has to later be ripped and redone."

Satan groaned and finally looked up from her hands. "For a little while, *one of you was gone*. I need a drink."

"I didn't know you drank," Bunny said.

Satan growled. "I started after you girls became the

Horsewomen."

Butterflye slid her scotch over to Satan. "Here. I promise I don't have any germs."

"Gee, Satan," Bunny said. "You really look down. Maybe you should send in the clowns. They'll cheer you up."

"What clowns do you mean?" Zoe asked.

"I'm not sure, but everyone knows a three-ring circus has clowns, and Hell has nine rings. So it should have lots of clowns."

Satan glared at Bunny. "You want to know where the clowns are? They're *right here!*" Satan fumed, turning red, back to her old self. "Look at Zoe's gunboat feet and Butterflye's whiskey-red nose and Sara Lee's Bozo-red hair. But *you*, Bunny, are the biggest clown of all!" Satan lurched to her feet.

"Well," Sara Lee said, "you certainly look like you feel better. I guess *we clowns* did our job."

"You've *never* done your job!" Satan grabbed fistfuls of her own hair and pulled. "A bunch of lab rats hopped up on drugs could do a better job than you four. Instead of spreading famine, war, plague and death, you spread moodiness, fashion-tips, sequins and coffee stains." She whirled on Butterflye. "Bug motels are *not* actual motels for bugs." She jabbed a finger in Sara Lee's face. "Why don't you just eat the rest of the world into famine?" She glared at Bunny then covered her eyes. "If I never see another shade of pink … I'll think there's a chance in Hell that God might forgive me!" She faced Zoe, steam billowing from her nostrils.

Zoe slammed a fist against the table, interrupting Satan's tirade. "Hey! I do my job pretty darn well."

Satan paused, shrugged, then said, "Eh." She took a swig of Butterflye's scotch. "You girls wait here."

"I take it Orcas's brother tried to kill you too," Butterflye said. "That's weird, because you actually try to do your job."

"Yeah, but I'm still a pain in her butt," Zoe said.

Satan bustled back through the crowd, knocking over different tables this time. She slammed a thick book on the table and sat.

"That's a copy of our wedding contract," Sara Lee said.

Satan heaved a defeated sigh and flipped open the cover. "Okay, girls, let's look for another loophole. I can't take *this* Hell any longer."

About the Redheads

Linda L. Donahue (www.lindaldonahue.com) was born in Burns, Oregon. As an Air Force brat, she traveled extensively while growing up. Now she lives in Garland, Texas. She has a BA in Russian Studies and a BS in Computer Science with a minor in Electrical Engineering from Southern Methodist University and a MAT in Earth Sciences from the University of Texas at Dallas. While she taught high school for 18 years, currently, when not writing, she teaches tai chi and belly dance. She also spends a lot of time taking care of animals, including cats, a rabbit and a sugar glider.

Rhonda Eudaly Rhonda Eudaly lives in Arlington, Texas with her husband and two dogs. She's ventured into several industries and occupations for a wide variety of experience. She writes the part of Death (Zoe) in the *Four Redheads of the Apocalypse* books. She's the author of *Tarbox Station* and has short stories in several anthologies and other publications, most of which can be found on her website - www.RhondaEudaly.com.

Julia S. Mandala (www.juliasmandala.com) was born in Kansas City, MO and lives in Plano, TX. She holds a B.A. in history from Kansas State University and a J.D. in law from Tulane University Law School. In addition to writing and being editor of The Fantasy Writers Asylum, she enjoys scuba diving, belly dancing and traveling with her husband, Larry.

Dusty Rainbolt is an award-winning cat writer according to her answering machine. She recently stopped writing on her cats because they move around too much and ink got on the furniture. She's the author of *Cat Wrangling Made Easy: Maintaining Peace and Sanity in Your Multicat Home*, *Ghost Cats: Human Encounters with Feline Spirits*, *Kittens For Dummies* (yes, one of the famous Dummies series), and *It's Cat Scene Investigator: Solve Your Cat's Litter Box Mystery*. She's also the author of a humorous science fiction novel, *All the Marbles*, an historical fiction entitled *Death Under the Crescent Moon*, and co-author of *The Four Redheads of the Apocalypse*, *Apocalypse Now!*, and *Redheads In Love* (written with three other redheaded authors). She writes the monthly feline advice columns, "Dear Hobbes" and "Ask Einstein." In her real job, Dusty is the product editor for *Catnip* published by Tufts University School of Veterinary Medicine. She also freelances for *Cat Fancy* and anyone else whose checks don't bounce. Over her cat writing career she has won 11 Muse Medallions and 23 special awards from the Cat Writers' Association.

Yard Dog Press Titles As Of This Print Date

Through Wyoming Eyes, Ken Rand
Turn Left to Tomorrow, Robin Wayne Bailey
The Twins, Selina Rosen
Wandering Lark, Laura J. Underwood
Wings of Morning, Katharine Eliska Kimbriel
Zombies In Oz and Other Undead Musings, Robin Wayne Bailey

Fantasy Writers Asylum (A YDP Imprint):

Blood Songs
Julia Mandala

Tale of the Black Heart
Linda L. Donahue

Double Dog (A YDP Imprint):

#1:
Of Stars & Shadows,
Mark W. Tiedemann
This Instance Of Me,
Jeffrey Turner

#2:
Gods and Other Children,
Bill D. Allen
Tranquility, Tracy Morris

#3:
Home Is the Hunter,
James K. Burk
Farstep Station,
Lazette Gifford

#4:
Sabre Dance,
Melanie Fletcher
The Lunari Mask,
Laura J. Underwood

#5:
House of Doors,
Julia Mandala
Jaguar Moon,
Linda A. Donahue

Just Cause (A YDP Imprint):

The Bitter End
Selina Rosen

Death Under the Crescent Moon
Dusty Rainbolt

The Ghost Writer
Selina Rosen

It's Not Rocket Science: Spirituality for the Working-Class Soul
Selina Rosen

Meditations of a Hoarder
Melinda LaFevers

Not My Life
Selina Rosen

The Pit
Selina Rosen

Plots and Protagonists: A Reference Guide for Writers
Mel. White

Vanishing Fame
Selina Rosen

Non-YDP titles we distribute:

Chains of Freedom
Chains of Destruction
Jabone's Sword
Queen of Denial
Recycled
Strange Robby
Sword Masters
Selina Rosen

Three Ways to Order:

1. Write us a letter telling us what you want, then send it along with your check or money order (made payable to Yard Dog Press) to: Yard Dog Press, 710 W. Redbud Lane, Alma, AR 72921-7247

2. Use selinarosen@cox.net or lynnstran@cox.net to contact us and place your order. Then send your check or money order to the address above. *This has the advantage of allowing you to check on the availability of short-stock items such as T-shirts and back-issues of Yard Dog Comics.*

3. Contact us as in #1 or #2 above and pay with a credit card or by debit from your checking account. Either give us the credit card information in your letter/Email/phone call, or go to our website and use our shopping carts. If you send us your information, please include your name as it appears on the card, your credit card number, the expiration date, and the 3 or 4-digit security code after your signature on the back (CVV). Please remember that we will include media rate (minimum $3.00) S/H for mailing in the lower 48 states.

Watch our website at
www.yarddogpress.com
for news of upcoming projects
and new titles!!

A Note to Our Readers

We at Yard Dog Press understand that many people buy used books because they simply can't afford new ones. That said, and understanding that not everyone is made of money, we'd like you to know something that you may not have realized. Writers only make money on new books that sell. At the big houses a writer's entire future can hinge on the number of books they sell. While this isn't the case at Yard Dog Press, the honest truth is that when you sell or trade your book or let many people read it, the writer and the publishing house aren't making any money.

As much as we'd all like to believe that we can exist on love and sweet potato pie, the truth is we all need money to buy the things essential to our daily lives. Writers and publishers are no different.

We realize that these "freebies" and cheap books often turn people on to new writers and books that they wouldn't otherwise read. However we hope that you will reconsider selling your copy, and that if you trade it or let your friends borrow it, you also pass on the information that if they really like the author's work they should consider buying one of their books at full price sometime so that the writer can afford to continue to write work that entertains you.

We appreciate all our readers and *depend* upon their support.

Thanks,
The Editorial Staff
Yard Dog Press

PS – Please note that "used" books without covers have, in most cases, been stolen. Neither the author nor the publisher has made any money on these books because they were supposed to be pulped for lack of sales.

Please do not purchase books without covers.